SWANGO

THE CELWYN SERIES BOOK 6

SWANGO

Lou Kemp

4 Horsemen
Publications, Inc.

Published By: 4 Horsemen Publications, Inc.

4 Horsemen Publications, Inc.
PO Box 417
Sylva, NC 28779
4horsemenpublications.com
info@4horsemenpublications.com

Cover & Typesetting by Autumn Skye
Edited by Joseph Mistretta

Library of Congress Control Number: 2024944608

Paperback ISBN-13: 979-8-8232-0426-2
Hardcover ISBN-13: 979-8-8232-0427-9
Audiobook ISBN-13: 979-8-8232-0636-5
Ebook ISBN-13: 979-8-8232-0425-5

Table of Contents

Cast of Characters:

Jonas Celwyn: Immortal magician and provocateur

Professor Xiau Kang: Automat, medical man, skeptic, and scientist

Bartholomew: Widower from Juba, scientist, and friend to Kang and Celwyn

Pelaez: Celwyn's obnoxious, untrustworthy brother, also a magician

Swango: Celwyn's acquaintance of dubious intentions.

Qing: Mechanical bird & lover of all things shiny and wonderful

Annabelle Pearse Swayne: Heiress and ward of Uncle Celwyn

Captain Patrick Swayne: Friend to Celwyn, married to Annabelle, master of Tellyhouse

Zander: An orphan rescued on the way to Prague

Otto: An orphan who joined them on their journey to Singapore

Edward Murphy: Their driver, also in charge of security at Tellyhouse

Tara McFein: Good witch and good vampire that Celwyn is enamored of

Valentine Soriano: Uncle to Tara and head of their family

Captain Nemo: Captain of the *Nautilus*

Granger: Nemo's Lieutenant

Jules Verne: Famous novelist traveling on the *Nautilus.*

Wolfgang Augustus Griffin: Father to Celwyn and Pelaez

Thales: Demi-god and capable of saving other immortals

Elmo Linssen, Tremaine: Celwyn's disguises while with the Nazi's

Lieutenant Dosher: Delectable female Gestapo agent

Corporal Frackler: Reports to Dosher

Corporal Porky: Reports to Dosher

PART I

Chapter 1

October 1877
Singapore

STUNNED, BUT ALIVE, CELWYN raised himself to his knees and fell again. His tunic stuck to his wound and blood ran down his leg. Off to the right, he spied a tiny ethereal figure hovering above the trees. Could it be Thales? Even before the man turned around, revealing a long white beard and a face older than time, the magician knew it had to be the immortal who'd saved his life.

Wolfgang Augustus Griffin stopped his attack. His face grew darker along with his rage, and his roar flattened the nearby trees. Celwyn didn't know what to do: from only feet away, his father tried to kill him, and on his other side, Thales approached with a ghost of amusement on his decimated face.

His father bellowed and pivoted back to Celwyn.

Thales lifted a hand and Wolfgang could no longer move.

In the dead voice Celwyn well-remembered, Thales told him, "I suggest you and your brother go. But first—"

Celwyn gasped. In a blink of an eye, Thales knelt over him and placed a hand on his chest, sending a chill flashing through him like he'd been shot. Celwyn couldn't look at him, afraid of what he would see.

When the magician focused again, Thales stood beside Wolfgang, thirty feet away. *Yes, it would be a good time to get out of here.* Celwyn rolled over and found Pelaez lying beside him, unconscious. With a last glance at Thales, Celwyn got to his feet and kicked his brother's leg. He kicked him again. When Pelaez opened his eyes, the magician told him, "Come on!" and yanked him upright.

The massive cloud of fire his father had brought upon them still crackled and burned the air. As clouds of smoke reached the ground Pelaez and Celwyn raced toward the water, and Wolfgang's bellows grew louder. The brothers leapt high over boulders, running for their lives.

"He's following us!" the magician panted. "Block him or ... we're dead—"

When they dove off the rocks above the headlands, the bay lay empty where the *Nautilus* should have been. For that, Celwyn felt thankful; Nemo must have heard his request to retreat when Kang and the others returned.

As a pair of sleek bonitas, Celwyn and Pelaez streaked through the water toward the nearest island. Their father could not detect them below the surface, but he would still search for them. The magician should have been utterly tired from the battle with his father and their flight afterward; it must be Thales helping him. *Why?*

Whatever he'd done, it began fading. Halfway to the first island, the magician felt his strength faltering while their father's wrath echoed louder across the water. He signaled Pelaez for help.

When Celwyn could go no farther, Pelaez's magic propelled them to where Nemo should be. His brother would also be tired, but he'd only joined the battle halfway through.

As usual, when the magician needed entry into the submerged submarine, he approached the underwater window of the bridge and tapped on the glass. Celwyn swam back and forth in front of it until Bartholomew yelped and pointed. Professor Xiau Kang rolled his eyes and alerted the Captain. The gongs sounded, and the *Nautilus* surfaced.

Minutes later, Celwyn and Pelaez stood in a puddle of water at the foot of the spiral staircase. Displaying his intelligence, his brother moved behind Celwyn as the others approached. The first to spot Pelaez, Nemo's Lieutenant Granger, couldn't help exclaiming how he felt.

"What the hell!"

The echo of the ship's gongs faded, and quiet reigned again. Perhaps too much so. The tension rose as

Captain Nemo, Granger, Bartholomew, and Kang confronted Pelaez; the man they blamed for the massacre at their compound in Turkey. Nemo's hand rested on his pistol as he stomped back and forth in front of them. Wearing an interested expression, Valentine Soriano flanked the automat, eyeing Pelaez like a medium rare steak. Bartholomew looked down on Pelaez with nearly as much venom as the Captain.

After treating them to his trademark smirk, Pelaez wiped the blood on his coat and waited. Before Kang checked, Celwyn stopped the blood from his own wound and suddenly wore a clean coat.

"Nice try, Jonas. I can still see your bloody trousers." Professor Kang aimed a thumb at them.

"How did you get away?" Bartholomew asked Celwyn, but his murderous gaze never left the top of Pelaez's head. He took a step forward, proving he had not forgotten Pelaez's crime.

In the years since they met, Celwyn had never heard so much anger in his friend's voice. And he wasn't alone; Nemo glared at Pelaez, speechless with fury, and clipped his words as if chopping them with an ax.

"When they ran back to this ship," Nemo waved a hand toward Kang and the others and told Pelaez, "I heard of your service to these gentlemen. Otherwise, you would be dead."

"My brother," Celwyn nodded at Pelaez, "supported me to this ship." He inhaled and wished he could sit down.

Kang asked Nemo. "Shall we go into the study, sir?"

"Follow me." Nemo led the way. Celwyn managed to walk by the bar and the man-sized globe before he collapsed on one of the sofas. With a squawk, Qing streaked across the room to nuzzle him and shrieked louder.

"I wasn't gone long," he told the mechanical bird.

"He knows something happened out there," Bartholomew said as Qing rubbed his beak on the magician's ear.

Nemo stood beside them, hands behind his back, and bored holes into Pelaez.

"Well, sir?"

Before Pelaez could answer, Celwyn said, "We were attacked and would have died if my brother hadn't intervened." The magician wanted his tea badly, but he first must defuse this situation.

"It is true," Kang said. "But it doesn't excuse what he did before."

Nemo let out a long breath and glanced at the line of bottles behind the bar. Without moving, Celwyn sent a tray of glasses and bottles around. After Nemo threw back a shot, he growled, "We have a much more serious situation than treachery, gentlemen."

"Sir?" Bartholomew asked.

Both the magician and Pelaez used towels supplied by the crew and Celwyn resisted using another towel on Bartholomew's face. The big man not only appeared angry and upset from the attack but still hadn't calmed down. His hands shook as he tried to sip his drink. Celwyn couldn't tell if it came from seeing Pelaez again or from what they just endured.

The whiskey had not relaxed Nemo either. Celwyn wouldn't have been surprised to see steam escaping from his ears.

"One-third of my crew is still ashore!" The Captain blew up. He gestured toward Singapore. "They are scattered everywhere. On leave. We need a plan *now*, gentlemen."

"We have one, sir." Like the *Nautilus*, some ideas arrived unexpectedly and floated just below the surface. The magician found it difficult to stand upright and hoped the automat didn't notice when he gripped the back of the chair; they didn't have time for his nagging.

With a look at Kang, Bartholomew stepped into the role of the worrier instead of his friend. The automat's mournful face looked worse now than an hour ago when Celwyn told him about his wife's murder—Xiau had been swallowed whole into a deep and quiet misery.

"What are you planning?" Bartholomew asked Celwyn, "How dangerous is it?"

Pelaez moved closer. "Do you need my help, brother?"

Celwyn didn't want his help. He didn't want to look at him. Most of all, he wanted Pelaez off this ship as soon as they retrieved Nemo's crew and left Singapore behind. In the months since the disaster in Turkey, Pelaez hadn't changed. He still dripped with sarcasm, and his voice made the skin of anyone listening to him ripple with foreboding.

Kang stood and addressed them.

"Jonas is exhausted from the battle and needs to rest. I suspect he has been wounded and is hiding it." He waited until he could go on. "I saw the fight with his father before he," Kang waved at Pelaez, "joined us. There may be little either of them can do for now."

"We cannot wait while they rest." Nemo stalked to the bar and back.

From his relaxed position on the sofa, Pelaez studied his nails as if he didn't have a care in the world.

Nemo saw him and gripped his pistol again.

"When are your men due back?" Bartholomew asked.

"Some today, the rest by late tomorrow. And that crazed madman is out there, still!"

Bartholomew watched as the automat withdrew into his melancholy again; his face fell, and he closed his eyes. The big man eyed Nemo. "We can't surface where Wolfgang last saw us? And where the crew expect you to be?"

"Precisely." Nemo inhaled several times and did his best not to bark again. It took an effort to keep his fists from flying into Pelaez's face. "Go on."

"Is there a distress signal from you that the crew would know?" Celwyn asked, "Perhaps one similar to the internal gongs that resound on this ship?"

"There is. They are all aware of it." Nemo's eyes flared with hope. "Where is this going?"

"Would the crew recognize your signal as a series of gongs ringing in indifferent timbres?" the magician asked as he tried to walk to the aquatic window and stumbled, settling for leaning against a chair. Under good conditions, expelling magic tired him. What he had just gone through had almost done him in.

"Yes, if they hear it, they know we are in distress, and they'll go north of the city and wait for us."

"I'd love to help, but it seems like there is still a spot of animosity against me." Pelaez sighed like a thespian villain. Bartholomew took a step toward him and lifted one of his ham-size fists.

"You bastard!" Nemo glared at Pelaez.

"Oh, pshaw. I didn't kill those people in Turkey." Pelaez flipped a hand to brush the idea aside. "They were already dead when I arrived."

Captain Nemo leaned into his face and ground out, "You burned the flying machine."

"Yes, I did. That was my pleasure."

Bartholomew went for him. No matter Nemo's ban on violence aboard the ship, Pelaez's insolence got to him. At over seven feet tall and built of solid muscle, Bartholomew could have broken Pelaez in two if got his hands on him. Pelaez flew backward, landing on the chess table, and knocking it over before executing another provocative bow.

"Not now—" Nemo yelled. Bartholomew and Kang had worked for months on the flying machine. It had been Captain Nemo's dream to build it.

Celwyn sent Pelaez a wordless warning and told Nemo, "My plan is a good one."

"Let's hear it," Nemo told him, but never took his eyes off Pelaez.

"Do you need my help or not?" Pelaez asked as the chess pieces reverted to the table one at a time.

"Yes, dammit." Celwyn inhaled and regarded the others. "My father will find us if either my brother or I appear above the water."

Jules Verne asked, "By your scent?"

"Yes." He turned to the Captain, "Sir, we will retrieve your crew." Celwyn sank into a chair. The automat eyed him, and the magician shook his head—he could last a few more minutes.

"I see you survived that unpleasantness," a deep and dramatic voice commented.

Celwyn had wondered where the vampire had gone. Valentine had presence. He'd also recently helped them at the Sulu Islands. Of anyone aboard the ship, he seemed much more deadly and quick-tempered. Despite the vampire's growing respect for Captain Nemo and the others, Valentine's restlessness grew by the day. He smoothed his mane of silver hair and made sure the magician saw the tear in his velvet cape.

"You owe me a new cape from our earlier escapade."

Nemo said, "Not now. I want to hear how Jonas will retrieve my crew."

Celwyn complied.

"It may sound strange, but my father hates the smell of eggs cooking. Absolutely abhors it. I propose that we cover the city with the miasma of rotting eggs. It will distract him and misdirect his sense of smell while looking for us. Meanwhile, this ship will stay as near land as possible while the distress signal is sent to your marooned crew."

"How?" the author asked.

"I will amplify the volume," Celwyn said, "while the *Nautilus* waits at the meeting point.

"How?" the author repeated.

"...the signal would come from this ship?" Nemo asked.

The magician shook his head and Bartholomew stopped boring holes in Pelaez long enough to say, "I hope this works. It is a horrid situation." He glanced at Kang. "We need to talk about Elizabeth."

With a pat on the automat's shoulder, Celwyn said, "We will," to Nemo, "I assume we will head for Prague from here?"

"Yes."

The magician started to laugh to himself as he pictured his father's reaction as a cloud of rotting eggs enveloped him. "To answer the question, I'm going to use every bell in every church in the city to ring out the signal. None of the crew will be able to miss it."

With a twinkle in his eye, Verne said, "I doubt that will surprise the crew, Jonas. Your magic has become a favorite topic of conversation aboard ship."

Like a balloon deflating, Nemo's expression changed from supreme annoyance to relief. "They will wait until dark to meet us." He raised a brow. "This will be quite an indoctrination for David. He is with the others ashore."

David had been one of the good outcomes from their foray at the Sulu Islands, and they were all happy he'd joined the crew. "Excellent." Celwyn told the room, "My brother and I must rest before the event." When the automat popped out of his chair, the magician added, "And, of course, after Xiau dresses my wound."

Chapter 2

BY MIDAFTERNOON, THE MAGICIAN returned to the study from a recuperating nap. Mid-way through it, Wye visited him. The wyvern did not appear injured from their encounter with Wolfgang, and Celwyn made sure Wye knew how grateful he was for his assistance. It was the first time the wyvern had smiled, with all his teeth—so long and white, Valentine would have been envious.

Everyone had gathered here just after dark, expecting to witness something extraordinary, except for Professor Kang, who sat by the map table staring at, but not seeing the maps under his hand. The magician patted his shoulder.

"Xiau, we will talk about Elizabeth when this is over."

The automat nodded but didn't look up.

Pelaez walked in, and after checking the mood of the occupants, said, "It will be sundown soon."

"So, it will." Celwyn agreed and joined him in the middle of the room. After Pelaez downed his wine, they faced west toward Singapore. The *Nautilus* had moved to the middle of the harbor and rested dozens of feet under the surface. Occasionally, the shadow of a small boat passed by overhead. Of all the fish, the spotted barramundi seemed the most interested in them, while Qing showed his preference for the veined catfish by pecking at them through the aquatic window.

"Are you ready?" Celwyn asked him.

Qing blinked, but didn't leave the window or squawk when Pelaez's pig appeared and rolled onto its side under the chess table. Verne moved as fast as he could back to the sofas. Everyone knew Pelaez's magic revolved around the pig, and it was not welcome aboard ship any more than Pelaez.

From his seat beside the globe, Bartholomew asked, "Which comes first? The smell, or the bells?"

"My brother will provide the odor first. It will be pervasive and go everywhere possible, since we do not know where Wolfgang is right now."

"When this is over, I have many questions about what occurred today." The big man told them.

"As do I," Valentine said.

"Same here," Verne agreed. "But I will wait."

The magician gripped Bartholomew's shoulder. "You are the bravest man I know. Thank you for your help during the attack." He turned to Pelaez. "Now, brother."

"As you wish."

Pelaez closed his eyes. Minutes passed in which only the ticking clock could be heard. From the doorway, Captain Nemo watched him through slitted eyes. Pelaez's transgressions would not be forgiven.

"Done," Pelaez croaked and cleared his throat. "It is done."

Immediately, Celwyn's violins entered the room as their music built, bringing clarity and strength for the job ahead. As their harmony balanced, turning pure and strong, the magician began clenching and unclenching his hands. Minutes went by while the music played on, turning softer and fading into the background.

Faintly at first, from far across the city, the steady sound of bells ringing traveled through the air and then the water to where the *Nautilus* floated. Cascading bells followed, becoming a cacophony as hundreds of bells resounded, repeating the same sequence over and over again. The noise became deafening as thousands of more bells arrived. Kang covered his ears. Verne wrapped his arms around his head.

When he raised his arms high, Celwyn's breathing slowed and, with a smile, he swiveled and saluted Captain Nemo. "It is done. Dispatch your boats, sir."

Without a word, Nemo saluted back and strode out of the room. The magician stood beside the automat, who shot him a quick look and resumed staring at his hands.

"Xiau, it is you I worry about. Does Nemo know what happened?"

When the automat shook his head, Bartholomew saw him and started for the door, presumably to tell the Captain about Elizabeth.

"Are you aware of what occurred?" Celwyn eyed Valentine. The vampire had been studying Pelaez with a voracious look intended to intimidate him, or it could be Valentine planned to do Nemo a favor of sorts.

"No." The vampire's eyes flared in irritation. "All I know is that Lieutenant Granger practically dragged me out of a wine shop and said that we had to get back to this ship." He widened his eyes at Celwyn. "Then you dropped the Professor and everyone else on top of us and ripped my new cape."

Each time Valentine mentioned it, the less Celwyn felt inclined to use magic to fix his damn cape.

Verne had perked up, inquisitiveness written on his face. As usual, the diminutive author looked gray all over, from his pointed beard to embroidered vest and shoes. He wore an excited expression, probably hoping Valentine would do something entertaining to Pelaez.

The *Nautilus* backed away from the city, and they headed north at moderate speed. Qing rapped on the window, and when they left behind a cloud of silvery sickle fishes, he pecked faster.

"Wherever the ship surfaces, make sure we're invisible, please," the magician told his brother.

Verne said, "Retrieving that many men will take a while, and it may be hours until the Captain joins us." He raised an expectant eyebrow.

"I believe they still want to know what transpired today," Pelaez drawled.

Kang gazed out the window, not seeing the kaleidoscope of colors and beckoning tendrils of the seaweed. "Tell them."

With a sigh, Celwyn related the news of Elizabeth's death, ending with the open question as to why. "For now, I would prefer not to talk about this several times. We will wait until the Captain joins us again."

Valentine asked a few questions about the telegrams and offered his services for any actions needed to avenge Mrs. Kang's death.

"We will remember, thank you." Bartholomew shook his head. "Again, we don't know why she was killed."

After a while, Lieutenant Granger arrived and stood at attention. "The Captain sends his regards concerning Mrs. Kang. He says it will be discussed as soon as all the crew are on board again." He cleared his throat and started for the door. "I must leave you to assist."

The magician jumped to his feet and blocked him, careful not to touch him. "Wait—"

Bartholomew pointed. "Ha—allow me to guess—the Lieutenant here has been around you too much recently, and your father might detect you on him?"

"Exactly." Celwyn sighed. To Granger, he said, "Please send someone else who has not had anything to do with us."

Chapter 3

ONCE AGAIN, EVERYONE GATHERED beside the aquatic window in the ship's study. Kang arrived last and settled next to the big man. Bartholomew studied him, then the others.

"You are all dealing well with our fright earlier today." Celwyn switched to Valentine. "I am thankful nothing else occurred except what happened to your cloak." The vampire saw that it had been fixed and showed his teeth in reply.

While they spoke, the crew entered to set up the dining table, saving Verne from staring up the corridor and patting his stomach.

"I am not calm, Jonas." Bartholomew set his jaw. "Not at all. Throughout the afternoon, I thought about what we went through." When he shuddered, everyone on the couch jiggled too. "I agree, let's wait for the Captain and discuss it just once." He sent Pelaez a confused and angry glance. "Just once."

By the time the rest of Nemo's crew had been rounded up and brought back on board, it only lacked a few minutes until midnight. The study had been a lively place while they waited. After the post-prandial cigars had been lit and drinks poured, Valentine started things off. His eyes glittered through the cloud of cigar smoke as he challenged Pelaez.

"Why don't you satisfy our curiosity and tell us about Turkey?"

"No."

A quiet but powerful voice stopped everyone. Kang had said little since Celwyn had rung the bells of Singapore, and his melancholy hung over the room like something tangible that wept, that they could touch. "We should wait until the Captain arrives."

Pelaez lifted a sarcastic brow at the vampire, subtle and insulting. Celwyn caught it and cringed.

With perfect timing, Nemo marched inside, followed by a crewman bearing a foldout table. Another man brought a dinner tray, bottles, and glasses. While they set everything up, Nemo rubbed his face in irritation, but not to the same degree as before.

"My digestion is already ruined. So please tell us what took place, Jonas."

After sending beverages around the room, the magician waited on his tea, not wanting to spoil it with what he had to report. Having Pelaez in the room and then reliving the encounter with his father made Celwyn thankful Tara couldn't see his furiously foul mood.

"It happened about noon." As he reported, Bartholomew and the others once more relived their fear and Verne turned pale. Celwyn continued, "Wolfgang appeared insane and out of control in a complete rage. The wyvern tried to help. When Father began beating the life out of me, Bartholomew shot him, and I got away." Celwyn addressed the big man. "You *are* the bravest man I know—the supernatural terrifies you, and yet you tried to save me. Thank you."

Bartholomew tried to wave it off, but Verne spoke up, "I felt so afraid. Then I saw Mr. Bartholomew fight his way through the fire and shoot."

"Just as my brother arrived, Father lifted Bartholomew into the air." Celwyn nodded at Pelaez. "We battled him together."

Throughout the recital, Kang remained quiet, sometimes alert and peering out from his world of grief.

"It was horrible!" Bartholomew gulped wine like it was water. "Flames everywhere!"

"What did the people nearby do?" Nemo asked.

"Run, mostly." The magician decided to finish the tale so he could stop reliving it. "My brother stood with me, pushing our father back—you'll recall that Wolfgang is much stronger than we are. His fury still drove him forward."

"Why?" the big man asked.

"We don't know." Pelaez shrugged.

"Between us," Celwyn almost grinned, "we tricked him again. If he hadn't been in a frenzy, he would have seen through it."

A crewman entered, whispered to Nemo, saluted, and left bearing his empty dinner tray. Nemo grunted. "We have retrieved another score of the crew. There are only a handful still outstanding. Go on, please."

"As you wish," Celwyn said. "Xiau was in shock at the news of his wife. We all were. But we had to move quickly. This time, we used a much simpler trick than the one we employed at the catacombs."

"Something that flies?" Nemo asked.

"A rather large raven," Celwyn nodded, "I flew away with Xiau and everyone on my back. My brother hopped aboard."

The sofa under Bartholomew shuddered again. "It was worse than the flights between the ships. We ascended much higher in the air, and I could hear their father roaring and saw the fire growing as we headed toward the bay."

"It was my first opportunity to fly with Jonas." A smile creased Verne's face. "Marvelous. Just marvelous."

"If you say so." Bartholomew raised a brow. "Wouldn't you call the ending rather abrupt?"

"We knew my father would follow us by smell, so my brother disrobed and dropped his clothing, a piece at a time, over the city as we circled above it." Celwyn said, "We expected Father would chase the scents on the ground and not look at the sky."

"It worked." Pelaez told them, "But ... I could only keep him from detecting us for a short time. The battle had taken much of my energy and nearly all Jonas's. Father caught up to us when we reached the headlands."

Celwyn entered Nemo's thoughts to silently ask, *"Excuse me, sir, did you expect Pelaez? You parked this ship in the same place as before … so he would find us?"*

With only a slight hesitation, Captain Nemo nodded.

Meanwhile, Bartholomew continued, "Jonas dumped us into the trees and confronted his father."

The author said, "While we ran as fast as we could back to the ship!"

"My contribution consisted of all of you landing on top of me, and I congratulate you on a unique and worthy entrance," Valentine drawled. "Although we ran for our lives, I was not afraid, only prudent—if I ever fought your father, I believe he is too strong for me to prevail."

"Good deduction." Bartholomew trembled again. "He kept throwing Jonas around like a rag doll and slamming him to the ground."

"Then what happened?" Nemo asked.

"The last thing I saw was the western sky above the city," Verne said. "A wall of flames emerged from the clouds, and the fire descended upon you." He studied Celwyn with concern. "I really thought the end had arrived."

Celwyn remembered the dive off the rocks well. He wasn't ready to thank or forgive Pelaez yet. "My brother and the others became quite heavy as we flew across the city." He smiled at the big man and almost received one in return. Instead, Bartholomew glanced at the automat with worry and laid a hand on Kang's shoulder.

Nemo's lips twitched. "My navigator nearly fainted when he saw an odd, green-eyed fish bumping the glass, Jonas." His amusement died when he looked at Pelaez.

Kang's voice sounded heavy with guilt and sadness.

"I loved my wife very much. I should never have left Prague." He hurried out of the room.

As Bartholomew started to get up, Celwyn said, "Let me."

The magician caught up with the automat just as he opened his cabin door. When he went to close it, Celwyn stood there wordlessly asking a question. Kang sighed and said, "Get in here, Jonas."

The magician took the empty chair, and Kang sat on his trunk. Minutes went by, each of them deep in their own thoughts. In Celwyn's opinion, their friendship did not need words, it needed music.

A trio of flutes entered. They played Elizabeth's favorite, and the theme from Schubert's *Der Graf von Gleichen* filled the room with the touch of a spring shower as it covered the automat in a veil of memories. Moments more and the magician spoke.

"Would it help if I made a copy of her for a while?"

Kang shook his head hard. "No—not yet. No. I am too angry."

"Not at yourself. We came back, and we did so much good this voyage."

The automat gulped and buried his face in his hands. "I know," he mumbled around his fingers, "Why? Why kill Elizabeth?"

"We won't know until we reach Prague."

Kang slammed his fists on his knees. "Is it because of us? Because of the flying machine?"

"I don't know, Xiau."

The background sounds from the submarine filtered through to them: a crewman walking by, the echo of a distant gong, and a squeaking door.

"You need rest. Perhaps to read. It would help."

"In this situation, you wouldn't." Kang told him, "You would just destroy another park."

"True."

"I would feel better if I returned to the study with everyone."

Celwyn stood. "All right. I'll go back and suggest we need more desserts this evening and tell them you'll rejoin us shortly."

"Thank you."

The magician controlled his anger until he was halfway down the corridor.

Of course, it was them. God dammit!

Chapter 4

WHEN THE MAGICIAN REENTERED the study, everyone still discussed his father, but none of them had Pelaez on the floor pummeling him—an improvement in the atmosphere. The magician produced a torte with strawberries and cream, an apple strudel, and a plate of chocolate cookies. "Xiau will rejoin us soon."

Verne edged closer, with nothing on his mind besides the torte. "Exquisite. I detect mint and ginger."

Nemo waited for the magician to settle on the sofa, then announced with extreme formality, "Everyone is aware that the atmosphere aboard this ship must be one of trust and adherence to procedure. I will not tolerate deceit." He swiveled. "Mr. Pelaez, now is the time to tell us exactly what happened in Turkey."

As Nemo spoke, Celwyn locked eyes with his brother and once again felt lucky that the ability to read thoughts only went in one direction. What he found in Pelaez's mind caused him to control his face; Celwyn now knew the answer to the previous debate; his brother could see into the future … brief glimpses that in his thoughts looked like photographs. For months Pelaez had known that they would come back to Singapore. He did not need to follow them.

Kang quietly returned and Nemo stared at Pelaez until he spoke.

"It is as I started to explain earlier. I did not kill anyone at the compound; they were all dead when I arrived. Yes, I detained your crewman while I burned that infernal machine you made. You must understand that I could have killed him, but did not."

On Celwyn's left, Captain Nemo's anger vibrated, and the magician noticed his death-grip on his fork. Pelaez should consider himself fortunate that he sat at the other end of the sofa with Verne, who probably wished him the least amount of ill will. If he couldn't eat it or use it as part of his novels, it lacked interest.

Captain Nemo ground out, "You left a grotesquely murdered body next to my crewman—an act designed to terrorize him."

When Pelaez would have shrugged, further inflaming the Captain, Celwyn jumped into the conversation. "Finish it. What happened? Who murdered them?"

"Many appeared freshly killed. I didn't see who did it … but wondered." His brother blinked at them. "As many of you have surmised, there are instances when I know of future events—previews—as it were. This wasn't one of them."

"I understand, but it doesn't excuse you." Bartholomew set his jaw.

"I suppose," Pelaez drawled.

His sarcasm caused the big man to rise until Valentine pulled him back again. Pelaez glanced at Celwyn. "No matter how guilty I might be of other crimes, as you perceive them, I have not erred in this instance. I did sense that someone else had been there."

Captain Nemo looked incapable of speech. The magician waved at Pelaez to continue.

"The witch had left, along with her horrid perfume." His brother pursed his lips. "And I knew we'd killed those mafia cretins, so … who was it?"

Duncan was already dead at this point. Celwyn sighed. "You are saying another warlock killed them all?" As he asked, a series of gongs resounded in the belly of the submarine. Nemo caught his eye and nodded; the rest of his crew had been retrieved.

As the engines under their feet rumbled, Pelaez said, "I don't know. But again, I felt the miasma of someone of great strength. So much so, I was glad I didn't encounter them."

Proving that even in the depths of despair Kang couldn't stop his logic, he said, "Jonas, I think the solution to this mystery is much closer to home." He selected a cookie and bit into it, chewing as he thought. "Earlier today, a 'supreme strength' attacked Jonas with unsurpassed fury. The compound in

Turkey displayed evidence of an eruption of killing—like someone in a rage."

"No." Celwyn shook his head violently. "No!"

Verne caught on too. "It makes sense, and I am merely a spectator to this." He told them, "That was not a warlock. It was—"

"Our father," Pelaez growled. "He killed them all."

"Why?" Valentine asked.

"It's your own fault," Pelaez said. "He must have tracked you there. Then killed anyone he met while he searched for us."

"It makes you wonder how that witch, Ginnie, got away," Bartholomew said. "Or if she left before Wolfgang arrived."

During the next few seconds, Celwyn felt his skin grow cold, and fear gripped him in a tight embrace. When he looked up, he encountered Nemo's gaze, finding kindness and understanding mixed with pity.

"Why?" Bartholomew asked, "Why would he be looking for you and your brother?"

Celwyn said, "I have no idea. Revenge for escaping from the catacombs before he murdered us all?"

Silence smothered the room until the ticking from the wall clock became intrusive. Kang finished a cookie, brushed the crumbs off his vest, and sat up straight.

"I believe there is a simple answer, at least partially, gentlemen." The automat addressed Celwyn. "Wolfgang has been trying to kill you for a while." At the magician's nod, he went on. "I postulate that the urge to do so recently increased because of something Thales said when we left them in the catacombs. Do you recall the details?"

"I do because I watched them through that—" Bartholomew gestured at the aquatic window. "While Peleaz and Jonas ran back to the ship, their father continued to stand underneath that enormous screen with Thales's image." He shuddered. "And Thales's voice echoed over it all."

Verne asked, "What did he say?"

"Something like… 'you never will have,' or similar." The big man shrugged.

Kang said, "I should have wondered about Thales before now."

"All of us should have." Captain Nemo frowned.

"Instead, you blame it all on me—" Pelaez complained.

"Don't start," the magician told him.

Nemo glared at Pelaez. "There is plenty of blame for you, sir."

"Bartholomew's expression grew darker. "And I am not convinced you didn't murder everyone there."

With another smirk, Pelaez inflamed the room. "In my letter to you, I explained why I had to destroy it."

Nemo's face bloomed a deep red. "If you hadn't—" he waved a hand at the others, "saved them today, you'd be dead by now!"

"We're going to Prague for Elizabeth's funeral." Celwyn tried to throw water on the fire. "That is all that is important right now."

The big man made the same effort by changing the subject. "We're traveling fast." He pointed out the flattened kelp as they rushed by.

The Captain seemed reluctant but calmed down. "Yes, I thought it prudent to leave the area once my crew had come aboard again." The ensuing silence demonstrated they all knew why. While Bartholomew could read the room, Verne could not.

"How did your father find us? How does he travel, considering his state of mind and his appearance?"

"Probably by railcar, with the livestock. He is comfortable around them. And he uses his magic when that is not enough." The magician's nose twitched. "After today, I can verify he hadn't bathed for a long time."

"I also wonder," Pelaez said.

"I do not know but suspect something." Celwyn eyed Pelaez. "He discovered you and followed you to Singapore."

The room fell silent, each lost in their own thoughts until Verne asked, "So, we can assume your father can't catch up with us at sea?"

"That is true to a point," Pelaez answered, "if he doesn't detect our scent."

Nemo stood and his voice held no quarter.

"Mr. Pelaez, we will leave you either in Djibouti or long before we near Africa. It will depend upon whether we chance going through the canal again at Suez. That will be determined soon." His voice turned colder. "I only offer this effort as compensation for assisting Jonas and the others while in danger. Your actions have not been forgiven. They will not be forgiven."

Nemo marched out of the room.

Considering the mood on the ship, the character of Pelaez, and Valentine's opinion that he should help their situation along with his teeth, it didn't surprise Celwyn what happened later that night.

The clock in his cabin showed nearly three in the morning when Qing jumped on his stomach and pecked at the magician's nose. "Ow!" Qing knew better. He didn't stop until Celwyn sat up and held the mechanical bird in the air.

"What is the matter?"

Qing squirmed away and hopped across the room to the wall they shared with Pelaez. At that point, Celwyn heard what he hadn't while he snored; from the next room came a thump and faint sounds of combat. In seconds, the magician reached Pelaez's cabin, where the rumble of Valentine's voice could be heard.

Celwyn blew open the door and rushed inside in time to see Pelaez dissolve himself just as the vampire's fangs touched his throat. He reappeared behind Valentine and wrapped an arm around his neck. They both froze at the sight of the magician in a fury.

"Stop it!" Celwyn did his best to keep his voice under control, but Kang came running from the study just as the magician lifted Valentine up and out of the room. "Which one is his cabin?"

"At the end, left side." Kang leaned around him. "Should I open the door?"

"I can." Seconds later, Celwyn tossed Valentine inside and swiveled back to his brother. "If you were not so damned obnoxious, this wouldn't happen." He held up a hand. "*Just shut up!*"

With a smirk at Pelaez, Kang followed the infuriated magician out the door and back to the study.

Chapter 5

OVER THE NEXT WEEK, THE *NAUTILUS* sailed westward, only stopping for maintenance and supplies. Verne and Bartholomew enjoyed a half day of hunting game, gathering eggs, and studying the fantastic colors adorning the parrots on the small island of Sandfal. Toward the end of the day, Valentine joined the party to refill his own personal supplies.

The days became a routine filled with the Professor's melancholy and the quiet around him. No matter who suggested it, Kang did not participate in the nightly bridge games or have the heart to play chess. Several times a day, the magician would come upon him staring out the aquatic window, but not seeing anything.

Sometimes, the automat would bury his nose in his books, but he took no notes and rarely turned any pages before his control broke and he'd hold his face in his hands. The magician grieved with Xiau and took turns with Bartholomew to sit beside him and provide comfort. Celwyn appreciated Qing more than usual during the automat's mourning period; the bird would perch next to Kang, blinking at him and occasionally tapping his watch with a gentle peck to remind him he sat there, and that as time went by the pain would lessen.

Because no one wanted to play bridge with Pelaez, and with Kang not able to, the games consisted of Nemo, Valentine, Bartholomew, and Verne. Having Valentine along had another benefit; the vampire could sniff out other beings, such as daemons, or if Pelaez felt the urge to masquerade as someone else. Unlike their last voyage with his brother, Celwyn was conscious and could detect him too.

At the moment, Celwyn watched the chess players from his position at the organ. Without thinking, his fingers moved across the keys with a speculative touch, fundamental and uncomplicated. One of his foremost thoughts centered on their impending passage through the Suez Canal. Soon, he would be in Beirut and hold Tara in his arms. He missed her very much.

It neared the ten o'clock hour when Captain Nemo returned to the study. He ignored Pelaez and nodded to everyone else. As he took his seat, he asked, "Shall we play?"

The magician studied the Captain and assumed Pelaez hadn't impersonated him. From across the room, the only way he could know for sure, other than asking Valentine, would be to sit so close to his brother he could smell his breath. Without going to that extreme, he would have to be vigilant; Pelaez might suspect they would rebuild the flying machine, and the bastard would be right.

To thwart his curiosity, the automat and Bartholomew had gone as far as placing their notes and correspondence in Nemo's personal safe in his quarters. The magician had added additional security to the safe; mostly as an audible alarm if Pelaez breached it.

"Mr. Soriano, it appears we will be partners tonight." Nemo nodded at him, and Verne shuffled the cards.

"Yes, it does." The vampire gestured at the door leading out of the study. "May I ask something? It has been touched upon and ignored out of politeness, but, now that the Professor has left us, could we discuss who would murder such a lovely woman as Mrs. Kang? I find it unbelievable."

Captain Nemo picked up his cards. "As do I, sir. We only know what Captain Swayne gave us in his telegram. At this point, we may be traveling in the opposite direction where further telegrams could await us. We would miss them."

"I see." Valentine sorted his cards, and his bejeweled rings shone in the lamplight. "This means we may discover nothing until Prague."

"Exactly." Nemo frowned at his cards. "Four clubs."

"You have the bid. On another subject, how many days is it until we know if we are going through the Suez?" Verne asked.

"Probably tomorrow when we stop in Hurghada." Nemo frowned. "There will be newspapers available that list water levels and, of course, the weather conditions." He played a card. "We may be delayed several days if we pass through the Red Sea and find that the conditions have changed."

Pelaez called out from his chair by the bookshelves, "I know I am a pariah in this room, but could someone explain what you are talking about? This ship must be too big to go through that canal."

Everyone gazed at Celwyn, and he obliged. After all, he still felt responsible for his brother, and for whatever the bastard did. When Celwyn finished a recital of how they went through the canal the first time, his brother asked a few questions and fell silent.

Bartholomew sorted his new cards, looked at his bridge partner, and intoned, "Five hearts." Verne tried to grin at him and passed. The big man groaned.

During Celwyn's explanation, Kang returned and sat apart from them, reading. As Valentine shuffled cards, the automat put down his book and stood. For the first time in many days, he did not seem as consumed with grief and guilt. Kang glanced at the others before saying, "We touched on this a few days ago. Could we discuss Wolfgang for a moment? How did he find us?" Celwyn hid a sigh of relief; his friend had started to crawl out of the other end of his tunnel of grief.

As usual, the Professor displayed supreme logic. He faced Pelaez. "Why did you come to us in Singapore?"

"To apologize, of course, and beg for your forgiveness." Pelaez blinked at them in surprise.

Celwyn doubted it. He remembered one of their earlier suppositions that Pelaez sought them because he feared someone and wanted to hide below the waves. This situation would qualify. Between his brother and mourning for Elizabeth, the atmosphere aboard the *Nautilus* remained tense, and the sooner Pelaez could be unceremoniously dumped ashore somewhere, the better. With a quick check of the automat, he caught the slight shake of his head too. "We'll let that go for a minute. What about the first question?"

"I can only speak for myself." His brother executed an elaborate shrug. "I spent a moderate amount of money and time to track you. Initially, I waylaid a messenger as he left your residence in Prague. From the information he carried, I determined that you were still at sea, so to speak, on this ship. It was months later when I figured out you would be in Singapore."

Bartholomew's eyes widened. "You know where we live?"

"But of course." Pelaez grinned at him with a hard eye. "And all about Mr. and Mrs. Swayne, the orphans there, and your household staff." He flipped a hand. "Anyhow, I made my way across the Mediterranean to the ports you most likely would have stopped in. On the docks, I sometimes encountered talkative drunks—anyone bribeable. Then, as I traveled east, I described the three of you and several times received information."

"Just as we thought." Bartholomew shook his head.

"When I couldn't find you after Beirut, I determined that you had gone to the Red Sea and beyond."

Bartholomew said, "Oh, lucky us."

Or my brother could have seen something in the future that directed his actions, the magician thought. He did tend to lie. And for the first time, the magician wondered if Pelaez hid a sinister purpose other than destroying the flying machine. Would that alone account for him traveling around the world after them and conveniently helping them here and there?

Pelaez appeared pleased with himself. "When I reached Singapore, I experienced a setback. No one had seen you there. After another week passed, I caught a glimpse of you—predictably at a pastry café before you disappeared for several weeks." He leaned forward and asked confidentially, "Where did you go?"

Celwyn's spirits dropped. If Pelaez could predict their movements, his father could too. No wonder he'd found them.

"Go to hell!" Bartholomew glared.

As the magician listened to the exchange, he accepted the fact they would have to be disguised any time they left the ship. Dammit. And no more pastry cafés.

Captain Nemo ignored Pelaez and the conversation. In the most pleasant voice that he had used in any room that contained Pelaez, he said, "A profitable hand for you, Jules. I believe it is your deal."

Before Verne finished shuffling the cards, the magician realized they still didn't know anything new since the evening began.

# Chapter 6

As the *Nautilus* turned north into the Gulf of Aden, the day dawned clear and warm, and she surfaced hours later south of Djibouti. Boats containing some of the *Nautilus* crew rowed to shore. Their purpose: to pick up supplies and periodicals.

It lacked an hour until dinner when Granger appeared in the study with a collection of newspapers. Kang left his book behind and joined Bartholomew in dividing them up. The automat wasted no time in consulting the back page of *Nahda* and reading it to them.

"This is dated three days ago. Water levels are above sixty feet between midnight and two in the morning. The moon will be three-quarters by the fourteenth. High tides expected."

The author frowned. "My report is similar but states a lower water level. What about yours?" He asked Bartholomew.

"Let's see … water levels at fifty-five feet. Otherwise, the same as Xiau's."

Celwyn raised a brow at Nemo's lieutenant. "I believe we need 45° of draft … if I remember correctly."

"That is true." Granger grinned at him as they remembered their previous experience in the canal. "The Captain will form an opinion and speak with you later. As you know, the last time we went through became an exciting occasion for all."

"After the canal," Pelaez raised a lazy brow, "it would be less than a day to Alexandria?"

Celwyn heard him and wondered if his brother could be trusted—even a little. Yesterday, he had approached Nemo about using Pelaez to help elevate the ship through the lowest levels of the canal. Nemo had growled, saying he wouldn't ask the man for a favor. Celwyn speculated … if it was Pelaez's idea, then he wouldn't have to ask him. Going through Suez would put Pelaez in Alexandria that much sooner, which he wanted.

"From here, it is less than three days to Suez. Alexandria is about 30 miles further."

Nemo stared at Pelaez.

Off and on since the altercation in Pelaez's room, Celwyn had wondered how Valentine had gotten in there. He didn't question the attack itself, just that it took so long to occur.

At least the vampire didn't hold a grudge about his unceremonious removal from the scene, courtesy of the magician. An informative crumb resulted from the confrontation; Celwyn now knew how his brother fared in a serious hand-to-hand fight, not the obnoxious ones they'd had as children. Pelaez had no fear of Valentine. In Celwyn's opinion, he should have been at least more cautious. The day before they reached Suez, he had another example of how his brother's mind worked and a reminder to beware of him.

They'd finished breakfast and a lively debate buzzed in the study about something scientific, when Bartholomew stopped mid-sentence, yelped, and crawled off the back of the sofa to hide behind the map table.

The others reacted in a similar manner, except for the magician. He not only could see what had happened but knew the source of it.

Valentine had burst into the study holding handfuls of his silver mane and in the next few seconds, they watched the rest of his hair fall to the floor. Completely bald, he cried out and then bellowed, bringing the hallway guard on the run. The vampire stood in front of them in tears.

"Look! Look at me!" the vampire howled. "My *hair!*"

With a withering look, Celwyn told his brother, "Put it back."

The next step would be extreme vampiric violence. "But—"

"Do it—" Celwyn growled. "*Now.*"

After his hair reverted back, perfectly combed and in place, Valentine swiveled to Pelaez. In a blur, he jumped on top of him. Pelaez flung him off again. Blood dripped down his neck.

"Hell—" Celwyn inserted himself between them. This time, he wrapped Pelaez in steel bonds and rolled him into a ball. He remained between them. When Valentine charged forward again, the magician flung him against the wall. "I'll take care of this. He is only here *one more day.*"

He repeated that louder as a mirror appeared inches from the vampire's face. "You look better than before. Go to your cabin—please—if all we've gone through in the last few years means anything to you." Celwyn locked gazes with Valentine until the fire in his eyes faded, and he bowed.

"As you wish. I acquiesce because of my niece, Tara."

After he left the room, Verne and Bartholomew remained as far as they could from Pelaez except for Kang, who stood over him with curiosity, probably wondering what Celwyn would do to him.

The magician squatted down to Pelaez's level.

"I'm going to leave a block around you and reinforce it the rest of the day ... if I must. And it will be a good one. Do you understand?" When his brother didn't move or say anything, Celwyn asked, "Remember how you wanted to be dropped off in Alexandria? And offered to help us through the canal?"

Something important must be in Alexandria, for Pelaez nodded.

"When I'm sure you won't make this mistake again, I'll release you before we reach there."

<hr>

At breakfast the next morning, Pelaez murmured, "From the discussion yesterday, I understood that we prefer to go through the canal, and not go around." He buttered a toast before continuing. "And the description of the problem detailed how it had been an ordeal for my brother to elevate this ship, even while being towed by a much larger vessel."

"That is true." Valentine agreed from his position by the sofa. The vampire had no problem conversing with Pelaez after their altercation and even went as far as smiling at him at times. *Hmmm.* Celwyn shivered and eyed his brother and then the vampire.

Pelaez smirked as they waited for him to speak. He nodded to a crewman to pour coffee.

"Wouldn't it benefit everyone if I assisted my brother, and we continued through to Port Said? You will be rid of me sooner, and I will be on holiday in Alexandria days earlier. It has been too long since I visited their bazaar." When no one said anything, he asked, "Does this meet your approval, Captain?"

Nemo didn't want to, but he grunted and said, "Yes."

While Pelaez took an afternoon "nap," Celwyn and the others met in the turbine room. This time Valentine came with them. The magician doubted they would have very long to talk without Pelaez's intrusion, but they had to try. Nowhere aboard the ship was safe from his eavesdropping.

The magician supplied chairs and placed a wall of silence around them. At his nod, Captain Nemo spoke.

"Mr. Soriano, do you wish to travel to Prague with us?"

"As you know, Miss Redifer had been severely injured." The vampire pursed his lips and didn't hesitate to pour a glass from a bottle that suddenly appeared at his elbow. "It all depends on how much my niece has improved, and I won't know that until we reach Beirut."

"What we find in Spain may be more than we can handle without your help. We just don't know." Kang sounded and looked stronger than the magician expected.

"Spain will be discussed in detail after Pelaez is off my ship," Nemo said. The turbines behind them continued their steady whirring; their mechanical music comforting. Whether Miss Tara McFein would remain in Berlin or accompany them seemed just as uncertain as their upcoming confrontation. Meanwhile, the magician wondered why his brother had not interrupted them yet.

Valentine said, "I suspect it would be hard to explain my presence at your home in Prague." He winked at the magician. "However, I'm sure you can recommend a good hotel."

"Probably." Celwyn sighed, trying not to imagine Mrs. Thomas's reaction to a real vampire sitting next to the figurines in her parlor. It would be memorable. Not to mention the traditional history that existed between vampires and witches; what if Valentine became annoyed and started feasting on the local witches that protected Tellyhouse? Then Celwyn would have the wrath of the coven upon him too.

The magician produced his tea. With his first sip, things seemed better. He thought it satisfying how that phenomenon worked. As the turbines continued whirring in tandem, smooth and dependable, they reminded him of this ship. Nemo remained deep in thought, while Celwyn controlled the urge to silently visit him and find out why. When the magician met the automat's eye, he received a sarcastic nod of approval of his restraint. *Pfft. Was he that easy to predict?* But Celwyn enjoyed what he saw; Xiau was getting back to normal—at least until they reached the sadness that awaited them in Prague.

"Do you think Pelaez will try to find the new flying—" Valentine began.

The magician shook his head.

"We can't even be sure he isn't listening now."

The night before they arrived in Beirut, a jovial atmosphere accompanied their dinner after an appetizer of lamb meatballs with lemon and capers. Nemo judged the wine. At his nod, the crewman poured.

"That was an exciting passage through Port Said last night," Verne said. "Fortunately, your brother helped."

"We're just blessed to be rid of him." Kang asked, "What will Pelaez do in Alexandria?"

Celwyn said, "Annoy the citizens, probably." Earlier, the magician had watched Nemo's mood visibly brighten as the skiff containing Pelaez pushed away the *Nautilus*.

"This sauce is new." Bartholomew turned to the magician. "Do you expect to see your brother again?"

"I don't know," the magician said. "He tried to quiz me about our plans as we approached Alexandria. Of course, I checked his thoughts as to why."

"Of course." Kang chewed and raised a brow at him.

"I only saw what he planned to do in the city, and nothing else—his version of subterfuge, in case I looked, perhaps?" Celwyn wouldn't have been surprised.

"Perhaps." Nemo said, "We will be on guard."

"He knows we will go to Prague, but nothing about Findbar Island, unless he's been extraordinarily lucky."

Celwyn had just sampled a medley of squash laced with turmeric and garlic. It suddenly tasted like paper—it looked like one of the dishes their chef Fatima had made for them at that first, wonderful dinner in Turkey. Weeks later, she had been murdered.

"Have cheer, Jonas." Nemo sounded optimistic; he'd unloaded Pelaez. "He is no longer on the *Nautilus*."

Celwyn held up his glass, thinking they only had educated guesses that his father, not Pelaez, had murdered everyone at the compound in Turkey. "Here, here. May our journey be a swift one." He did not know the proper salute for a voyage of bereavement and revenge.

After their toast, the automat brought up a painful subject. Lit by the fire in his eyes, anger once again smothered his grief.

"I have reviewed all the telegrams from Prague we have recovered so far," Kang said. "There will be many of them everywhere we stop. Patrick grew desperate to reach us. He blanketed every telegraph office between here and Prague." He stabbed a berry and ate it.

Captain Nemo asked, "Do we know anything else from your research?"

"Yes and no. The bare fact is that my," the automat stopped and after a second continued, "that Elizabeth was murdered. Patrick is upset, understandably. He needs us."

"I feel so sorry for everyone who knew her, and for Xiau." Bartholomew put down his fork. "How long will it take us to reach Szczecin, sir? Or should we wire the Conductor to bring our train to Odessa?"

"If all goes well," Nemo studied them pointedly, "and you can refrain from attracting warlocks or worse, we would be in Szczecin in about two and a half weeks. You would arrive in Prague the same day. Odessa would be a few days sooner, but you'd take those days to travel back to Prague afterward. Odessa also means you would miss a visit to Findbar. At the rate we're traveling, I'm not sure if we wouldn't arrive before a telegram would."

"Which means the Conductor couldn't improve on our time because he would still have to get the train ready for a longer trip," Kang speculated.

"And by redirecting him and some of the other staff away from Tellyhouse, we'd leave Patrick with less protection for a longer time," Bartholomew said.

"Which begs the question; what do you wish to do, sir?" Celwyn asked Nemo. "Do you want to await us on Findbar until after the funeral and we have caught the murderer—"

"After he is hanged—" Bartholomew interjected.

The vampire waved a jeweled hand. "No, torn up by yours truly."

Celwyn hoped this wouldn't develop into a contest like it did over the honor of killing Captain Dearing. "After the murderer is caught, do you prefer to pick us up and then continue to Spain?"

"I do not know yet." Nemo frowned.

Celwyn checked the others, seeing a variety of worry, revenge, and, in Verne's case—fear. "Perhaps deciding if you want to finish the flying machine first would help?" He savored a final bite of trifle and silently thanked the Scottish for the invention. "I, for one, am open to whatever everyone decides. My personal preference? Avenging Elizabeth's death first."

"Thank you, Jonas," Kang lowered his brows. "This is worse than Jane Austin's tale of choice."

"Before I make a decision," Nemo pivoted, "Professor, please tell us of anything else you gathered from the telegrams."

The automat lifted his shoulders and let them fall. "I do not know how they killed her, but in the messages we picked up today, Patrick added one thing of interest. He asked if we knew of a man called Gaspard, and he stated Gaspard killed her."

Bartholomew gaped and stared. The magician did as well. The big man spoke first.

"Gaspard was one of Talos's automats on the *Primero*. I remember him because he wanted to shoot me."

"I swept him into the sea with the rest of them." Celwyn cursed. "He must have clung to something when the ship sank. Dammit." Every time the magician thought he'd finished Talos and his automats, they returned.

Kang fought for control while Bartholomew steadied him with a hand on his shoulder. "It appears he survived." The big man asked, "Why kill Elizabeth? How did he find her?"

"It is one of the many questions to be answered in Prague." The vampire shrugged. "I'm not sure if I'm simplifying this too much, but if it is just one automat, perhaps you do not need my assistance until the conflict in Spain?"

"It is possible there are more of them who survived when Dearing's ship sank." Captain Nemo watched a crewman pour coffee and then eyed the magician. "What if Gaspard spotted us when we took you and Bartholomew out of the water? He would have also seen us retrieving Dearing too."

Verne's eyes skittered everywhere except upon Nemo. The fish wiggling its way by the window offered him no help. "It might be good if I went home to see my wife while you are in Spain."

"That telegram from Patrick stated that Gaspard had been looking for me," Kang said.

"Oh my." Bartholomew's eyes widened.

Verne asked, "I wonder why?"

"This is useful information," Nemo said. "It goes to the question of whether or not you require my assistance in Prague."

"I agree." Celwyn wished they weren't at the dinner table so he could walk while he talked. "However, it is also time for you to meet everyone at Tellyhouse formally; in my opinion, we will be partners for many years to come." He smiled a hard smile. "While in Prague we could take turns destroying whoever murdered Elizabeth, and you could participate."

Kang said, "I also agree, sir. It is time for your introduction to everyone at Tellyhouse."

"Count me in." Bartholomew's expression showed his nervousness. "I can't wait to see you two explaining all this to Mrs. Thomas." He reminded Nemo, "She is the housekeeper of Tellyhouse and no one to be toyed with."

"Don't we know it," Celwyn said.

"How is the information about Gaspard useful?" Nemo rubbed his brow. "Because it narrows down the motive for the murder to us. It is specifically connected to the flying machine, or possibly the Professor's work on atomic power. We won't waste time looking for a motive in Prague."

"It could also be revenge for killing Talos." Verne blinked at them.

Chapter 7

Alexandria, Egypt

THE BAZAAR OF ALEXANDRIA HADN'T changed much over the years; to Pelaez, it still smelled like cumin and donkey dung. He kept an eye on the ground as he walked through the crowds and made his way to the west side, where the best kabobs would be.

His stomach grumbled; he must indulge in them today—he wouldn't be here long. With a smile, he remembered how elated Nemo had been only hours ago as Pelaez climbed into the boat that would take him ashore. Pelaez smiled his smile some have said looks like an amused corpse. *We'll meet again very soon, Captain.*

While his stomach continued to grumble, Pelaez negotiated for a lamb kabob and moved under the overhang of the booth next door to eat it and wait.

Just as he finished wiping his fingers, he sensed a presence and smelled danger too. When he swiveled, the garish dress of a vagabond met him, along with intense scrutiny from the eyes of someone much more complex than a simple beggar.

Pelaez greeted him. "Good afternoon."

The beggar clicked his chipped teeth as if they did not fit his mouth. His gaze traveled across the crowd and farther away as he beckoned Pelaez to step into the shadows between the stalls.

"Yes, it is a wonderful afternoon. Do you have my information?"

"But of course. Do you have mine?" Peleaz looked closer ... yes, those were fake teeth fitted over the man's real ones. How cute. He studied everything from the man's fingernails to his toes, looking for a clue to his identity. The odor he'd detected reminded him of a cleaning solution.

"You have such a lack of trust. By the time your brother and his party reach Spain, I'll have a great deal for you, but their immediate goal is revenge for the Professor's wife's death in Prague."

Pelaez suspected he'd put his foot in it. "I already know this. Did you obtain my information or not?"

"Yes. They are building it on an island. I'll reserve the location until we conclude our business. Your turn."

It wouldn't take much effort to throttle this bastard and hang him with the chickens in the booth next door. Pelaez eyed him benignly. "After Prague, they will go to the Castell de Ferro in Spain. That is all I know."

"When?"

"My guess is after they kill whoever murdered Mrs. Kang. Their ship travels about 200 miles a day. That might help you." The occupants of the *Nautilus* had learned not to talk anywhere on the ship about their confounded invention, thinking he would hear them. For other things, they were much less circumspect.

"It does." The beggar watched him with a peculiar form of curiosity as if he wished for tweezers and a specimen bottle.

"The name of the island?" Pelaez felt his patience evaporating. As the beggar's smile widened, something slammed into Pelaez's head, and the lights went out.

Chapter 8

The study of the *Nautilus*

As a thoughtful silence filled the evening, Kang's melancholy returned, and the magician caused a plate of cookies to replace his dessert bowl. When the automat looked up, he met Celwyn's look of empathy with a small nod. Meanwhile, Nemo continued.

"We can't afford to lead anyone to Findbar until this is settled." Nemo paused to let them digest that. "I will go to Prague with you and suggest you send a telegram to request they meet us in Szczecin. The more I think about it, your train is as flamboyant as you are and could be followed to Odessa. Have your conductor take a circuitous route to Szczecin and be sure his crew says nothing to anyone."

Bartholomew said, "The same secrecy for Tellyhouse too, please. Only Annabelle and Patrick need to know until we arrive. That will put Mrs. Thomas in a snit, but it can't be helped."

"Lovely. I expect we will once again be wearing wigs and unfashionable suits to avoid detection." Valentine sighed. "Captain, will you be in disguise when you board the train in Szczecin?"

"Yes. I'm not sure who will accompany me to Prague." Nemo said. "Afterwards, the *Nautilus* will continue to Findbar and wait there."

Kang's sadness gave way to logical determination. "We should collectively compose a circumspect letter to Tellyhouse and a telegram with different information." He turned to Bartholomew. "Don't you and Annabelle have those silly nicknames for each other? We should be able to use them to disguise our plans in case our messages are intercepted or talked about."

"You are suggesting we sign the telegram with a silly name." Verne nodded to himself. "Good idea."

"You should hear the name we use for Jonas too." The big man grinned.

That brought a look of amusement to the vampire's aristocratic face. "This will be interesting. Perhaps, we can treat it like a game of charades."

"Possibly." Kang and the others stood aside for the crew to remove the dining table. "The first telegram will consist of nonsense, perhaps even a reference to a past problem we can link to our current situation. Or we can refer to that play we saw last year, the one full of intrigue and subterfuge—something that will alert Patrick for Annabelle to our purpose."

"What play?" Verne asked.

"*The Pigs in the Attic*," Bartholomew answered. "Jonas slept through most of it, but Annabelle couldn't stop talking about the costumes."

"The first telegram will also tell them we're on our way to Egypt, or similar. Our enemies will not leave Prague until they know exactly where we intend to go."

"I admire your devious mind, Professor," the vampire said.

"I learned it from Jonas." Kang yawned. "Anyhow, the next telegram will seem innocent and in it, Bartholomew will talk about sending them a science project, and describe it in detail. The boys will notice and tell Patrick that they have already completed it, further alerting them."

"It could even mention that an experiment will be sent to general delivery, and to pick it up there—" Celwyn said.

"Excellent." Kang nodded.

Verne said, "Or it would go to that bookstore we love."

"Ezekiel's." Kang sat up straighter, more confident. "The message will tell them to meet us in Szczecin."

"This is all to prevent the interception of our messages by Gaspard," Verne said.

"Yes. We should be the ones choosing when and where you'll meet that man." Nemo stood. "I must leave for the bridge. We have resolved our dilemma, gentlemen."

Chapter 9

Beirut

Two days later, birds flittered through the acacia trees and accompanied the magician and the vampire along the walkway to the Paix Sérénité clinic. Beside them, rosebushes bloomed in every color of pink, and a cloud of delicate moths preceded a nurse as she passed by them on the path.

As they stepped inside, another nurse directed them to Miss Redifer's room, and when they approached the door, Celwyn's heart raced. *Would Tara be here?* He straightened his tie and ran a hand through his hair.

Entering the room, they found Miss Redifer sitting up in bed and her color much better. A few scars marred her neck, but overall, the beautiful vampire appeared near-normal. Her pale blonde hair had been piled on top of her head, and icy blue eyes lit up at the sight of her uncle.

"My dear," Valentine embraced her. "You look so much better!"

Celwyn well remembered the day they rescued her from the pirates. With a smile, he recalled what befell the bastards afterward.

"I am so glad you are here." She spied the magician. "I must thank you, Mr. Celwyn. I owe you my life."

"I am happy to be of service and regret what occurred. Your uncle will tell you some very good news concerning those villains." He couldn't help but ask, "May I inquire about Miss McFein—"

From behind him came a contralto he knew very well.

"I am here."

Celwyn whirled and instantly she was in his arms. He buried his face in her hair and inhaled. "I missed you," he whispered.

Tara McFein, a vampire and witch with golden eyes, had captured his heart. She stood barely over five feet tall, yet fit him perfectly. He wound one of her curls around his finger and inhaled her unique perfume.

Valentine cleared his throat. "I say, we are still here."

Tara disengaged from the magician's arms. "It is wonderful to see you, Uncle." She pecked his cheek. "I am very glad you have returned."

Miss Redifer snorted. "I think you are more pleased by Mr. Celwyn's arrival." She adjusted the ribbons on the bed jacket she wore. "I want to hear everything that happened after you rescued me. I understand I left the pirate ship on the back of a bird?"

Celwyn laughed. "Yes. You handled it much better than Bartholomew does."

"Uncle, can you tell Simone about everything while Jonas and I take a walk in the gardens?"

"But of course."

Tara took Celwyn's hand, and they escaped.

By the time they came back, Tara knew generally of everything that had occurred on the *Nautilus's* journey to the Sulu Islands, Hong Kong, and the horrible encounter in Singapore. Certain parts caused her concern until Celwyn assured her he had recovered.

Their discussion moved on to the situation in Prague, the probable battle in Spain, and other things. Tara asked a few questions, and as they approached Miss Redifer's room again, she asked, "Do I have an invitation to join you on the *Nautilus*?"

The magician said, "Of course. Valentine does, and you are held in high esteem by Captain Nemo." He touched her chin. "You have changed his mind about women on his ship."

"But has he changed his mind about vampires?" she asked as they entered the room.

"If you are referring to the Captain—" Valentine showed his teeth. "Let us just say we respect each other." He arched a brow at the magician. "Did you tell her about Prague and Spain?"

"I did."

Miss Redifer watched them with an amused eye. "You seem to attract danger, Mr. Celwyn."

"Xiau says so too, but he attracts it multiple times over. That is part of an ongoing debate."

"I heard how you rescued Tara in London. How is that fantastic man, Bartholomew?"

Celwyn made a note to himself to repeat that description to the big man himself. "He is well and sends his best wishes. He would like to visit you here before we leave." That brought a smile to the patient's face.

"He should do so this afternoon. Nemo plans to depart early tomorrow." Valentine regarded both of his nieces. "We must confer."

"At least, I have that trunk full of clothes I left on the *Nautilus* months ago." Tara leaned into the magician's side with a sigh of relief.

Chapter 10

AFTER LEAVING VALENTINE BEHIND, and best wishes for Simone's recovery, they alit from a hire cab and passed into the cooler shadows between an olive merchant and the ocean boardwalk. The air over the city spread a veil of intrigue and earthy fragrance, and they strolled along another few blocks until the houses and passing pedestrians became fewer. When they reached the berm above the beach, they stopped.

"I thought it would be a nice change to arrive by boat."

Tara cocked her head at him and scanned the waves below. "I do not see one."

With a bow, he took her hand, and they floated off the dune, over the water, gradually descending until they landed in a small riva, a gondola type of boat. He pointed to the stern end. "Tara" had been painted on it, christening the craft.

"Although traditional and romantic, I would prefer to just enjoy your company, not to row. So, I will propel us another way." As Celwyn spoke, their boat swiveled and headed toward the northern coast. "The *Nautilus* is several miles away."

"Can I assume Valentine's trunk will be delivered to him when Bartholomew visits Simone this afternoon?"

"Yes. It also wouldn't hurt for your uncle and Nemo to have a respite from each other, no matter what he says." Celwyn produced a pair of crystal glasses and a bottle of champagne. As he poured, he asked, "Do you like Schubert?" At her nod, a chorus of strings arrived, the music warm and dream-like.

"Watch your hands, young lady. We are no longer invisible."

"Why?" She giggled.

"So that the crew can spot us and help us aboard."

"We'll see. You look like you need pinching." She smiled.

"Possibly." Then the magician remembered something. "Could you direct Bartholomew to a good flower shop for when he visits Miss Redifer this afternoon? If I made them, they wouldn't last after we left. A jewelry store too, please?"

"Of course. The florist on Amatouri Avenue is well known. Speaking of treats, I brought some nourishment with me, but did my uncle procure any for the trip ahead?"

Celwyn waved at the crewman on the platform of the *Nautilus*. "I'll make sure Bartholomew consults Valentine and they will take care of it." He wondered if Tara imagined which flowers she liked, so he visited her thoughts just to check.

Instead of flowers, he found her concentration upon a man with luxuriant whiskers, a wide forehead, and serious eyes. Tara considered William Butler Yeats a sensitive man as she relived a scene where they sat on a leafy park bench, whispering together and laughing. Celwyn didn't know whether to back out of her thoughts or what to do.

Even worse, she sat beside him on a boat ride designed to show her how romantic he felt toward her. *How stupid of him!* He felt hurt and angry. *Damn.* The magician had assumed Tara shared his affections. Had she developed them for someone else?

Nemo held dinner until Bartholomew returned from his visit ashore. As everyone took their places, the Captain faced Tara.

"It is good to have you with us again, Miss McFein." He waited until the magician pushed in her chair and asked, "Should I assume the absence of your uncle means he will remain in Beirut, and you will be with us for our journey to Prague?"

"Yes, it does." She unfolded her napkin. "Miss Redifer is healing and will be ready to travel soon. Valentine plans to take her to Milan where many of our family reside. He will meet you in Palermo when you are ready for him." She watched Celwyn from under her lashes. "I know little about what will happen in Spain."

The magician pursed his lips and glanced at the Captain. Since they came aboard, Celwyn had studiously avoided invading her thoughts, yet he itched to know more about his rival. Meanwhile, he would demonstrate his regard for her. How could she help but choose a handsome green-eyed devil such as himself?

Nemo told her about Doctor Jurik Lazlo and the paintings. She asked several questions, and then said, "I heard about what happened in Prague. I am so sorry, Professor."

"Thank you. I am extremely angry and worried about everyone at Tellyhouse. Had you heard of this Gaspard?"

"No. When Talos and Dearing imprisoned me, they said nothing about him. I am so sorry."

Celwyn patted her hand. Tonight, she sat so close to him he had trouble concentrating. With a sigh, he realized the idea of Keats saddened him more than he initially thought. She caught his sigh and raised an inquiring brow. He could only offer a limp smile, not an answer.

"Are there questions the rest of us can answer for you?" Nemo asked as the crew delivered platters of appetizers and poured the wine. After Tara declined, Nemo raised a glass and said, "To our journey to Prague and to Miss McFein's return."

After the toast, Tara said, "Thank you, all of you. Jonas gave me a summary, and I would like to know what else occurred in Singapore. I have a feeling that the level of danger had been softened for what I was told. Perhaps to save me from worry."

Nemo arched a brow at Celwyn, and the rest of them snickered at the magician's attempt at subterfuge. "Well, it was a memorable situation. Should I assume Valentine had not written to you about the Sulu islands?"

She shook her head. "Just quick telegrams talking about when he would return to Beirut and sending his wishes to Simone." Suspicion clouded her eyes. "What happened? My uncle said Dearing did not exist anymore. He seemed pleased, but that is all."

The soup bowls had been removed and platters of Seabass and vegetables appeared before them before the Captain answered.

"Miss McFein, what you have not learned yet will take a while and not be pleasant to hear," Nemo said. "If you could wait until after dinner, I'm sure everyone will supply the details. One of them is that Pelaez is featured in the situation, and I do not want to hear his name again while I am enjoying my dinner."

Tara's eyes had widened as far as they could go. "I understand, and will be patient."

Chapter 11

OVER POST-PRANDIAL CIGARS, whiskey, and conversation, Tara listened to their adventures. She also thanked Bartholomew for his bravery and again offered condolences to the Professor. Her sympathy for Celwyn about his father rivaled her reaction to what the slaves and prisoners had endured.

"What befell the slaves was horrible and again for those poor people on the island because it went on for so long." Tears filled her fine eyes. "What happened to them all?" After the others told her, she toured the room, talking as she walked. "So, we have covered everything that occurred before Hong Kong, and the instance of the daemons who were destroyed in front of you."

"Yes," Bartholomew assured her as the clock behind them chimed the hour, a reminder it would soon be time to play cards.

"We should tell her about Thales and his relations," Kang said.

"All right," Celwyn said. It would keep her from asking why he sighed. "Much of this is supposition that fits the facts." He gazed down his nose at Kang. "Please keep the teasing down until I finish."

"Of course he will." Verne laughed.

"I admit, I should have seen all this before, but did not." Celwyn made a point of controlling his temper.

Kang packed his pipe while Verne slipped his notebook into his lap for stealthy note-taking. Celwyn removed the ink from his pen before he spoke.

"As a child, I saw little of my father until he began my magic lessons. Pelaez continued his magic studies also. This occurred long before Father went insane. Throughout it all, we saw his disinterest in us, or in anything. It felt as if he had been ordered to teach us, unwillingly handing down our legacy, as it were."

Kang nodded. "That matches his actions the last hundred years or so after that."

"Probably," Celwyn said. "He had never been fatherly to either of us after my mother died, and then he left England to become the alchemist for King William. Word spread of his activities, and my brother and I became tainted with his reputation."

"You were shunned?" Bartholomew asked.

"Feared and whispered about." The magician shrugged. "Whatever. We finished growing up and went our separate ways. By then, our father had disappeared."

"Pelaez continued to search for him," Kang said.

"Yes. As many of you know, my brother discovered Father living in his own filth in Paris. Later, in a crazed rage, he tried to kill me." Celwyn inhaled until his fear subsided. "I am still afraid of him."

Bartholomew said, "And now things seem to have escalated. He is actively hunting you."

"Yes."

"After our experience with him at the catacombs," Verne speculated, "he apparently spent months tracking us down."

"But we don't know if he found Pelaez or just followed him to Singapore the other day. We only have Pelaez's word for it." The Professor's frown deepened.

As they watched Qing disassemble one of his magical frogs, the magician half-way listened to the voices of the past he usually ignored. The mechanical bird concentrated on pulling off the toes of the frogs.

"During my exploration of Pelaez's thoughts, I decided my brother is innocent of anything connected to our father," Celwyn said. "But he still has many crimes to account for."

"Quite so," Nemo said.

The magician's brows drew together. "I discovered nothing about Father's motives in Pelaez's impish mind. In fact, he seemed just as surprised when Father attacked us that day."

"It makes you wonder." Kang's expression matched Celwyn's.

"Someday I will forget about it, but right now it is most vivid. For those of you who haven't heard," Celwyn nodded at Verne and Tara, "Thales's appearance in Singapore saved us, just as Wolfgang readied to kill us."

Verne furiously tried to make his pen work and slammed it on the table. "But Singapore is thousands of miles from the Verde Islands. How could he—"

"I wondered also," the automat said. "Yet, as a demigod, should we be surprised that he did?"

"No. I'm just thankful he arrived." Bartholomew turned to the magician. "I saw you talking to Thales after your father knocked you out of the sky."

"I would not call him a friendly person, but Thales seemed relieved that I still breathed." Celwyn couldn't control a deep shudder. "And he also gave me another 'present.' It began right after he hovered over me on the beach and told me to get the hell out of there."

"What was it?" Tara asked as Qing flew to the magician and snuggled him.

"Here and there, night or day, I have begun to see strange scenes in my mind." Celwyn hadn't mentioned it until now because he didn't want them to ask why, or listen to guesses as to what it meant. "The scenes feature almost anything, including Thales ... or my father, and many strangers. When I said I consider it a present, I meant it. The pictures are all from the past, sometimes from a thousand years ago, and make no sense at all. When they make sense, I'll inform you."

"Do you hear anything with them? Accents? It could help identify them." Tara mused.

After Celwyn shook his head, Kang examined him like a new specimen. "But that is not all, Jonas."

"Why would Thales do this?" Verne asked.

"Remember how he pressured my uncle to assist you at the catacombs?" Tara asked. "At the time ... I wondered why. And—" Her eyes grew wide.

Celwyn brushed a curl off her forehead. "Exactly. He told us to find Wolfgang and pass along a simple message; 'go see Thales.' Why would a demi-god have an expectation that a violent-crazed madman would obey the summons? It took me until the other day when I lay at my father's mercy and ... behold! Thales appeared in a place so far from his lair. That is when I knew, even though I wanted to deny it. I think the reason Thales appeared in the catacombs was that he couldn't wait for Wolfgang to go to him."

"He told you that?" Nemo asked.

"No, the other day he just looked at me intently, and told me to get out of there."

"Seemed like a great idea at the time," Kang drawled.

"Thales is Wolfgang's father," Tara said with a measure of distaste and fear. She regarded Celwyn. "That makes him your grandfather." Qing left the magician to waddle over to her and sit at her feet.

"I'm afraid so."

"That *is* it." Kang rubbed his chin. "Wolfgang thinks Thales is old and may skip him when it is time to bestow his knowledge and talents on his successor." By now, Bartholomew studied the magician as aghast as if the magician had frogs crawling out of his nose. Celwyn stared at the automat and cringed when Kang added, "And give them to you."

Tara still held the magician's hand. "I agree with these conclusions."

"There is an ironic side to this." Bartholomew barked a gallows laugh. "These suppositions mean Pelaez is expendable."

That brought a gaggle of chuckles. Kang sobered. "Probably. But even without Thales's type of inheritance, it makes sense as the only reason your father keeps trying to kill you: jealousy and anger."

"We just don't know why Grandpa is ignoring Wolfgang and concentrating on you," Bartholomew said. "Or when he plans to give something else to you. It must be soon to account for your father's tenacity."

Celwyn sighed. Qing walked across the top of the sofa and hopped onto the magician's shoulder. He squawked his opinion in Celwyn's ear. "What?" The magician asked him as the bird scraped his beak across his chin.

"Things are never dull with you gentlemen." Nemo merely repeated his oft-recurring statement.

Tara said, "I like that, and perhaps we could add, 'and always dangerous too.'"

"I think I'll retire for the evening," the magician announced and pecked Tara's cheek. "Good night, all." Normally he would have said good night in a private and intimate way, but all he could think about was that damned Keats.

Celwyn buttoned his collar to keep Qing inside and headed into the corridor. He'd placed everything from his pockets on his table when he heard a soft knock at the door. There could only be one person who knocked like that. He felt his heart seize, knowing a difficult conversation would ensue, not romance.

When he led her inside, Tara turned into his arms and embraced him.

"What is wrong?" She whispered it into his chest and then reared back. "Qing tried to peck my nose."

"Sorry." The magician undid his collar and the mechanical bird swiveled between them, not making a move to get out of the way. "Here." When a green snake, as long as a finger, dropped onto his trunk, Qing chased it.

"What is wrong?" Tara repeated.

"I have a question. Do you still work for that Essex Club in London?" She hadn't already been interesting enough as a vampire and witch, she also spied for various royal houses and others. The Essex Club, comprised of the finest men of letters in Victorian England, had asked a favor of her last year. That Keats was one of the members.

"No." She tilted her head back to study him but made no move to disengage from his arms.

Celwyn recognized that by not volunteering more, she waited for him to make a move. While he thought of what to say, she smoothed the skin around his brow and kissed it.

How could he ask her something he had no right to know about?

"I've never seen you at a loss for words. It must be serious."

Would she be angrier if she knew he'd visited her thoughts, or less so if it was a misunderstanding?

Tara disengaged from him and headed toward the door.

"Let me know when you're ready to talk about it."

When her hand touched the door, he spoke.

"Are you ... are you involved with that Keats character?"

Tara whipped around, her eyes blazing. "Excuse me?"

"I asked—"

She opened the door and looked back. "Why do you ask? Or should I say, how did you know to ask?"

The door slammed behind her.

Chapter 12

Prague

BEASTIE, THE RUSSIAN WOLFHOUND who thought of the world as a toy, bounded down the driveway of Tellyhouse with Otto in pursuit. Edward pulled on the reins of the carriage and swerved out of his way. From experience, he knew the dog would not stop—even though the team of horses could have trampled him.

"Beastie!" Patrick yelled out the window of the carriage.

The hound loped up to the carriage, put his paws on the window, and licked his face.

Otto arrived out of breath, tugged on the dog's collar, and they ran the other way toward the back of the estate. As Patrick climbed down, Edward unloaded the packages they had acquired.

In his hand, Patrick held their mail and telegrams from the adventurers. Every day, either the Conductor or Patrick went with Edward to retrieve their messages. They had done so for weeks since a messenger had been hit over the head and left in the bushes down the street. At least Gaspard had not killed him.

How did he know Gaspard had done the deed? One of Francesca's witches described him and reported the attack. Afterward, she relieved the assailant of what he had stolen before returning it to Tellyhouse. Patrick suspected the witch had also done something to the thief, but did not want to know what.

During the drive home, Patrick verified the age and originating city of today's telegrams, noting they did not come from the Professor or the others. Damn. When he stepped inside the front door of Tellyhouse, Edward headed out again to take the carriage to the stables; dusk came early these days. Soon, it would be Christmas and a somber affair in a house of mourning.

He walked down the hall and into the parlor, detecting the scent of a roast and perhaps a pie for dessert. Mrs. Thomas stood in the middle of the room in full voice and was not pleased. At over six feet tall and built like a coal miner, her sweet face deceived those who did not respect her wishes. The crusty and ancient footman, Sully, measuring at least a foot shorter, worshiped her—when she allowed him to.

"The last two deliveries of coal have been dismal. We must change suppliers." She consulted her clipboard. "I also need to hire another scullery maid. Libby sent word this morning she had found another position." Mrs. Thomas directed an annoyed glance outside. "No wonder. With guards and witches everywhere. Blasphemous."

Annabelle heard Patrick approaching the parlor and struggled to her feet. As of mid-November, she had reached the three-quarters point through her pregnancy. Today's dress of cornflower blue camouflaged her condition and emphasized her beauty. Her eyes twinkled—indicating she did not mind the housekeeper's list of complaints.

"I missed you, my dear," Patrick embraced her and turned to Mrs. Thomas. "Good evening. I'm sure you agree that the witches' spells are valuable in protecting this house and our staff."

"I do." Her gruff voice rattled the windows. "I just don't like it, sir." She regarded him. "I see you have the mail. Do you have any news?"

Patrick maintained his calm and easy manner, but her question caused him to relive their tragedy. Again, he clearly saw Mrs. Elizabeth Kang's body as it lay upon the cobblestones outside the front door. After sending dozens of telegrams, they still didn't know if her husband knew about it.

Chapter 13

The Mediterranean Sea, near Paphos

A S THE EVENING BRIDGE GAME ON the *Nautilus* progressed, his annoyance at the author replaced Bartholomew's nervousness about Wolfgang; Verne had decided to drink a second bottle of Bordeaux and his bidding went downhill concurrently.

Tara handed Celwyn another cup of tea and received a kiss for her trouble. Things had been tense since the other night, but they still spoke.

He raised his eyes to Kang, meeting his stare and concentrated expression.

"Is everything all right?"

The automat blinked several times. "Just that I am angry still."

Captain Nemo threw a card on the table and Bartholomew scooped up the trick before making a comment. "I am more concerned about your father finding us again and finishing the attack."

"We need to confirm why he attacked." Professor Kang frowned. "There is one place we could expect to find an answer."

It took the magician a second to understand, and when he did, he shook his head. "No."

Tara looked a question at him. Over the top of her head, he saw Bartholomew's confusion.

"We never found out why Thales wanted an audience with your father."

"We've been rather busy, Jules," the magician reminded him.

Bartholomew gathered the cards closer to be shuffled. "Purely from a tactical point of view, we should consider that as long as your father is intent on killing you, he will pursue us. We don't know when he'll strike and some of us could also be hurt. Optimally, we should avoid that."

"I certainly agree," Nemo said.

"Wolfgang would eventually discover Findbar and our new prototype as he searched for you. Just because he is insane..." The automat checked his new cards and directed a disappointed look at the big man before addressing Celwyn. "Just because he is insane, it does not mean that your father is without guile. He is a danger we cannot ignore."

The clock behind them chimed loudly, and the magician managed a wry smile. "That means you and Bartholomew can't complain when I disguise you before we go ashore. Correct?"

Bartholomew exclaimed, "Aw... Jonas—"

"Pfft." The automat glared at his cards. "Five hearts. All right."

"As soon as we are done in Prague, I recommend that we go back to Thales's lair and discover what he knows. We don't want Wolfgang showing up at a crucial point in our efforts in Spain." As Nemo spoke, he did not sound happy at the prospect.

Celwyn glanced at Tara, who would soon become quite annoyed. He privately enjoyed the fire in her eyes and small bursts of annoyance. In the next second, he would know if it would be a conflagration.

"Thales's island is not too far from our destination in Spain, true?" Tara asked.

"Yes," Captain Nemo said. "And there is a certain risk in going there, but it is necessary." As soon as he spoke, a cloud of melancholy descended over him. With a ghost of a smile, he told the magician, "Perhaps Thales will bestow even more of his gifts upon you."

"I still dream about those catacombs." Bartholomew agreed despite his uncertainty. "That was quite an adventure."

Celwyn realized something unexpected had just occurred; for the first time, Nemo had used humor to tease him. The magician celebrated, showering the study with a storm of tiny stars and a lively Baroque melody.

Nemo addressed Tara, "Miss McFein alone does not seem to cause us as much concern as you gentlemen do."

Yes, she does. Celwyn worried about her all the time. He gazed at Tara, remembering their encounter with Talos and Dearing in the Tower of London and how it all turned out. If he mentioned her involvement with the Essex Club from a few months ago, and the intrigue around it, Nemo would revise his perception of her innocence when it came to unwanted danger. If the magician mentioned it now, she may never speak with him again.

Qing had been watching from his perch in front of a bust of Shakespeare and left the bookcase to screech at them on his way to the game table. When he landed on Bartholomew's shoulder, the big man tried to shoo him off. Qing squawked in Bartholomew's ear and flapped his way to the bar. The game continued as the bird took a step toward the crystal decanters.

Verne said, "The Captain doesn't like that."

Qing scraped his beak across a decanter and fluttered his way over to Celwyn.

While pretending not to hear the scratching of crystal, Nemo said, "We have had enough for tonight. Tomorrow we will arrive at Spelman Island where once again you may hunt game while the ship performs her maintenance."

"There will be eggs!" Verne rubbed his hands together.

Kang said, "I'm still curious about Thales."

"His appearance in Singapore may mean nothing," Celwyn told him.

"Or it means everything." Bartholomew nodded.

The automat's voice became serious. "It is time I tell you of something that I have deduced. Haven't you wondered about Thales's interest in Jonas and his dislike of Pelaez? Neither of them had met him before. And isn't his need to keep track of Wolfgang suggestive?"

"Yes, I wondered." Nemo narrowed his eyes at Celwyn. "And with the latest revelations, I believe in the same deduction." He saw the automat nod and continued. "In my opinion, *you* are part of something Thales plans to do." His stare at Celwyn intensified as if he peeled away his scalp to inspect his mind. "Perhaps directly related. Why else would someone who has been so disconnected from you suddenly be so intent on contacting you? Why now?"

A little less than five days after leaving Beirut, the *Nautilus* cruised into the waters off Palermo. They had made good time, averaging 300 miles a day.

Through the top few inches of the aquatic window, they viewed the last of a spectacular sunset that painted the ship in gold and pink. Below it, the sea had already turned a deep midnight blue. In the distance, the lights of the city twinkled as the submarine sank below the waves and motored toward the northern coast.

After dinner, Tara brought one of the books on the Frumentarii (notable Roman spies) over from the bookshelves and settled beside the automat, who perused two of his own books. Kang devoted the hour after dinner to pleasure-reading. His scientific journals occupied him in the dead of night while everyone else slept. Tonight, he held *The Princess and the Goblin* which he picked up in Singapore, along with an annotated copy of Dumas's *Three Musketeers*.

The automat peered at Tara's selection and said, "Greene's illustrations are exceptional. He incorporates the nuances of the Roman cultural period rather well."

"I agree," she said. "And I have always wondered if I would have an opportunity to read this. Doriori describes Nero's spies and their stories in intricate detail."

"A busy dictator, certainly," Verne said from his position at the chess table. Qing waited inches away, his diamond gaze on the author's shiny pen glinting in the lamplight. Nemo walked into the study, beckoning Bartholomew to join him at the game table.

"I thought that we could forgo bridge this evening." As Nemo spoke, the others couldn't help a relieved glance at Verne, the player most likely to make his bridge partners twitch. "Instead, we should discuss a few things."

"Certainly, sir." Celwyn caused a tray of refreshments to circle the room, along with wine for Tara. It felt so good to sit next to her tonight, even a week after she rejoined the ship.

When everyone had served themselves, Nemo began.

"Most of you know that when we stopped in Beirut, we heard encouraging news from the monks concerning the slaves. Before we reach the North Sea, we can also expect messages about the hostages from the Sulu Islands."

"Yes, we did. The news mentioned Andros Town in the Bahamas." Bartholomew asked, "What kind of life the slaves will have when they arrive there?"

"That is the good part; the slaves will receive grants of land for their own farms, and money to start them. Most likely, they will enjoy a full and busy life." Nemo lit a cigar and inhaled in satisfaction.

"Excellent news," Celwyn said. The discussion went on with predictions of what awaited the slaves until the big man slapped the table and changed the subject.

"Over a month ago, Patrick reported everyone at Tellyhouse was in danger. It would be nice to know that has changed. It is bad enough what happened—" Bartholomew stopped and gazed at Kang.

"Patrick is strong, organized, and purposeful," Celwyn said. "He would have made sure of their safety after the shock of the attack."

"I hope so." Captain Nemo blew a smoke ring and then ground out his cigar. "It is still possible my inquiries about this Gaspard will bear fruit."

"Do you have an idea of when we'll arrive in Prague?" Tara asked.

"If all goes well, and we do not attract attention from your father," Nemo nodded at Celwyn, "or entities who are after the flying machine, then we will reach there a dozen or so days from now, just before Christmas."

The magician sent the big man an innocent look. "I nominate Bartholomew to write to Annabelle and inform her there will be several guests and suggest she is the one to tell Mrs. Thomas when it is time to do so."

It didn't take long for Bartholomew to figure out Mrs. Thomas's reaction. But they saw a rainbow of sorts—the automat smiled.

The magician yawned. He wasn't bored, but not entertained either... Something to liven their evening would be nice. He concentrated on Wye, and between the sofas, the green vapor announcing him took shape above the table.

With a yelp under his breath, Bartholomew made ready to run, and Celwyn held his arm. The wyvern's appearance surprised the others just as much, but their fascination with him overrode their fear. Nemo even ventured closer to the table as Wye solidified. His scales glimmered in the low light, and his fat body rolled over the sides of the table. When the wyvern's tail slid to the floor, he swished it, causing Verne to lift his feet high.

"Good evening." Celwyn tilted his head, noting Wye's eyes had a rather mischievous glint tonight.

"What have you been teaching him?" Kang asked.

"Mostly to improve his arrival speed, and to listen when I say it is time to leave. He came close to being eaten by Father the other day."

Qing squawked and swooped across the room to the wyvern. They'd become fast friends.

"Valentine mentioned wyverns are sometimes deadly and may turn on their owners." Bartholomew inched his way off the sofa.

"I heard that too. But Wye just seems devoted at this point. I want him to learn to defend you too."

Celwyn noticed Bartholomew stopped his retreat. "Would you like to get to know him?"

"Not right now." The big man settled for watching their visitor.

"I will." Tara put out a hand within biting range—and Wye had a full set of teeth that Valentine envied. "Do you think he could be jealous of me since we … are close?"

"The opposite. He seems happy." Celwyn put an arm around her shoulders while watching the wyvern. No change, except Wye continued to study everyone in between his adoring glances at the magician.

Professor Kang stood and quietly circled the table to approach Wye from the front. The creature's eyes rotated, following him, and then he showed his teeth. The automat didn't back down and came closer until he stood only inches away, nose to nose. For the first time, Celwyn heard a noise of contentment from Wye—something like a purr if a wyvern could purr. Kang murmured to him and patted his head.

"Nicely done," the magician commented as the automat returned to his seat. "I've been talking to him when Qing isn't in the way and making progress." The bird heard him and went back to chewing on the wyvern's scales.

"At least your pets are entertained." Nemo listened to the gongs and glanced at the wall clock. "You should know that I've made a change in our plans. Initially, I will remain with this ship, and Jules and Lieutenant Granger will go with you to Prague." Nemo eyed the author. "For security purposes, my lieutenant would stay there along with Miss McFein until we are sure of the situation. We do not know how many of Talos's men survived, or if they are in Prague." He regarded the room with the kind of intensity Celwyn felt relieved to see; Nemo's concern meant he considered there could be dozens more automats. "At the same time, I must verify that Findbar and our endeavors are secure."

"I agree. Tellyhouse is huge and we need to make things safe there," Celwyn said. "The Conductor and our footman, Edward, are good men." He stroked Qing's shiny feathered head. "We will prevail." His voice turned colder than the North Sea as the bottles on the bar rattled and shook. "Whoever killed Elizabeth will pay." Until now, Celwyn had hidden his anger to keep from further upsetting Xiau, but the time for their revenge had come.

Wye's tail switched violently from side to side, clearing away everyone's feet.

"He still reacts to your moods, Jonas," Bartholomew said.

The automat frowned. "And he wants to help with whatever upset you." Kang raised a brow at the magician. "How do you do that? First, Qing is not happy unless you're here, and now you've spoiled the wyvern too."

Bartholomew laughed as Celwyn shrugged again and addressed Wye. "Thank you, but we're fine."

"Like I said," Nemo drained his glass, "Nothing is ever dull with you."

As peace again reigned, the quaint grinding noise of Qing chewing on Wye's scales returned. The conversation resumed.

"We still do not know the motive for the murder." Bartholomew sighed.

"But soon you will." Nemo paced to the chess table and back again. "I promised to tell you about Doctor Lazlo. You have been more than patient. When we arrive at his stronghold, it will be imperative that you are all prepared." He swallowed his emotions until he could talk again. "My wife, his sister—" Nemo sat down again and used a handkerchief to wipe his brow.

"Sir, if this is—" Bartholomew began.

Nemo waved it away. "Thank you. It is beyond what I can endure, but to guarantee our success, you must know." He faced Tara. "Miss McFein, you have not heard any of this. Your uncle spared you from it." He proceeded to summarize all the Lazlo information they knew.

After listening to Nemo, Tara's expression turned inward, and she kept resolute eyes upon them. "Whatever happens, I am with you." She faced Kang. "What occurred with Dearing … that was what made the connection for you?"

Nemo excused himself and brought in the three pictures. In a few words, he explained the background.

"All this time," Bartholomew said, "It sounds like Dearing didn't know what he had, other than his thievery of the paintings."

"Yes," Nemo agreed, "however, if we hadn't retrieved the pictures, Lazlo would have used another way to get my attention." When he saw Verne writing furiously, he laid a hand across his notebook. "Not a word, Jules. Nothing, until I say so."

The author licked his lips. "Of course." But his glance at Celwyn proved that up until this moment, it had not been so. The magician decided a reminder was in order; he told Wye to leave them.

With a low snarl, the tiger Verne had last seen terrorizing Prince Leo on their train joined them, padding toward Verne at the chess table. The animal's eyes glowed a beautiful green, and the feral smell of its breath hung in the air as it growled and lay down at the author's feet.

Verne tried to stand up but couldn't. Like Nemo, the tiger laid a paw on top of his notebook, and this time shredded the page. When he flung the pieces at their feet, Verne squealed.

"Remember, Jules, nothing." Celwyn intoned as the tiger faded away. In its place, a playful kitten bumped against the author's ankle and rolled over his shoe.

"Yes! I understand."

Kang yawned. "Subtle, Jonas. At least you didn't dangle him over a waterfall this time."

"It would be much easier if you stopped gossiping," the magician told Verne.

Nemo had watched the display with interest. "It is likely the occupants of Tellyhouse are still in danger. No reporter or editor can be trusted." He eyed the author. "Why do you wish to go to Prague? You could wait for everyone at Findbar instead."

"I want to visit the library there, also the royal museum and castle again, for my new book."

Tara, like Bartholomew, couldn't tolerate discord between friends. She made a request of the room. "Describe Tellyhouse and its inhabitants, please?"

Bartholomew complied. "It is a large property with beautiful gardens, a gazebo, and stables." He rubbed his chin. "I remember the Conductor had planted a vegetable garden when we left Prague last year. Both his helpers from the train work on the grounds of Tellyhouse in between train trips." With a big grin, he said, "There is a new addition to the house that sleeps in the stables with the horses."

"Beastie." A ghost of a smile crossed Kang's somber face. "He is a Russian wolfhound, quite big, and the boys are enamored of him."

"That would be Otto and Zander," Tara said. "I know some of their background and that they are good students."

"I've heard that, too," Nemo said.

After climbing up his leg, the kitten tried to make friends with Verne by bumping his chin and doing its best to be adorable. At first, Verne tried to ignore it but soon rubbed its ears. The magician controlled the urge to have it whisper to him.

"Last year you found Otto on your way to Singapore?" Tara kept the distraction going.

"Yes, we traveled there to retrieve my wife." Kang managed his response without his emotions interrupting. "Otto lived on the streets, and we discovered him under attack by a group of ruffians. Jonas chased them off, in a most colorful manner." He sobered. "Those days seem so uncomplicated now."

"Yes, it does, my friend," Celwyn said.

"I'm sorry I missed the wedding last year," Tara said. "I could have met everyone then."

Nemo said, "Someday soon we can arrange a limited tour of this ship for them—if Jonas erases their memories of it afterward."

"That will be wonderful." The magician grinned. "So, when we arrive in Prague, we will add a bed in the conservatory for Granger. And I'll refrain from pounding on the pianoforte while he is sleeping."

"He may not mind." Nemo shrugged, but his lips twitched, showing he knew better.

"Also," the magician looked at Tara, "Annabelle has a parlor upstairs that is beautiful and will easily accommodate a bed there." He studied the automat. "Unless you would prefer to sleep downstairs because of Elizabeth's absence?" Even though he had expressed the thought awkwardly, he gentled his voice.

Kang blinked rapidly. "I will think about it."

Bartholomew changed the subject. "When I write to them, I'll ask Annabelle to explain the guests to Mrs. Thomas." He tried to appear innocent. "I wonder what she will do..."

"I do too." Celwyn barked a laugh. "Blame it on me?" He sat up. "I know what would help... do we still have the phonograph player in the parlor?"

"Yes." The automat nodded.

"Good. At the Hague, the Mauritshuis Museum has a wonderful gift shop. I will find her a peace offering there." He told Nemo, "Good news for Granger, sir; our chef Ricardo is supremely talented. Your Lieutenant will be pleased."

Tara stood and took the magician's hand. "Please excuse us, everyone."

When they entered the corridor, Tara turned right toward her cabin. She opened the door and motioned him inside. "Sit, please."

After he did so, she moved in front of him, putting them on an eye-to-eye level.

"I've had enough of sad looks, half sentences, and you being evasive. *What* is going on?"

Celwyn couldn't have gotten away, especially with her hands on both sides of his whiskers and tugging on them. She also wouldn't let him break eye contact. Seconds ticked by, and he saw her jaw tighten. Then her foot started to tap, tap, tap.

"All right." He cleared his throat. Would she be angrier because he invaded her thoughts, or about what he saw that he had no right to be jealous of?

"Any time, my dear." She kissed his nose.

"Let's start with this. Do you have feelings for me?"

"Of course I do, silly."

"Only me?"

She tilted her head to the side. "Now we're getting warmer. I reserve my answer until you tell me why you are suddenly asking."

He stroked her hair. "Because I'm wondering if you have feelings for Mr. Keats." He saw the spark of anger entering her fine eyes and rushed on. "Because

I, err, visited … your thoughts while in a romantic mood, and … you were thinking about him." When she tried to pull away, he held onto her hand. "Please?"

At that one word, her anger drained away. "I am not romantically interested in Mr. Keats. Just you." She slipped away and held open her door. "But if you don't leave right now, I'll show you what I think of you sneaking into my thoughts. Out!"

Celwyn made it to the door, gave her a thorough and happy kiss, and started out.

"You are *so* frustrating!" Before the door slammed behind him, he heard her say, "And you have my heart, you irritating man."

Chapter 14

E LEVEN DAYS LATER, THE *NAUTILUS* cruised into the North Sea.

The remainder of their journey had been uneventful and successful. During their stop at the Hague, Captain Nemo sent Granger into town to return all the recovered paintings to the museum in Rotterdam. The magician went with him and purchased the choral recordings for Mrs. Thomas. Everything would be well at Tellyhouse. Maybe.

The submarine gradually ascended until she sat topside about eight miles northeast of the city of Szczecin. Grayish water sloshed against the aquatic window under a heavy bank of clouds, and rain fell in a steady stream as they donned slickers and climbed the spiral stairs.

"Qing is going with us?" Bartholomew asked as he stepped onto the platform.

"Yes." Celwyn followed him with the others close behind.

The bird greeted the big man as loud as he could.

"Ha. That will still not endear you to Mrs. Thomas."

Celwyn patted the bird's head. "Probably not."

They carried one bag each, and none of them contained clothes. With all the comings and goings, they had enough things at Tellyhouse—however, scientific books couldn't be left behind, nor the objects they picked up during their travels. Of course, they brought presents for the inhabitants of Tellyhouse. The magician had made a point of obtaining saffron and Spanish paprika for Ricardo and those Tunisian cigarettes he loved. For Edward, Jackson, Sully, and the Conductor, he again brought pouches of extraordinary tobacco from a little shop near Ceylon. When they smoked it, he wondered if it contained something other than tobacco, and would smile benignly as they burbled their thanks.

The activity increased. While the crew rolled out the floating pier, the magician counted the transport boats that had been made ready.

"One boat alone is dedicated for Xiau's books," Celwyn told Bartholomew.

"Pfft." Kang regarded him. "The teasing helps, Jonas. It is good to be here. Where is Miss McFein?"

"Deciding what to take with her."

Celwyn scanned the shore and Bartholomew joined him, passing over a second spyglass as he asked, "We don't want any company, do we?" In front of them, the beach appeared hospitable and the incline toward the trees gradual. A minute later,

Captain Nemo climbed through the hatch, followed by his lieutenant dressed in nondescript civilian clothes. Granger's excitement appeared evident as he too, scanned the shore.

The platform couldn't hold many other people, so Bartholomew swung down to the floating pier and helped the automat onto it.

"We'll remain in this area while you investigate the situation in Prague," Nemo said. "Eventually, we will head over to Findbar."

"That makes me wish to see the flying machine." Bartholomew sighed.

"Same here," Kang said.

Celwyn yawned. "I wonder if our ghost on Findbar misses me? You remember Mrs. Spencer."

"Don't remind us, Jonas!" Sweat beaded on Bartholomew's brow.

"I have never been so afraid!" Verne cried.

Tara heard them as Nemo handed her out of the hatch and onto the platform. She turned an inquisitive gaze upon the magician until he explained.

"We're not sure why, but Mrs. Spencer haunts the mansion on Findbar, and she has a fondness for broad swords."

"Like I do at times."

Celwyn tried to determine if she meant it, and gave up.

As the crew loaded the boats, the rain increased, and the magician added awnings to them. The wind stole the automat's hat and carried it out over the waves until Celwyn brought it back and continued checking the shore.

Although not probable, Pelaez could be here looking for them. Leaving him in Alexandria might be part of his plans; his brother would assume Xiau would come home to Prague to grieve and avenge his wife's murder and have a nefarious plan.

Right now, Celwyn didn't care. Instead, he speculated upon what Ricardo would make for their lunch.

It neared noon by the time they reached the Szczecin train yard to wait beside the empty berth the *Elizabeth* used. The rain had stopped, yet the clouds still hung low over the city.

As they talked and gazed down the rails, Celwyn did not mention his hunch about Pelaez, which caused Tara and King to take turns staring at him to guess what worried him. The magician knew it could be just his imagination, not a disturbing fact. While he thought, Bartholomew set off down the tracks to where they took a sharp eastward angle.

The magician smiled at Tara. "Excuse me for a moment, please." As she raised a beautiful brow, Celwyn stepped behind Kang and emerged as a sleek falcon, soaring high. When he went by Bartholomew, he called down, "Au revoir," and flew on.

Puffs of steam decorated the air above the city. Celwyn drew closer to it and congratulated himself; he had indeed found the *Elizabeth* chugging her way toward the coast. He circled the train and descended until he flew parallel to the dining car windows.

Otto sat at the pianoforte, and Patrick and Annabelle stood by the sofa gazing through the glass. The magician stared. *Oh my!* A most joyous occasion awaited them.

Celwyn hovered against the wind until Patrick spotted him and then sent him a silent message. "See you shortly." Patrick's mouth opened in surprise as the magician ascended again and swerved toward the train terminal. When Celwyn landed on Bartholomew's shoulder, the big man jumped.

Granger said, "Welcome back, sir. Did you see the train?"

"Droll as ever, Jonas." The automat rolled his eyes.

As himself once again, Celwyn bowed. "But of course. They are a few miles away; it won't be long now." He faced the big man. "You wrote to them that there would be guests?"

"Yes." Bartholomew straightened his cuffs. "There should be no surprises."

"I think they have one for us."

Before anyone could question the magician more thoroughly, clouds of steam appeared far down the tracks and the ground started to vibrate. Celwyn enjoyed teasing the automat to no end, but news such as this should come from Annabelle and Patrick, especially if Patrick told Annabelle of seeing a green-eyed falcon at the window. He glanced at Tara, enjoying her innate goodness. That did not describe her as well as she deserved, but in the next few minutes he hoped that the others, especially Annabelle, saw in Tara what he did.

As the train came into sight, Celwyn took her hand and he and Bartholomew wordlessly joined Kang, standing on each side of him. They hadn't planned the gesture, but it seemed like a fitting thing to do.

"We are here, Xiau."

Resolute misery filled the automat's eyes. He nodded, thinking of his wife.

Bartholomew said, "We always will be."

The *Elizabeth,* named after the real Elizabeth, had been derelict when Celwyn discovered her in India years ago. He had also acquired the services of an old reprobate, Sully, now the footmen at Tellyhouse. That day, he permanently refurbished the train using magic and enhanced the engines until she became the majestic machine that coasted to a stop in front of them amid billows of steam and screeching brakes. The wheels had barely finished turning before Otto and Zander came flying out the door and running to them.

Zander made a beeline for Xiau and Bartholomew while Otto skidded to a stop in front of Celwyn, tears filling his eyes. The magician hugged him, and soon Zander replaced Otto when the boys switched places. Meanwhile, with more care than usual, Patrick led Annabelle down the stairs.

Celwyn held Tara's hand and waited. Otto took his other hand and finally smiled. Just as the magician spotted Zander's black eye and wondered if he had been in a fight, the parents-to-be arrived.

"Oh, my!" Bartholomew exclaimed and looked at Kang to see if he saw the wonderful news too.

"Congratulations—" Kang bowed to them; the automat's despair momentarily forgotten. "When is the joyous event?"

Annabelle gazed at Granger and then Tara while Patrick answered, "Just after Christmas. It is so good you are here."

Bartholomew performed the introductions and received a variety of responses while the boys studied Granger with open curiosity. Nemo's man winked at them. Patrick and Granger exchanged a relaxed and military type of acknowledgment. So far, so good, the magician thought.

Annabelle had watched the ceremony with a noncommittal expression. When she fully faced Tara, everyone held their breath, knowing Annabelle's hatred of what the vampires had done to Telly. Tara's hand trembled in Celwyn's.

"Pleased to meet you, Mrs. Swayne," Tara said. Seconds went by, and Bartholomew appeared ready to intervene when Annabelle spoke.

"Well, it's about damn time we got to meet you. We're pleased to have you here." She sent a teasing glance at the magician. "Call me Annabelle and we will get along just fine." Annabelle hooked an arm through Tara's and led her toward the train. "I'll call you Tara ... if that is all right."

"Of course. I am also glad we're here."

"Bartholomew wrote that you prefer red wine, and we have some inside." She stopped and turned. "What are all of you waiting for? I'm not going to have the baby in the train yard."

"Oh, thank God," the magician whispered to Kang.

He managed, "As usual, your luck holds." Xiau elbowed him and lowered his voice. "Did you see Zander's eye?"

The boys still talked with Bartholomew and Granger. When Otto handed Granger his tablet, Nemo's lieutenant held it up. "You are asking if we are friends of your uncle and the Professor and Bartholomew. Yes, we are. And very happy to meet you." He ruffled the boy's hair.

Granger asked Celwyn in an undertone, "How long has he been mute?"

After Bartholomew scooped both boys up, at the same time, and headed toward the train, Celwyn said, "His early years are something he won't or can't talk about. We think he lost his parents somewhere in the Rhineland, violently. That could be the event that caused it."

"I see. You know, we haven't discussed what to tell them of the *Nautilus*." They fell in line behind Kang and Verne to follow Bartholomew inside.

"We need to do so." The magician waited for Granger to proceed him up the stairs. "Annabelle and Patrick will have opinions on the subject in addition to your concerns." As they entered, Celwyn searched for Tara and found her sitting next to Annabelle, both seeming comfortable with each other ... but he wondered about the look in Annabelle's eye. It could be more teasing, or something else.

The Conductor entered the car from the kitchen and greeted them.

"It is very good to have you back, sirs." He couldn't help a worried look at Kang and a curious one at the other guests. "We will have a smooth trip to Prague." After greetings and handshakes, he said, "After my helpers finish loading your luggage, I'll help shovel coal. We're going to fly back!" He touched his cap and left.

Patrick invited Granger to sit down. Extra chairs had been added, forming a circle of coziness in front of the windows with the bar nearby. The author didn't need an invitation and, along with Patrick, poured drinks for everyone.

With rigidity, as if he would shatter if he moved, Professor Kang gazed out the window, and the train began to slowly roll forward. As the engines rumbled louder, he turned around. Being on the *Elizabeth* brought back poignant memories of his wife and his resolution to be strong crumbled. Bartholomew reached him first and urged him into a chair.

Annabelle made it to her feet and took his hand. "We are all so very sorry." Her voice wobbled. "It has been months, and we're still devastated. We miss her so."

From their position at the dining table, the boys watched, unsure what to do. Kang noticed and said, "Get over here, you two." After he hugged them, he told the boys, "I won't be able to get through this without all of you." Zander wiped his eyes, and Otto needed to as well.

Bartholomew cleared his throat. "We have missed every one of you."

"We wished for your return from this trip more than any of the others." Patrick glanced at the automat. "You can imagine that we have much to talk about."

"I'm sure you didn't expect extra guests during this time," Granger said. "I am sorry to impose upon you."

With a shake of her blonde curls, Annabelle said, "I assure you, Mr. Granger, you are not imposing. You'll soon know why." She eyed Celwyn. "As for you, Uncle Celwyn, it is about time everyone came back in one piece." She confided to Tara, "He attracts danger like bees to honey."

"I have noticed." Tara chuckled. "But, like the Lieutenant says, we are imposing."

"Not at all. The chance to tease Uncle Celwyn can't be missed. I have been wanting to meet you and … we must resolve what happened to Elizabeth." Annabelle tried to relax. "It is safer to have you at Tellyhouse than anywhere else."

"I agree." Patrick nodded.

"If I may," Granger sniffed the air, "what is that wonderful aroma coming from the kitchen?"

Patrick patted his stomach. "We have an inspired chef in Ricardo. I'll see if I can steal him and the porters for introductions. Excuse me." He headed toward the kitchen.

"They would have been out here to greet everyone, but the meal is probably at a finishing stage right now." Annabelle yawned and tried to cover it.

"It is pork roast." The magician elbowed Bartholomew.

The big man lifted his head and inhaled like he judged a cake-baking contest at the fair. "Perhaps … or a soufflé…"

"Oh, for God's sake you two—it is Trout Almondine in honor of our arrival." Kang almost smiled. "Ricardo knows it's my favorite."

Their chef led Jackson and Muldoon into the room. The porters bowed as Ricardo introduced them. None of them expressed curiosity about the guests, but they certainly looked like they had some. Especially Jackson, who couldn't keep his eyes off Tara.

"Luncheon is nearly ready, and we must leave you. It is very good to have you back with us." Ricardo raised a brow at Celwyn. "Mrs. Thomas is in a state over your return, sir." Ricardo couldn't quite hide his amusement as he retreated to the kitchen with the porters.

"Ha, ha. Jonas." Bartholomew chortled.

Annabelle enjoyed the situation, too. "That is not my problem, but it will be interesting when we walk through the door and she sees you. Perhaps we can sell tickets."

"And have popcorn." Patrick winked.

"By the way, beginning tomorrow, you three will take over the lessons for the boys. All subjects." Annabelle hesitated as her eyes clouded over with sorrow. "In addition to what else you must do."

With the talk of food, the boys left whatever they had been whispering about and checked the dinner table. Patrick saw them. "Why don't you two wash up for lunch?"

"Excuse us." Zander bowed, and they ran toward apartments at the rear of the car. After the door closed behind them, Celwyn waved a hand and locked the door.

"Quickly please," Annabelle addressed them. "How many of our telegrams did you receive? Patrick has so much to tell you and we don't know what you already know."

"We retrieved Patrick's initial telegram on the twelfth of last month and found duplicates of the message in Algiers, Barcelona, and Bombay." Bartholomew took a deep breath. "A newer message awaited us in Tunis and other stops. But in each of them, the text only mentioned the fact of her death and Gaspard. Yes, we know some of this, but prefer to hear it directly from you first."

"Certainly. And you should know that about the time I sent the last message, Zander sustained an injury to his eye," Patrick said.

"An attack?" the automat asked.

"Yes, and connected to what happened to Elizabeth and Edward that day." The door at the back of the car rattled and shook. Patrick lowered his voice. "I better wait until later to tell you everything else."

"Agreed." Kang glanced at the compartment door. "That washing up didn't take as long as it should. They are old enough to be curious about our trip and everything else." The door rattled again. "I doubt they cleaned their faces."

The magician unlocked the door and turned to Tara and Granger. "Anyhow, our housekeeper is a forceful personality. She rules the house like Attila the Hun. And I am usually in the doghouse with her."

"As you should be." Kang sounded more like himself. A bit of the old Xiau fought his way out of the pit of melancholy he lived in.

Chapter 15

EVEN IN A SMALL GALLEY ON A bouncing and swaying train, Ricardo produced a masterpiece; from the perfectly broiled trout in sauce to the mushrooms and truffles to the six-layer lemon tart. As if it were any meal, the boys gobbled the fare as fast as they could.

Not hiding his interest, Lieutenant Granger read the labels on every bottle of beer that Muldoon served him and remarked on the one from America.

"Yuengling. From the Eagle Brewery. I had no idea it existed."

"This is the first time I've seen any beer on this train," the magician said.

Bartholomew pointed to the bottles. "In the letter about our arrival, I included a request for the kind of draft I've seen the Lieutenant drink and thought it would be good to try, along with others. I am pleased with it." He nodded at Tara. "Ricardo has beverages of choice for us all." The magician sent him a silent thank you; he had been so caught up in their problems he had forgotten her personal needs.

"An excellent meal," Verne said. "It appears these young men were famished." Otto wiped his face and grinned at him.

Zander wiggled in his seat. "We are building a surprise for you in our old classroom. May we be excused?"

"You did not eat your carrots. And you will eat your vegetables tonight," Annabelle said. "You are excused."

After they raced away and the compartment door closed again, Celwyn said, "That saves me the trouble of blocking what they hear until we reach Prague."

"Will it be that bad?" Patrick asked.

"Parts of it, yes. But we must hear what happened here first, please," Bartholomew said.

Before they could say anything, Muldoon and Jackson started to clear the table. Kang stopped them. "Please tell Ricardo we enjoyed a most superlative meal. I'm sure you both contributed to it too." A train heading toward the coast passed the *Elizabeth*, loud and fast. "If you could please bring out a tea service, wine, and coffee in a few minutes?"

After they had returned to the kitchen, Patrick got comfortable and began his report.

"This has been a horrible few months, and I hope to never go through it again." To Granger and Tara, he said, "We will need your help also."

"I've had the last several weeks to come to terms with Elizabeth's death, but not how she died." Kang set his jaw. "Spare no detail, no matter how small, and do not shield me; my anger knows no bounds."

As he spoke, the *Elizabeth* rumbled past acres of wheat and frozen ponds. Clusters of sheep milled about in the near distance. The train blew her whistle as she rattled through Weigan, the town where over six months ago Celwyn had disembarked to rush to London and free Tara.

"First, we received your telegram saying you had sailed away on the submarine to rescue Miss Redifer." Patrick hesitated before going on. "To complete the picture, can one of you tell me about that, please?"

Bartholomew complied, finishing with, "You should know that Miss McFein and her family have helped us significantly through some dangerous situations. Her uncle destroyed the vampire who killed Telly and removed Mrs. Karras for her part in their attacks."

"Oh!" Annabelle cried, and Patrick grabbed her hand. "I didn't know." She gave Tara a grateful look.

Tara addressed them, "We are an ancient family … and a good one. Fiercely loyal too." She glanced at Celwyn with a look he could not interpret. "There are rogue vampires whose blood lust has made them immoral, and most dangerous to innocent people. Because of that, we think that some of it," she checked on Bartholomew's level of nervousness before continuing, "we think it may be contaminated blood causing their actions." After she finished, the big man blinked rapidly but remained upright.

Annabelle did her best, too. "I understand." She nodded at Tara. "Why did the pirates kidnap Miss Redifer? Is she all right now?"

Muldoon came through from the kitchen with a cart full of beverages, including a pitcher of milk. When he had been thanked and left again, Celwyn remembered more about the porter from last year. He considered Muldoon as honest as he could be, an ex-military man with an open face and nary a hair on his head. The magician wondered how he felt about the comings and goings at Tellyhouse when they happened to be in town.

"In the interest of time," Bartholomew spoke faster, "I prefer Miss McFein answers those questions a bit later. It is a long story and the attack on Elizabeth and the danger here are current. I can tell you that Miss Redifer is recovering in Milan and Mr. Soriano is with her."

Verne shook his head. "She was most fortunate to live."

Celwyn poured coffee for the author while Bartholomew uncapped a beer for Granger; their version of avoiding answering questions and making the automat do it.

"Very well," Kang said. "It is at least two hours to Prague, so here is an abbreviated version of our activities. Perhaps we can find a way to keep the boys occupied tonight so we can finish discussing the trouble in Prague."

"We will think of something," Patrick said. "What happened to you can't be worse than what occurred there."

After Kang finished the tale, Celwyn kissed Tara's hand and held it up. "Tara threw herself in front of the knife Ginny slung at me. She saved my life."

"Were you badly hurt?" Annabelle asked.

"Yes, but I recovered fast." Tara regarded the magician. "And I'm usually luckier than he is."

"We found Gaspard on that pirate ship with Talos and Captain Dearing," the big man said. "Jonas appeared to them as a raven bigger than this train car. He swept the automats and pirates into the sea."

"Everyone? Including Talos and Gaspard?" Patrick asked.

"We thought so until very recently, but can only confirm Talos," the Professor said. "I have his power disk, and the rest of him is at the bottom of the North Sea."

"That leaves Gaspard unaccounted for. Didn't Talos die in the Arctic Sea years ago?" Patrick raised a brow.

"We thought so, but Dearing retrieved his disk and had him rebuilt," the magician said.

"That is too bad." Annabelle pushed her empty milk glass toward Kang. "Hit me again, please." She asked, "Did Gaspard know you knew the Professor?"

Kang said, "I've never met him. However, my brother Talos could have told him of me."

"And about your work on atomic research," Celwyn said.

"That seems likely," Swanger grunted. "It is a relief that neither Dearing nor Talos wanted your flying invention. It does not lessen the danger, though. Gaspard wants to finish what Talos started."

That deduction deserved another beer, and Celwyn provided it. The Lieutenant did not hesitate to drink it. The magician enjoyed seeing the man relax and not be as serious as when on duty.

Kang pointed through the window at a cluster of buildings a mile away. "That is Mieszkowice. Which is less than an hour to Prague. Patrick, tell us everything else that happened, please."

"All right." He glanced at Annabelle. "Are you ready to hear this again, my dear?"

"I wish to hell I had a cigarette."

Verne reached into his pocket for his Gauloises. Annabelle stopped him. "No, thank you, Mr. Verne. My doctor doesn't think it's a good idea. Oh—" she gaped at Tara open-mouthed.

Patrick saw her expression and for the first time since they boarded the train, he smiled. "Miss McFein, my wife is speechless because she just realized that you could help us. If you would be so kind."

"I would be happy to. How?"

"We have a problem," Annabelle said. "My husband has a small amount of vampire blood from an attack by Mrs. Karras. It happened years ago." Tara stared back at her until Annabelle continued. "We need to know how it will affect the baby, and what to do. We've been desperate to find out."

The magician also remembered Mrs. Karras and her merry band of vampires, especially when they attacked him last year.

"From what I know, it will be fine, and I am at your service."

Just as Tara spoke, Bartholomew opened a bottle of champagne and the loud pop brought Jackson running in. By request, he retreated again to fetch the rest of the staff and more bottles to celebrate their homecoming and the baby news. Annabelle sighed.

"My doctor didn't say I couldn't indulge, but it upsets my stomach along with carrots, of all things." The *Elizabeth* blew her whistle and gained speed, leaving Mieszkowice behind with its extensive stables, churches, and quaint red roofs.

After everyone had toasted the impending addition to Tellyhouse, Ricardo collected the champagne glasses and herded the staff out of the room again.

"I better hurry up before the boys return." Patrick finished off his glass and sobered. When he got to the part about the murder and what happened to Edward, Celwyn felt himself losing control, sending the chandelier above the dining table spinning, and the crystal on the bar rattled like an earthquake shook the train.

"Hold on." Kang grabbed his arm. "We need to hear this."

"You are a braver man than I, Xiau."

"Of course, I am. Now, calm down."

Patrick continued, "The police arrived and their doctor fixed Edward's head. You should know; the Conductor has been stalwart through all of this." His voice wavered. "It was horrible. Professor, I am so sorry."

It took a moment before Kang could speak. "It still is. Please continue."

"Tell them about the notes," Annabelle said.

"Yes, Gaspard left one in the carriage with the body. Edward found it. When Gaspard killed one of the guards, he left a similar one."

"You can't be everywhere Jonas," Bartholomew told Celwyn.

Everyone else concurred, with one exception; Patrick.

"Although I have come to the same conclusion, I must ask that we look at this carefully." Patrick glanced at his wife. "We have the boys and Annabelle to protect, and everyone at Tellyhouse is vulnerable. They have been in danger for months."

Annabelle went to him and touched his cheek. "This has been a strain on you, my dear." She kissed his brow and told the others, "We are relieved we can share this burden with you. When Zander was hurt—" Her voice broke, and she buried her face in Patrick's chest.

After a moment, Tara asked, "Mr. Swayne, tell us, please."

"Zander was waylaid a block from home, struck in the eye, and the messages he had picked up were stolen from him."

"By God, what does he say about this?" Kang demanded.

Annabelle said, "He is better now, and he wants a 'rematch.'"

"Good to hear, Ma'am," Granger said. "I would be honored to teach him and the other lad how to box if we are here long enough."

Patrick's expression of relief demonstrated he loved the idea. He'd already taught them how to wrestle, and with things like they were, he had plenty to do. Annabelle's reaction did not seem as sure. Celwyn would talk with her; he'd seen Granger in action. Celwyn's own approach amounted to flinging their enemies aside instead of punching them, but both methods worked fine.

"Go on," Kang said.

Patrick inhaled. "After they took Elizabeth's body away, the police interviewed us and the staff. I sent Edward to the coven to increase the protection spells on the house."

Granger jerked around, open-mouthed.

Bartholomew saw him. "The local coven assists us with security. Jonas's old friend Francesca oversees them."

"I also hired a slew of guards, and everyone at Tellyhouse knows not to leave without at least one of them." Patrick handed the notes over. "Here are copies of what Gaspard left us. The police have the originals."

The magician's anger rose as he read them and passed them to Tara.

"If we had been here—" He couldn't go on, and he shouldn't—Xiau would blame himself.

Tara provided a distraction. "Please finish the story. Has anyone else been hurt?"

"Zander's attack was the last," Annabelle said.

Silence descended upon them as the train rounded the crest of Mount Kladno and started the descent into Prague. She blew her whistle without stopping, signaling any train beginning the climb upward.

Verne had been as quiet as an untrustworthy mouse throughout their journey and stood at the window, seeming happy to return to the city. He caught the magician's eye and winked.

"What else do you know we haven't heard?" Bartholomew asked Patrick.

He shrugged. "I have the feeling Major Jardin, the policeman in charge of the case, would work on it if he had a solid clue. Otherwise, it will sit."

"Is there more?" Kang frowned. "Do you think anyone is watching the house, or has anything odd occurred?"

"Yes, and no," Patrick said. "A few times a week, I feel eyes upon me but cannot spot anyone. Annabelle is not allowed out without several guards. Please talk with the Conductor or Edward. They may have seen more—Oh." He slapped his head. "The day after the attack on Zander, someone waylaid our messenger and stole his messages. So, now we pick them up at the post office ourselves. We think Gaspard had been looking for telegrams from you."

Wonderful. When he spotted the spires of St. Vitus, Celwyn said, "We don't have much time left. Have you explained our guests to Mrs. Thomas?"

Annabelle laughed, and not nicely. "We didn't. You three can do it." She patted her stomach. "I have enough to worry about." She addressed Tara, "Again, I feel better that you are here. Do you enjoy embroidery?"

While the magician stifled his reaction, Tara pursed her lips and carefully did not look at him. "I have never tried it."

"I will teach you." Annabelle beamed.

Tara would be more likely to hide the embroidery needle in her hat as a weapon and garrote an enemy with the thread, Celwyn thought. When he silently checked, he found her wondering how she could avoid needlework and not offend Annabelle.

"Let's look at the situation." Kang surveyed them. "Some of you have seen Gaspard, some have not. We will need a good likeness of him made, and copies for everyone, so we will know who we're looking for."

Celwyn couldn't help himself. As the air grew fuzzy between Kang and Bartholomew, he turned away so he wouldn't alert them. When the lifelike effigy of Gaspard touched Bartholomew's elbow, the big man yelped and said, "That is exactly what he looked like, Jonas—now make it go away!"

It disappeared in an instant. "Thank you." Kang rolled his eyes at the magician. "We still need a drawing to refer to and one to give the police, if it's better than what they have. Until then, hopefully, Bartholomew won't spend his time checking in corners and under tables for that thing." He held up his hands and dropped them. "Good grief, Jonas!"

"Do you think it is just Gaspard we are after?" Tara asked. "Was he the only automat to survive the sinking of the *Primero*?"

Celwyn appreciated Tara's imaginative nature. No one else had posed the question.

"When Jonas swept the automats into the sea, we assumed they would sink. They can't swim, are made of metal, and wouldn't need air." The automat shrugged. "If they fell into deep water or undersea trenches, they would never leave that part of the ocean. I admit, it is possible they could land on a flat seafloor. They would wander in different directions without finding land. But a few of them could have walked the dozen miles to the coast."

"We just don't know." Bartholomew frowned, and he relaxed again.

"Next," Kang said, "we need to know exactly what the police have done. I should submit to their questioning to discover that and determine if any of it is useful in finding Gaspard."

"Would you work with the coven going forward?" Tara asked.

"Yes," the magician replied. An odd thought occurred to him; *did Tara know Francesca or anyone at the coven?*

Professor Kang asked him, "Is Francesca in your debt?"

"I think we're even."

The door leading to the classroom and apartments rattled. Celwyn unlocked it, and Zander stuck his head inside.

"We have a surprise to welcome you home." His smile warmed the room like a sunburst in the atmosphere of mourning and vengeance. "Close your eyes."

Celwyn obeyed, and immediately they heard a low whirring sound. Qing did too and wormed his way out of the magician's collar.

"You can look now—" Zander said.

On the floor between the dining table and sofa, a foot-long mechanical frog lurched and hopped with a gurgling squelch. The boys walked behind the frog and, in between giggles, they watched it with the kind of seriousness that Bartholomew and Kang reserved for the flying machine. Otto held a small black box impaled with a stick that he steered with.

Qing tilted his head at the creature and inched his way out again.

"I see that damn bird is back." Annabelle regarded the frog. "You *made* this?" she asked them.

Otto wrote on his tablet and Zander read it aloud, "We borrowed some of Bartholomew's books. We've been working on this for a long time!"

The whirring noise increased with the frog's speed, and Qing had to waddle faster to keep up as he hopped along behind it. Qing amazed him again; Celwyn realized the mechanical bird imitated the mechanical frog. When Otto stopped the frog, Kang squatted beside Bartholomew to study it. Soon, they peppered the boys with technical questions. The joy on their faces did everyone good, if only for a while.

Chapter 16

The Kolejiště of Prague

WHEN THE BRAKES OF THE *Elizabeth* engaged, the screech of metal on metal filled the air along with the flare of flames and she slowed. As she neared the terminal, Zander stood at the window beside Celwyn, chattering about everything they had done while the magician and the others had been at sea.

Celwyn asked him, "Are you afraid because of that—" he pointed to the boy's faded black eye. "Does it hurt?"

"No." The lad stared at him with sparks lighting up his eyes. "At first, I felt afraid, and it hurt. But now—just ... just furious." He kicked the wall next to the window.

"We are here, and we're not leaving again until whoever hurt you and Miss Elizabeth are taken care of." Celwyn hugged him. "We will find them."

"What are you going to do?" As Zander asked, Otto reached them and Celwyn included him in the hug.

"We don't know yet." The magician and the boys grabbed at the wall to keep from falling as the train bounded onto another track and slowed still further. "We will need your help."

"How?"

"Protect Aunt Annabelle. While we go after the bad men, we must be sure she and everyone at home are safe. Can you two do it?"

Otto nodded vigorously, and Zander joined him.

"Good." He hugged them again, and they watched the citizens of Prague parading by on the streets.

"Who are the people who came back with you?" Zander asked.

"Friends that have helped us in dangerous situations. They will help us now too."

Otto handed his tablet to him. After Celwyn read it, he blushed.

"Err... yes I like Miss McFein very much."

The boys giggled and ran to Annabelle to tell her the news.

⌣

After they descended from the *Elizabeth* and stepped into the weeds of the train yard, they found Edward, the carriage, and a second carriage Celwyn had never seen before. Sully, their footman, stood beside it, waving his hat.

The magician greeted him and walked up to Edward and shook his hand. They had developed a strong friendship, although an infrequent one. As their driver and head of security, Edward Murphy played an important role in their household, and Celwyn could see that the recent events had taken a toll on him. The first time that the magician had met Edward, he had thought them close enough in height and features to be twins. Not anymore. A long scar ran from Edward's hairline to his ear and his eyes mirrored the man's overwhelming worry. When Celwyn had been attacked and nearly died, Edward had been just as upset.

"It is good to see you."

It had taken a while, but when they didn't have an audience, the magician had convinced the man to stop calling him "Sir."

"It is good to be back, even in these circumstances."

Bartholomew joined them and shook Edward's hand. "Good afternoon! How are you?"

"I'll be forthright with you; I am in a terrible humor and expect to be until we exact our revenge. Nothing else will matter." Edward controlled his quivering fists. "Is that the Lieutenant Granger we've been hearing about, and Miss McFein?"

"It is. Come over, we'll get everyone introduced." Celwyn led the way and made the introductions.

After greeting Granger, Edward said, "I have many questions. But first, Mrs. Thomas..." he checked behind them as if he expected a trail of tiny devils running up to them, "is waiting for us. We can leave the cart here for the Conductor and his crew to use."

"Good plan. The Professor and Bartholomew's new books won't fit in the other cart."

"True." Bartholomew smiled. "I've never seen the other carriage before. It is bigger, and sometimes we need something like that."

Edward shot a glance at Kang as he joined them. "Mr. Patrick arranged for it while our usual one was ... with the police. And we will need more seats this afternoon." To the Professor, he said, "My condolences, sir."

The automat blinked and thanked him.

As tactful as ever, Verne said, "We heard one of your guards had been killed inside your usual carriage."

Edward flushed. "It has thoroughly been cleaned since then, sir."

"Not to fret." Celwyn gave him an encouraging nod and Verne an itch in his underwear. "We'll talk later when we can get away from Mrs. Thomas. Is the Conductor aware of everything that occurred here? We haven't had a chance to talk with him yet."

"Yes."

"Excellent."

"What is wrong?" The automat asked Verne.

"Nothing—" The author squirmed and backed up to the carriage and wiggled like a bear against a tree.

The magician tossed his bag and Bartholomew's into the cart, and when Kang handed his over, he said, "Don't throw it—there are presents in it for the boys."

The big man passed over more bags to Edward. "If I'd known Annabelle was with child, I would have bought all the baby toys I could find."

The automat elbowed him. "Indeed, you would have. Did you notice Zander is exactly as tall as Otto is now?"

"Yes, if we'd bet on that, I would have won. What did he say about his eye?"

The magician inhaled his rage. "The boy is angry and a touch afraid." He nodded to Granger, who joined them. "We will hear about Zander's ordeal later in detail, which may provide clues to our enemy."

After Celwyn ushered Tara and Annabelle, who still chattered about the merits of embroidery, into the carriage, the automat consulted this watch. "It is nearly five and already dark. We'll wait until tomorrow to visit the police."

"Get in. I'm going to ride up top with Edward." The magician leaned inside the cab and asked Granger and Tara, "Have either of you been to Prague recently?"

Verne still squirmed. "It is a charming city. Especially the bridges and churches."

"I visited here a few years ago before Tellyhouse came to be." Tara's eyes twinkled at Celwyn, making him wonder what brought her here.

"Never," Granger answered.

"Then I'll ask Edward to take the long way home." The magician glanced at the other carriage. "And let

Sully know our plans so that he doesn't worry. The city is most beautiful during the holidays."

I'll need a heavier coat too, he thought. The magician provided one before he climbed up to the driver's seat. Edward still wore his unease and an even heavier coat. As the loading of the carts continued, Celwyn congratulated himself on developing a way to talk with Edward and enjoy the city again.

Chapter 17

BY THE TIME THEY REACHED Tellyhouse, Celwyn had listened to a firsthand account of the murder of Elizabeth and the subsequent attacks. He and Edward compared descriptions and confirmed it was definitely Gaspard they sought for the crime.

On Celwyn's part, he gave Edward everything about their trip. As he talked, Edward drove with his eyes on the road and monitored the other carriages. Prague did not have a reputation for polite coach drivers; instead, reckless speed had many admirers, and shouts of colorful language abounded everywhere. As they turned down the street toward Tellyhouse, Edward's brow furrowed.

"If you don't mind me asking, is Miss McFein a vampire?"

"Yes. Her family assisted us in the catacombs last year. They did so again this year in the Far East. They are not to be feared. Her uncle, Valentine Soriano, helped us greatly. And last year, they took care of Mrs. Karras and her pack of vampires even before I asked." He smiled to himself. "Most recently, Tara saved my life."

With a dark look, Edward said, "I remember what Delgado did to Telly and what that woman did to you. Miss McFein is here to help with this Gaspard, too?"

"She is. Along with Lieutenant Granger. We just don't know what we're up against. And now, we must double our efforts to protect Annabelle. Do you know anything more?"

"Not really." He jiggled the reins. "The Conductor and I do a great deal of surveillance and get reports from the witches."

Celwyn asked, "You suspect it is not enough?"

As Edward drove up the driveway to Tellyhouse, the other carriage stayed close behind them. "We see shadows and hints, but nothing solid."

Celwyn swung down from the high seat. "We also need to keep an eye on Jules Verne and his gossiping. And the Professor, for other reasons—such as being careful. We will talk." Then the magician looked behind him.

All the lights in the house had been turned on. Like an annoyed gargoyle, Mrs. Thomas cradled a rolling pin as she waited on the front porch. Behind her, a line of maids and other staff he didn't recognize stood at attention. They must be cold. Leftover drifts of snow crouched like bunnies under the rose bushes and denuded trees. Everything appeared the same, yet different, each time they returned to Tellyhouse.

"Thank you for your company, Edward," the magician swiveled and bowed to their housekeeper. "Good evening, Mrs. Thomas. It is nice to see you again." Every time the adventurers came home, it signaled a dance between them and Mrs. Thomas; one usually fraught with her irritation at their absence and placated with apologies.

Qing chose that moment to stick his head out of Celwyn's collar and squawk in the housekeeper's face.

"I see you and that damn bird are back. Sir." She swiveled and started barking orders easily heard across the street. "Let's get moving, Sirs and Ma'ams. I have things to do and it's too cold out here. Move!"

Celwyn enjoyed Granger's reaction to Mrs. Thomas, especially when Tara had to tug on his hand to get him to walk by her and into the house. Tara had already been warned about their house-keeper and hid a grin. Annabelle hooked an arm through the magician's. Leaning around him, she confided to Tara, "You'll get used to Mrs. Thomas and appreciate her." She pointed at the magician. "Mrs. Thomas missed him, even while thunderously angry that they had not returned."

Tara ventured, "She seems formidable. Does she know about me?"

"Nothing yet. I thought Uncle Celwyn should be the one to tell her."

"You learned that from Xiau, don't you?" Celwyn kept track of how often Bartholomew and Kang made him deliver controversial news. Tara chortled.

They headed inside and to the parlor. The others followed and the second carriage moved up to disgorge the rest of the passengers. Otto carried their mechanical frog as if it were the crown jewels.

When Annabelle said, "Stop," the boys skidded to a halt. "It is your bath time. Upstairs, please."

"Yes, Ma'am."

Ricardo had ridden in the other carriage and rushed by them on his way to the kitchen while expertly avoiding Mrs. Thomas.

"That reminds me." Celwyn took Tara's elbow. "I'm going to escort you to the conservatory." They started down the hall again. "You may have your preferred nourishment there without questions and gawkers. It is high time you received it."

By the time they reentered the parlor, everyone had settled comfortably while Granger and Bartholomew stood by the fireplace exchanging remarks about a new lager they sampled. Verne studied the bookshelves until Kang joined him to point out new tomes of special interest. When Patrick arrived, he appeared tired, but game for whatever the evening held.

"Annabelle is upstairs resting. I insisted. But she will be with us at dinner."

"I detect an enticing aroma. Pork roast?" the magician asked. 'Pork roast' had rapidly become an inside joke between them as a way of talking about food.

Kang sniffed the air. "Perhaps. Ricardo's helpers probably worked on the preparations for dinner before we returned." He pivoted and gazed through the archway to the dining room. "Once the leaf is put in the dining table, I believe we will all fit."

"We have some information for our guests." Patrick cleared his throat. "Annabelle and I request that you not stand on ceremony. If you need something, just ask. Explore anywhere you want. Nothing is out of bounds. You've met Mrs. Thomas." A ghost of a smile crossed his face. "She is highly organized and will solve anything."

"If you're brave enough to ask." Annabelle smirked.

"She thinks Jonas is a bad influence on the rest of us, but worries about him." The big man couldn't help but check the hallway behind him.

Verne said, "She has always liked me."

"Oh?" Kang stared at him. "Even the time we brought you home drunk after we found Mrs. Karras outside your hotel room?"

"Then it is best we do not remind her, no?" The author shrugged.

Qing squawked and Celwyn undid the button on his collar. "Try to behave."

With a squeak of happiness, the mechanical bird landed on his favorite perch atop the armoire and next to the bay window. The longer he and Mrs. Thomas did not encounter each other, the better.

"Wine, my dear?" The magician settled beside Tara on the sofa and produced a tea service.

"No, thank you. Tellyhouse appears quite large."

"It certainly is," The automat said. "The grounds are beautiful, and you will see them tomorrow when it is light out."

The floor shook as Mrs. Thomas marched in. By the time she came to a stop in the middle of the room, they all sat up straighter. Celwyn introduced everyone formally.

"Thank you." She pinned the magician with a look. "Welcome back. It has been a horrible time here. I expect you to stay until everything is back to normal. And I do not," she glared at Bartholomew and Kang as well. "I do not like having witches around here or armed guards."

"Yes, Ma'am," Professor Kang, the diplomat, said. "We plan to take care of everything."

As he spoke, her irritation broke. "I am so sorry about the missus, sir."

When he could talk again, he said, "Thank you."

Into the somber silence, Bartholomew spoke. "We are relieved to be home and plan to be here until everything at Tellyhouse is safe again."

"I look forward to that." Mrs. Thomas swiped at her eyes. "Until then, I have some announcements." She consulted her clipboard. "Mr. Verne, you will sleep in the room on the third floor next to Bartholomew. It has an excellent view of the gardens. Miss McFein—"

"Yes?" She raised her hand.

"You will sleep in Miss Annabelle's parlor. It is a beautiful room on the second floor."

"Thank you."

"Mr. Granger."

He almost saluted, but instead said, "Yes, Ma'am."

"You will be in the conservatory on the first floor with Mr. Celwyn. The room is enormous. He will not disturb you with his piano playing." She checked her clipboard. "Dinner is at eight. However, it might be a tad late tonight because of your arrival." She studied Granger. "You do not strike me as needing protection, but Mr. Patrick has guards ready to accompany you and the others as necessary." She glanced at Tara and pursed her lips, a little confused, but not sure why.

"Thank you for your usual efficiency," Bartholomew said.

"You are welcome." As she started for the door, she pivoted and said, "I admired Mrs. Kang greatly. Get the bastards who did this." She blinked fast and held her head high as she strode out, rattling the magician's teacup with each step.

"Like a cyclone," the big man commented.

Annabelle pulled an envelope from her skirt and handed it to him. "This came general delivery for you a few weeks ago. Who is this from?"

A twinkle lit up his eyes and Bartholomew opened the envelope. "Mrs. Esther Peabody is a widow we rescued with the hostages in the Sulu Islands. A most fascinating woman."

As he read, Verne grinned. "She is strong of purpose and as the Americans say, 'sweet' on Bartholomew."

"Oh?" Annabelle teased. "What does she say?"

"That she is settled in Lisbon and will write more later." He stuffed the letter in his pocket and eyed the grandfather clock. "We have about two hours until dinner, probably less before the boys arrive and want our attention." Without missing a beat, he asked the magician, "What did you learn from Edward?"

Annabelle's arched brow promised there would be a bit more discussion about Mrs. Peabody.

The magician agreed. Even though he preferred to keep his attention on how wonderful it felt to sit next to Tara, he reported everything Edward had said and finished with, "We do not know if Gaspard is working alone, or with others."

"Nor, where he is," Tara said.

Patrick held up a hand. "Before I forget, for any side trips you must make, we have acquired a two-person caleche if the main coach is not here. Sully can also drive it for us." He looked at them. "I am available to help with whatever you want to do, but it is best that I stay here to protect Annabelle and the boys."

"I agree," the magician said.

Sounding like his old self, Kang said, "From a logical standpoint, I have some suggestions. Did any of you have any to suggest first?"

"Here is mine." The magician caused several plates of cookies to appear in front of them.

The automat tried to be stern but grabbed a cookie and continued, "All right, then. First thing tomorrow, I will go to the police and find out what they know."

"Of course," the magician inserted, "Bartholomew and I will go with you. You are what Gaspard is after. Don't argue."

"If you must." Kang finished the cookie and started on another. "I also recommend that any time Lieutenant Granger leaves the house, that he is in disguise." When Granger appeared ready to ask why,

Kang added, "It will make it easier for you to investigate; you won't worry about anyone recognizing you and connecting you to us."

"Interesting." Tara shrugged. "This sounds like the choice is to wait and be attacked or become bait."

"Specifically, Professor Kang will be the bait, and Gaspard will not be able to resist the opportunity." Bartholomew glanced at Kang. "Everything he said is all true, but until we know how many of them there are, it might be a risk to invite their attention." He raised a questioning brow at the magician.

Granger understood. "You have a plan."

"We do." Bartholomew rubbed his hands together, just like Nemo did at times. "We suggest that Jonas disguises Edward as himself and you and Bartholomew accompany the Professor tomorrow. Jonas will be flying behind you, as a bird of his choice, to see who is interested in you. If all goes well, he will follow them to their lair."

"That sounds reasonable," Verne said.

Tara nodded. "It makes sense. What will I do?"

Celwyn had that answer ready. "In disguise, you will also be watching the police station and tracking Gaspard or anyone he is working with. It will have to be a different disguise, not the same one they saw in London when they attacked you. Why? Because there is no guarantee our enemies will stay together when they leave the police station."

"We must have a script for what Xiau will do." Bartholomew tapped a finger on his knee as he thought. "He would go to the police station and directly home again. Correct?"

The magician laughed. "Think about it ... yes, Xiau would head home." His amusement grew. "But they could also see him go elsewhere."

On a list of what the big man feared, effigies occupied the top spot—like the one of Gaspard he'd already made. The usual discussion ensued where the automat worried and fussed about Celwyn's magic. When things calmed down, Granger asked, "Perhaps those ideas will work—but what are we expecting from it?"

While everybody pondered that, Zander and Otto thundered down the stairs and into the parlor.

"Do they look clean to you?" Patrick asked Bartholomew.

"Well—they don't smell."

Zander laughed and landed on the sofa next to him. Otto sat beside the automat and handed over his tablet. Kang read it and hugged him. "I miss her too."

Zander's attention had moved to Tara. He stared. She smiled at him, and he blushed.

"Pleased to meet you, and your brother," she said. "I hear you haven't had Beastie very long."

"You need to meet him!" He edged to his feet and Otto did the same.

Bartholomew held up a hand. "After Beastie has his dinner, the Conductor will bring him in to meet everyone. Why don't you two tell us about the mechanical frog you made?"

They did so until Jackson arrived to set the table for dinner. Minutes more and Annabelle came downstairs, patted a yawn, and settled beside Otto.

"Did you finish your homework?" When the boys exchanged a look, she asked, "Or were you doing something else?"

While Zander did some explaining, Otto scribbled and handed his tablet to Granger. It surprised him, but he did not hesitate. "He asked 'if Miss McFein and I have known you long.' Yes, we have, and we are enjoying this visit too." Granger answered with caution and sent Kang a glance. "We hear you are very strong."

Zander flexed his muscles, and the magician grinned at his earnestness.

"I am ready. For anything. So is Otto. Tell us about your trip, please."

Kang related a sanitized version to them. Otto listened, spellbound until he scribbled a question. Zander read it aloud, "Why didn't your ship sink?"

The magician looked away, hoping the automat could handle that one—he personally couldn't explain it without describing the submarine. Granger tried.

"I work for Captain Nemo, who sails the *Nautilus*. It is a special ship. It can go below the waves sometimes."

Jackson approached them and bowed.

"Dinner is served."

Granger sighed his relief.

As Celwyn escorted Tara to the table, he sent both Bartholomew and Granger a question and whispered the same one to Kang. They all answered the same way.

"What are you whispering about?" Annabelle asked as Patrick pushed her chair in.

Celwyn got Tara settled and unfurled his napkin. "Just making sure everyone agrees that the boys are old enough to hear more about things that happen when we are not here." He turned to them. "Do you remember when I told you a little about magic? And how you said you wouldn't tell anyone?"

They both nodded. Zander said, "We can keep a secret."

I hope so, he thought. "All right, then." The magician proceeded to introduce them to the *Nautilus*. He had just finished when Jackson arrived with the first course. By the time they began sipping the minestrone, Otto's eyes shone like twin beacons, and Zander bounced in his seat.

"You must promise again not to tell anyone." Celwyn verified each boy's thoughts and saw agreement.

"When can we see it?" Zander whispered.

Granger shrugged. "I will have to get permission. I hope soon."

As dinner progressed, the lads held the floor, full of ideas and questions. Annabelle put a stop to some of the outlandish ones, such as having their own uniforms for the visit to the submarine. Celwyn enjoyed the conversation, hearing the distracting normalcy in what they said.

Of a sudden, Zander asked, "What are you going to do to the man who hurt Miss Elizabeth?" His voice wavered and his stare challenged each of them in turn.

As smoothly as if they'd rehearsed it a dozen times, Bartholomew answered, "We will turn him over to the police."

Probably a lie, but a good and necessary one, the magician thought. Verne finished a bite of the bread and said, "I believe they still hang murderers here."

Annabelle gasped, and Kang kicked the author under the table and said, "It may be prison for him. Either way, he will not hurt anyone again."

Chapter 18

AFTER BREAKFAST THE NEXT morning, Professor Kang, Bartholomew, and Granger (disguised as Celwyn) left the house. They made no effort to hide Kang's identity. Tara had already departed dressed as one of the housemaids. In different wigs, she would be stationed at each of their stops throughout the day.

The automat didn't even wear a hat, leaving his elfin ears on full display. As a handsome fly, Celwyn rode on Edward's collar as they pulled out of the driveway and rolled down the street. For some of them, their itinerary included Christmas shopping. Everyone agreed: destroying Gaspard would be a wonderful way to celebrate.

Hours later, Kang followed the others out of the police station and his irritation showed in the way he stalked, not walked.

"Major Jardin has done nothing to be proud of and lately has done less than that. The trail to my wife's murderer is cold."

As they climbed inside the carriage, Bartholomew held the door open and nodded at the police building. "At least they won't be in our way." The big man sat heavily next to the automat. "And it allows us to do as we please."

As Celwyn slipped inside the carriage window and transformed back, Granger flung himself backward. The curtains on the right side of the carriage remained shut, but an enemy could not miss Kang if they looked through the other window, which they'd purposely left open.

The magician aimed a thumb outside. "No one is inordinately interested in us." As he spoke, Granger's hair grew a bit longer. "I do look even more handsome when my hair just touches my collar."

"It makes you so much more modest too," Kang said. "Our enemies might be confused as to why they suddenly can see all of us. It'd seem like Christmas to them." He grinned. "Let us go shopping!" His enthusiasm brought out other smiles until they drove by Rosalie's Pens and Stationery and his gaze changed. "Elizabeth used to love that shop."

"I hope Gaspard finds us soon." As they drove on, Granger pointed out a nativity scene with actors and barn animals. "If you don't mind me saying so; although this is a beautiful city, I do miss the *Nautilus*."

"Same here, and the flying machine, but do not tell Annabelle and Patrick that." Judging by his dreamy expression, Bartholomew proceeded to enjoy some memories of Findbar. "Above all, do not tell the boys. They would demand to see it."

The rest of the morning passed uneventfully as they drove slowly between a variety of shops. All the while, Kang kept an eye out for Tara and found her at each establishment as planned. When they left Henry's Fishing and Hunting Store, Kang felt especially pleased with the hip waders he had bought for the boys. After this business, they would enjoy a fishing expedition, perhaps a trip to Lake Hlucin— when it warmed up, of course.

They had just passed a Hindu temple when Kang pulled his coat closer, and asked Celwyn, "Are you getting tired of waiting in the carriage?"

"Somewhat."

"Are we going to do this for the next five days until Christmas?" Bartholomew asked.

"Let's hope not," Kang answered as they turned onto Gertova Street at a moderate speed.

By the time they saw Tellyhouse again, they had picked up Tara and waited while Granger sent Captain Nemo a telegram reporting no progress. Verne seemed the most jovial of them all, remarking that he had finished much of his holiday shopping.

Chapter 19

O N CHRISTMAS EVE, TELLYHOUSE buzzed like a large beehive with frantic activity and good cheer. Mrs. Thomas had finally hired all the housemaids, scullery maids, footmen, and anyone else she desired. She also appeared much too busy to worry about Tara and settled for a few curious glances here and there.

By mid-afternoon, the gloom of rain clouds had darkened the house. Annabelle waddled around the parlor lighting pine-scented candles and appeared very pregnant.

In the days since they returned to Tellyhouse, Tara never left Annabelle's side for very long. Kang deduced that she wanted to ease Annabelle and Patrick's worries over the baby's birth. Or she could be worried about their enemies and want to remain close. The automat did not voice his second deduction that Miss McFein suspected their enemies planned something.

From his position on the parlor sofa, Jonas kept an eye on them as he listened to Otto practicing the piano in the conservatory.

Bartholomew said, "He is getting better every day. When is his piano teacher due here?"

"Patrick says not until this Saturday because of the holiday," Kang answered. "Why?"

"Elementary." The magician regarded the automat. "So that we can quiz him about who waylaid him the day Elizabeth died."

"Ah," Kang said.

As Annabelle settled into a new position next to Tara, she asked, "Do you hear that thumping from above?" When Tara bobbed her head, she explained, "Lieutenant Granger is teaching Zander how to box. My husband has taught them how to wrestle. I do not approve. But I have been convinced it is necessary."

"May they never need to use those skills, my dear," Verne said. "I hope this unpleasantness is resolved soon."

Another thump made Qing squawk. He had been vocal since returning to Tellyhouse, and Mrs. Thomas's annoyance grew with each of his outbursts.

"Is Qing bored?" Bartholomew asked.

Annabelle snorted. She did not appreciate the mechanical bird. One of his habits included attacking her earrings. In Qing's opinion, anything shiny would do.

Patrick wandered into the room and collapsed on the sofa next to his wife.

"The bird is bored?" he asked.

"I can fix that." The magician eyed Annabelle and Patrick. "I'm going to show you something that interests Qing very much. And I am showing you now, so as not to scare you or the baby later."

"I have figured out what it is," Kang said. "Tell them why first."

Bartholomew, instantly suspicious, sat up.

In the next second, the automat felt something tingling on his ears, courtesy of the magician. Elizabeth used to giggle or hide a smile every time he did that.

"What Xiau is hinting at," Celwyn said, "is that you're going to see something that could appear any time, even when I am not expecting it."

The tingling stopped and a purplish frog the size of a thumb fell into the automat's lap, and he swatted it away.

With a grin, the magician gestured. "What happens next is *not* my magic. I just invite him, sometimes."

On the empty table in front of Annabelle, a green haze formed. The magician kept his voice low. "Please do not be frightened. His name is Wye. He protects me, and he will protect you."

The mist solidified as the wyvern took shape. His slick green scales became distinct, then iridescent wings tucked close to his fat body. The wyvern lay on his side, teeth showing, and emerald eyes fixed adoringly on the magician. Kang noted that this time the wyvern only measured two feet long, no more.

Annabelle grabbed Patrick's hand and held on. Tara nodded encouragingly at them. "There's nothing to fear. He is devoted to Jonas."

When Qing let out a squeak of joy, they all jumped. In a blur, Qing landed on top of Wye's side and bounced up and down. The wyvern's eyes rotated to glance at him and went back to Jonas while the mechanical bird sat down to chew on his scales. In the silence, it sounded loud. Minutes went by until Otto came into the room, showing no fear, just wide-eyed fascination.

The wyvern yawned and rolled onto his back, dumping Qing on the floor. The bird shook himself and jumped back on top of the wyvern.

"Not to worry, Wye doesn't mind," Celwyn said.

Annabelle licked her lips. "I guess that damn bird isn't all that frightening."

Mrs. Thomas's voice floated through the open door, and then her serviceable shoes started to descend from the second floor. By the time she reached the parlor, Wye had gone, and Qing sat on the magician's shoulder innocently nibbling on his collar.

"My, my ... you all look as guilty as Zander does when he hides lizards in his room." She put her hands on her hips and regarded them without any trace of humor. "What is that on your ears, Professor?"

Kang felt it, removed it.

Bartholomew pushed the empty cookie plates behind the couch pillows. "We were hoping to sample some of Ricardo's Christmas cookies." As he spoke, Zander and Granger appeared behind the housekeeper.

"Cookies!"

Her voice softened at Zander's enthusiasm, but she kept a suspicious eye on the others, especially Celwyn. "I suppose that would be all right as it is almost Christmas, and as long as the Missus drinks some milk with them."

As she marched out, Annabelle made a face. "Milk."

Otto scribbled on his tablet and handed it to Zander.

"He wants to know what he saw. I want to see it too."

Celwyn patted the air. "Wait until the cookies arrive. Mrs. Thomas would not be amused if she discovered something she shouldn't. Not at all."

Granger asked the big man, "Tomorrow is Christmas, which must be a special time here?"

"I hope so. This is only the second holiday that we have been in town for. Last year, Jonas had been attacked, and we took off to meet you and *Nautilus* in Odessa."

"I certainly remember that." Celwyn winked at them.

Kang wanted to inquire after Granger's family but hesitated. *What if he had none like Bartholomew? Or had also lost his wife*, he thought. *Like me.*

Jonas must have mirrored his thoughts. "We will all miss Elizabeth, Xiau. She will not be forgotten."

"Never," Bartholomew said. "When you are ready, I will tell you of what happened the time she went with me to Ezekiel's Books to find a present for you."

Annabelle said, "And I have one about the day she had spent rearranging your bookshelves and realized she had skipped the letter 'H.' And had to redo much of it."

The automat smiled. "When I came home that day, she had a clump of dust on her nose and got very grumpy with me and my books."

Chapter 20

J ACKSON ARRIVED WITH A CART FULL of cookies, milk, and more tea and coffee. When he placed the cookie platter in front of the boys, Celwyn waited until the porter exited before dividing the plate in two and putting one of them in front of the automat.

Yes, Christmas made things merry. The parlor had been transformed with garlands festooning the windows, candles everywhere, and boughs of holly over the door mantles. A baby doll wrapped in rough cloth lay in a make-shift manger with small farm animals that Annabelle had found in town. Christmas crackers, candles, strings of popped corn, and tiny toys, such as a soldier with a drum, British flags, and ribbons, decorated the tree.

As the phonograph played "O Little Town of Bethlehem", Patrick and Annabelle danced to it.

Gently. The room felt warm from the fire, and fragrant with boughs of pines.

"Ricardo is making a Christmas goose with all kinds of dishes and cranberries." Bartholomew sipped from a mug. "I heard this from Jessie, the new scullery maid."

"Did you know the Americans' contribution to eggnog is putting a goodly amount of rum in it?" Verne smiled at him.

Annabelle laughed as the song came to an end and Patrick returned her to her chair.

The magician relaxed and put his arm around Tara while he tried to remember such a wonderful Christmas Eve and couldn't. Instead, he recalled being marooned on a mountaintop near Kharkiv with Count Wachinsky and Prince Oleh while they fought over a lady. It didn't come down to a duel, but close to it. The arrival of a foul-tempered dragon resolved the situation.

The clock on Tellyhouse's wall had just chimed the eight o'clock hour when Jackson announced dinner. After Patrick helped Annabelle to her feet, Otto took her hand to escort her into the dining room. Before the magician reached the table with Tara on his arm, he showered the room in veils of festive stars cascading from the ceiling. Granger noticed, his face flushed from the eggnog, and Bartholomew laughed at whatever they had been talking about.

Celwyn slapped Verne on the back. "Did you find everything you needed at the library this morning?"

"I did. Mr. Bartholomew kindly went with me."

"After today, the museum is closed until Friday, but you will have an opportunity to visit it then for as long as you need," the magician said.

"How did you know—" Verne regarded him, "No matter how you knew, it is appreciated."

As they took their seats, Celwyn asked Mrs. Thomas, "Is everything ready for what we planned for after dinner?"

He'd remember tonight's frown as one of her best. "It is." She humphed. "Like I said earlier, it isn't proper, and I just pray that the neighbors do not find out." She growled an order at Muldoon and dinner began.

Professor Kang licked his spoon. "I'm wondering if this turtle soup is even better than yesterday's offering." As he spoke, they heard a knock at the door. Sully bustled up the hall to greet whoever graced their porch on a snowy winter night when everyone should be inside by the fire.

Sometimes Celwyn's premonitions amazed him, and others he expected, such as now. "Excuse me, please." He hurried into the hall in time to hear Sully addressing the visitor.

"They are at dinner, sir. If you—"

The magician crossed the remaining few feet to the door and tapped Sully on the shoulder. "It is all right. This gentleman is expected." Celwyn thought fast. "Come inside, Mr. LaMer."

A medium-sized dusky-skinned man in a long winter coat and black beard stepped inside. He knocked the snow off his shoulders, and Celwyn shook his hand but said nothing, well aware that

Tellyhouse represented a veritable hive of gossip that could rival Buckingham Palace. Sully shut the door and watched them starting back up the hall, where the magician bowed their guest into the dining room.

A broad smile filled Bartholomew's face, and he shot to his feet to shake the man's hand. Lieutenant Granger did more; he snapped a salute and shook Nemo's offered hand.

Celwyn turned to Jackson. "Could we have another place setting, please?" He needn't have asked; the porter was already headed for the door.

Tara squinted and lowered her voice. "Good evening, Captain."

Nemo bowed and kissed her hand while Bartholomew performed the rest of the introductions in an undertone, well-aware of the need for circumspection.

"Just now, I gave the Captain's name as Mr. LaMer to Sully, and that might be wise for us all to use, especially around the staff."

"Good grief," Kang said. "LaMer? That was the best you could do?"

Verne pursed his lips. "The Sea, it fits."

When Jackson returned, Mrs. Thomas stomped into the room, stopping long enough to bestow an annoyed look upon Celwyn's head for upsetting her routine. As Jackson arranged the place setting, Bartholomew retrieved another chair, and Celwyn asked Nemo, "Do you have a bag?" When he nodded, the magician swiveled to Jackson. "Could you ask Sully to take this gentleman's luggage to the conservatory, please?" He'd remember to add another bed, a comfortable one.

"You'll be happy there," Bartholomew told Nemo. "The room is spacious."

Annabelle blinked her curiosity at the Captain. "We had hoped to meet you, sir." She looked happy. "We are celebrating many things tonight. Having you join us is especially wonderful."

"I am pleased you are here also." Patrick indicated the others. "We heard so much about you."

"How did you find us?" Bartholomew asked. "How did you get here?"

Nemo tasted the soup and his frown smoothed out. "I traveled all day, switching trains and back-tracking to be sure I hadn't been followed." He finished his soup. "There has been no time to dine."

"We are having a feast!" Zander declared.

With an amused twinkle in his eye, Nemo said, "I can see that young man." He told Bartholomew, "The Professor left your address with me in case of an emergency."

"We also discovered a blessed event when we arrived." The magician nodded at Annabelle and Patrick.

"Ha. Uncle Celwyn is hinting for me to explain." Annabelle patted her stomach. "I am due to give birth in another week. It is our first." Patrick leaned over to kiss her cheek. "Miss McFein will be here to help also."

Captain Nemo frowned. "Perhaps you do not need the stress of having all of us here and the danger we attract."

"Never fear," Kang said. "Annabelle wants us here, so she knows where we are. Also, we will take over the boys' school lessons." That brought a circle of smiles. "She won't have anything to complain about until we leave again."

"Correct," she said.

"Sir," Granger said, "It is good that you are here."

Nemo nodded. "We usually have a small celebration on the ship, nothing as festive as this," he gestured at the mountain of presents, the tree, and the garlands.

Talk around the table wandered from the snow outside to the boys' studies. When Zander asked Captain Nemo if he had ever seen a mechanical frog, Nemo checked with Celwyn before saying, "Yes, a long time ago. Why do you ask?"

From beside him, Otto handed over his tablet.

"You built it, you say? Yes, I would love to see it."

The frog had to wait. Tall praises and high spirits resounded everywhere as Patrick carved the goose, the loudest of which came from Bartholomew. Jackson opened more bottles of wine. Talk resumed with the conversation on anything except Elizabeth and their activities to find her killer.

As they left the table, Celwyn and the big man headed for the conservatory, and by the time they returned, Mrs. Thomas had assembled all the Tellyhouse staff in the parlor. More chairs filled the dining room as everyone took their seats.

"Ho! Ho! Ho!" Bartholomew called from the doorway. "Merry Christmas!" He toted a bag as big as himself, and behind him, a tall, whiskered elf lugged another bag.

The boys pointed and giggled at Bartholomew's red suit and suddenly large belly. With exaggerated drama, the magician modeled his tunic and tights to whistles as the teasing increased. Tara laughed and winked. From Ricardo to the Conductor, the upstairs maids, and Abe, and Andy and Sully, their enjoyment grew as they sipped eggnog and accepted presents from Santa and his oversized elf. Mrs. Thomas even unwound long enough to smile at Bartholomew's antics.

The Professor ferried plates of cookies around the room while Verne managed to get the phonograph going again.

With squeals of surprise and joy, paper and ribbon flew. Jackson held up a handsome tie and cufflinks and beamed. Flossy showed Annabelle her new hair ribbons and matching dress, exclaiming, "How did Santa know I love blue ribbons?"

"I think that big green elf told him," Annabelle confided with an eye-roll worthy of Kang. She studied the magician and added with speculation, "I wonder how he knew?"

Celwyn just grinned at her, not admitting to an unauthorized foray into the maid's mind. God knew how that got him in trouble with Tara. He took over passing the plates of cookies while Nemo and Kang sat down in a quiet corner to catch up. The magician swiveled; Qing remained atop the armoire, his eyes glittering like twin diamonds, and very interested in the crowd below. Mrs. Thomas also kept a wary eye on him, and, at times, switched her scrutiny to Nemo. Mr. LaMer nodded back at her like a wise owl.

Verne thanked Celwyn and Santa for the beautiful new fountain pen and then put a choral rendition of "Silent Night" on the phonograph. Without getting up, the magician added more candles to brighten the party while Annabelle regarded her innocent glass of milk and sighed. Soon, the baby would take all their time and milk would not bother her as much. A few feet away, Mrs. Thomas held up the recordings from the museum they'd found for her. The pleased expression across her face lasted until Bartholomew's announcement.

The big man tapped the side of this glass with a spoon.

"May I have your attention, please? Tomorrow is Christmas, and we wanted you all to enjoy the holiday. Everyone will have the day off tomorrow. You may leave right after breakfast. Or you may elect to stay here and relax. But if you leave, one of the guards must accompany you until you board your bus or reach your destination."

"Oh, thank you!" Flossy, the upstairs maid, exclaimed. "I will see my mother."

"If the guards are busy, Santa and I are also available to escort you," Celwyn, the elf, said. "We will make arrangements to bring you back after the holiday."

"I need to pack!" Flossy couldn't sit still. "Excuse me, and thank you." She flew out of the room and down the hall.

Ricardo approached Santa and his elf. "Sirs, although this is very generous of you, Mrs. Thomas does not appear happy about it. Most of the big houses do not allow their staff off work like this."

Bartholomew told him in an undertone, "We will speak with her. Again."

Ricardo did his best not to glance at the house-keeper. "If you say so. But how will you eat? Mrs. Swayne cannot cook." He raised his eyes heaven-ward. "Perhaps you remember? We discussed this after she started a fire in the kitchen."

"Mr. Granger can cook, and I will be here to help," Celwyn assured him. "Please enjoy your holiday. We will be fine."

Still doubtful, Ricardo followed the others out of the parlor to finish their chores and get ready for their time away. Verne asked Celwyn, "How *are* we going to eat?"

The magician held up a hand. "I will make what-ever we need with Granger's help. He said he knew his way around the kitchen, so we will survive." He eyed Mrs. Thomas in the corner, glowering like a large grumpy fairy. "We should figure out how to convince her to go somewhere and enjoy herself."

Bartholomew laughed. "The answer is right over there." He pointed at Sully. "Our footman is sweet on her, and she will go on an outing with him if he is persistent enough."

Celwyn laughed and glanced at Kang. The automat seemed animated as he talked with Nemo, and soon Bartholomew joined them. From their gestures and smiles, the magician assumed their talk had evolved to the flying machine. Otto jabbed Zander in the ribs, and with wide-eyed fascination, they approached the scientists and Nemo. Zander sat on Bartholomew's lap and Otto glued himself to Nemo's side.

"Are they too old to believe in Santa?" Tara asked as she hooked an arm through his.

"Unknown." Celwyn shrugged. "Do you and Valentine have a celebration for the holiday?"

"Yes, but many times we are out of town. I expect a letter from him and Simone soon."

The record on the phonograph magically repeated itself as they watched the snow fall outside the picture window. Qing studied the flakes, too, and enjoyed it in his own way; the brightness of the snow made the details of the scene quite clear as a rabbit hopped across the snow and disappeared into the hedges.

"The boys are twelve and fifteen, and they spent most of their early years on the streets cold and hungry." Celwyn wiped away a tear. "Bartholomew has been talking about building an orphanage here in town. It would also be a school."

"That would be lovely and useful." Tara nudged him and whispered, "I've never been kissed by an elf."

The magician smooched her thoroughly. "I feel like I've ignored you since we arrived." Over Tara's shoulder, he could see Annabelle's amused expression as she gazed at them. The magician made a new tea service behind the bookshelves, intending to wait until everyone looked the other way to bring it over. When Kang spotted it, he delivered the tray.

Ricardo and Jackson would not bat an eye, but some of the staff hadn't been exposed to the unexplained.

"You're lucky no one saw you do that," Kang said and went back to Nemo. Granger had joined them for the discussion and soon hid a yawn as he listened to their science talk.

Jackson stroked the fire, and sparks flew as Muldoon brought in another cord of wood and built up the fire. "This should last you through tomorrow." Jackson pointed upward. "The bedroom fireplaces are stocked up also." He located Bartholomew, who had again refilled his cup of eggnog, and his speculative frown at the magician showed he considered Celwyn the most sober of the bunch. "Is there anything else we can do for you tonight?"

"No, please enjoy your holiday, both of you." The clock chimed the eleven o'clock hour. After the porters left, Celwyn noticed that, except for Mrs. Thomas and Sully, the rest of the staff had gone to bed. He sent the footman a silent suggestion that he take Mrs. Thomas on a carriage ride along the river tomorrow.

Tara snuggled closer to him and, when her gentle snoring came, it reminded of him how she fell asleep next to him the night of their escape in London. A few feet away, Patrick yawned and took Annabelle's hand, ready to head up the stairs, slowly.

As he surveyed the room, Celwyn spotted Zander and Otto and pursed his lips. This would be interesting; it appeared he had the chore of getting the boys ready for bed. How hard could that be?

Chapter 21

A Merry Christmas Day at Tellyhouse

BY NINE THE NEXT MORNING, THE guards had escorted the Tellyhouse staff to their destinations. Once they dropped off their charges, the guards had also been granted the rest of the day off. A few of the staff elected to stay behind, including Edward and the Conductor. The redheaded twins Abe and Andy departed on their holiday while singing off-key Christmas carols and passing a bottle between them. As he watched them through the window, they both shuddered, feeling the cold outside.

An hour later, Sully finally convinced a reluctant Mrs. Thomas that it had stopped snowing for now and that the weak sunlight overhead would make their buggy ride along the river most pleasant. The Conductor ferried them to the hire park for their outing and returned, stating he might be needed for an emergency. The only urgency Kang foresaw would be if Bartholomew ran out of rum for his eggnog. Last night had been the big man's first sample, and he positively loved it.

Throughout the morning, everyone lounged in the parlor listening to the phonograph or Otto's attempt to play *The First Noel* on the piano. It seemed a difficult piece for him at this point, but the lad stayed with it, sometimes discordantly. The sound caused Bartholomew to squint painfully from under his hangover. While Zander sat at his feet sketching him, Kang peeked; it looked like an excellent likeness. Today, the big man wore his usual well-fitted suit and tie, but the lad drew him in his Santa costume and giggled as he worked.

"Where did Lieutenant Granger and the Captain go?" Tara asked.

Bartholomew murmured, "Edward drove them to the telegraph office at the train station after he dropped off Lucy and the other new maid—that I haven't been introduced to—for their day off. There is only one telegraph office open today, and Nemo wanted to send a message to the ship."

"Why did Verne go with them?" Kang asked. "For something to do, or—maybe he planned to meet someone. Like a reporter."

The magician said, "Granger will keep an eye on him. And," he checked his watch, "they will be back soon. The Lieutenant is scheduled to help prepare our luncheon." A grin came with that. "It seems he doesn't trust my culinary skills."

"What are you preparing?" The big man asked with obvious suspicion.

Kang laughed. "Eggnog." The automat realized it seemed much easier to smile and laugh in the last few days. He didn't stop thinking about Elizabeth, but his sadness had begun to lift.

When he stopped laughing, the magician answered them. "Eggplant with sauce, mozzarella salad, and cold ham."

"That will be interesting, I'm sure," the Professor said.

"Wait and see, Xiau." Celwyn eyed the Christmas tree. "I wonder if one of those presents is a headache remedy."

"That will not help Bartholomew." Annabelle watched Patrick massage her feet. "When are you going to open your presents, Uncle Celwyn?"

If anything, the automat thought, she appeared even more pregnant today. Of course, he did not express that thought.

"When is the baby due, precisely?" Kang asked.

With an annoyed look, she demanded, "You three bet on this, didn't you?"

"I would appreciate you waiting until Monday for the event." Bartholomew giggled. He couldn't help it. "That is only three more days."

"Oh, you do—" She spied Otto smiling as he joined them and showed Zander his tablet. The boy read it, shook his head, and held up two fingers. "You too?" Annabelle sat up. "Uncle Celwyn, did you encourage that?"

The magician stopped the string of endearments he'd been whispering to Tara long enough to ask, "Encourage what?"

"You have the boys betting on when the baby will be born!"

Patrick patted her shoulder and murmured, "Maybe you shouldn't exert yourself, dear."

As he continued to reason with Annabelle, Zander announced, "Otto thinks it is today. I have Sunday. Uncle Celwyn says it is today too."

"Out with it, Professor, what day do you have?" the mother-to-be demanded.

"Tomorrow. It seemed logical." Kang shrugged.

Patrick couldn't help himself. "Why?"

"Because—"

Zander yelled, "Look—they are back!" He ran out of the room and up the hall.

After Edward brought the carriage to a stop, Granger and Nemo alit from the back and waited for Verne to climb down. Otto waved at them from the window, and Granger waved back.

With a scowl, Annabelle asked, "Are they in on the wagering?"

Not hiding his grin, Celwyn stood and stretched. "Not yet."

Tara said, "Just ignore them. How are you feeling?"

"Like a prized stallion running a race." She put her shoes on with some help from Patrick and looked at Bartholomew. "What does the winner of your wagering receive?"

Before he could answer, Zander led Nemo and Granger into the parlor.

Kang greeted them and asked, "Did you see anything unusual out there?"

"No." Nemo shook his head. "We took our time also."

"Welcome back." The magician told Granger, "I believe we are due in the kitchen to prepare lunch."

"We are. Excuse me." Granger pivoted and followed Celwyn out of the room.

Annabelle called after them, "I'm not done with you yet, Uncle Celwyn—"

After lunch, Bartholomew and the Conductor cleaned up the dishes and shooed Edward back to the parlor when he tried to help.

Kang said, "You've been driving all day and deserve to enjoy your holiday, please sit down."

Tara moved over and gestured for Edward to sit next to her. The automat noticed their driver seemed a bit apprehensive, nervously licking his lips, but also seemed fascinated with her. He handled his first exposure to a vampire—one not trying to kill him—rather well. For her part, Tara engaged him in a conversation about his travels through the wilds of Alberta. As they talked, Verne stayed close by at the parlor desk writing, and occasionally looking up to listen to everyone.

Annabelle eyed the hallway. "The boys are upstairs showing the Captain and Patrick their creation and can't hear us. Is there any news on finding Gaspard?"

"No. Just what you already know," Kang said, "I'll feel better when we retrieve the house staff." Behind him, the Christmas tree still twinkled, alive with candles and tinsel, but with most of the presents opened, it appeared near naked. Even Nemo had been surprised by a vintage map of the Shetland islands courtesy of the automat.

Granger modeled the jacket the magician had given him and wondered aloud how the magician had known he liked a jacket with wide lapels. Celwyn had responded that all he had to do was watch the Lieutenant's face every time he wore his own like it.

It neared four in the afternoon when Bartholomew asked Annabelle a question that drew a frown from Patrick and a whoop of glee from the mother-to-be.

"I promise not to exert myself. The only thing we must do is keep the boys from seeing us." She looked at the magician, "Arranging that is your punishment for betting on the baby."

"I understand." Celwyn bowed with contriteness. "It shall be done."

Minutes later, he sent both boys to the stables with the Conductor to take care of Beastie, including a long walk. The oversized wolfhound had been banished after an incident last night and needed company.

"All right." As the boys ran out of the parlor, the magician turned back to Annabelle. "You have an hour. And don't be surprised if Mrs. Thomas returns before then and you have to explain yourself."

"I'll take my chances." Annabelle settled across the card table from Bartholomew under the window. "I can see from here when they drive up."

Kang didn't agree, considering how they concentrated while they played.

Nemo joined the table, and while the big man shuffled the cards, he intoned, "Place your bets."

The Professor noted Celwyn's expression, which mirrored his own. The last time they had watched Bartholomew and Annabelle playing poker had been years ago—right after the big man had been shot while guarding her. Patrick did not enjoy playing cards but seemed satisfied to perch nearby and keep an eye on his beloved.

"Raise." Annabelle told Bartholomew, "You might as well fold, you have nothing my friend."

"Ha. I raise five cents."

Lieutenant Granger tossed coins in the pot and Nemo hesitated. Kang wondered if he had ever played poker with a very pregnant woman before. Especially, a feminine one such as Annabelle.

If they had any reservations about her condition, she disabused them of the notion by announcing, "God, I would kill for a whiskey. Hit me." She tapped the cards.

Bartholomew didn't bat an eye and handed her a card. Play progressed and Annabelle's pile of chips grew over the next hour. The Christmas Day sun began to set, and Swang realized the Conductor would be bringing the boys inside any minute. Good. He didn't want them out of the house after dark.

With a nod to the table, Edward said, "I enjoyed this very much. But I must leave you for a bit." He stood. "Mrs. Thomas expects me soon. There's no telling what kind of humor she will be in after a day in Sully's company." That brought a few smiles and as he turned to go, he added "On the way back, Ricardo and at least one of the maids should be at the downtown bus stop waiting, too."

"I hope Ricardo doesn't think he has to prepare supper," the magician said. "The Lieutenant and I have it under control."

"Pfft," the automat said.

"The luncheon you made tasted surprisingly good." Nemo frowned at his cards. "I'm sure dinner will be also." He checked the room and asked in an undertone, "Did you actually make everything we ate, or—"

"Yes." Granger said, "We really cooked everything, although the vegetables seemed to be ready rather fast along with the salad." He shot a glance at the magician who batted his eyes innocently.

Just as Annabelle put away the poker chips, the boys and the Conductor came in the side door. She kept a wistful look on the card table until Celwyn whispered, "Perhaps we can play again tonight after the boys are in bed?"

"I would love that, but you'll have to slip Mrs. Thomas a sleeping draught first." Annabelle allowed Patrick to make her comfortable on the sofa again and picked up her embroidery.

Chapter 22

DARKNESS HAD BECOME COMPLETE by the time Edward returned with his charges. Celwyn could hear Mrs. Thomas from down the hall quite clearly as he and Granger worked on their dinner of shepherd pies. They had a system; the magician put in potatoes and other ingredients, while Granger added the beef, butter, and seasonings. Before they started, Celwyn had made a pile of pastry sheets for topping each of the pies. To accommodate Nemo, they planned a rack of grilled shrimp and roasted potatoes.

Ricardo rushed into the kitchen and stood there open-mouthed.

"*Mon Dieu!*"

The magician grinned and gestured at the trays of pies. "All we have to do is bake them, the salads are already done—" he stopped when he saw their chef's face.

Ricardo's stuttered, "I-I—"

Mrs. Thomas rushed through the door and had no problem expressing herself.

"Look at that mess! And now you have made another mess!"

She wanted action, so Celwyn waved a hand turning the kitchen into a sparkling clean room. That upset the housekeeper even more. She began panting and gasping for air until he patted her back. When she could, she raised a shaking finger. "Look at the floor!"

The magician realized he'd been walking in the bag of flour they'd dropped. He also noticed they hadn't put away the luncheon dishes before adding in a mountain of them to the pile.

Ricardo had paled. "How … h… how are you going to bake the pies? You have let the fire in the ovens go out—" he spotted one of the scullery maids trying to sneak out of the room. "Ginger! Ask Edward to bring in wood. Hurry—" It took more urging to stop her gaping at the suddenly clean kitchen.

"Sirs!" Mrs. Thomas stamped her foot. "Get out of here. Now!"

Granger wasn't slow. He wiped his hands, threw the towel on the cutting table, and trotted out behind the magician, bestowing his most charming smile and words of apology to Ricardo before running out the door.

When they reached the parlor, Annabelle and Patrick already roared along with the others. "We could hear Mrs. Thomas all the way here—" she laughed until her face turned as red as Santa's suit.

"They probably heard her in the belfry of the Castle." Kang rolled his eyes and asked as drolly as he could, "My, my, Jonas. What did you do?"

Celwyn sank down next to Tara on the sofa. "Well. Ricardo err ... noticed we let the fire in the oven go out. Mrs. Thomas saw a bit of a mess, and I had not cleaned up the bag of flour I dropped. And had been stepping in."

Bartholomew leapt to his feet. "Oh, no—I didn't finish the dirty dishes from earlier." He started for the door.

"I would not go in there," Granger advised. "Your housekeeper is extremely annoyed."

"I—cleaned most of it up. That caused the last explosion from Mrs. Thomas."

Annabelle roared louder and grabbed her stomach.

Verne left the parlor desk and approached them. "But ... what about our dinner?" The author had his priorities.

Granger and Celwyn exchanged a look. "Ricardo will have the ovens going again, I trust," the magician said.

After a knock at the front door, Sully admitted Jackson. The porter headed down the hall, and Kang asked, "Edward brought you home?"

"Yes, sir," Jackson said. "He told me I would be the last one in for tonight." They heard the yelling escalate from the kitchen. "Excuse me—" and broke into a trot.

"Be careful," Kang warned him. "Mrs. Thomas is in a temper, and it's Jonas's fault."

To change the subject, Granger fished out a coin and flipped it to Celwyn. "You win. Counting everyone, we made one pie too many."

The magician nodded and then asked Patrick, "Where are the boys?"

"Bathing." Patrick raised a sarcastic brow, recognizing the question as a diversion. "They landed in the horse stalls after one of their games."

———

The aroma of the shepherd's pies cooking gradually perfumed the parlor; a promising sign that dinner would occur. Edward brought in a cord of wood and Bartholomew helped him take it upstairs. Jackson had plenty to do in the kitchen. Into lulls in the parlor conversation, Ricardo's shrill voice could still be heard climbing a scale of outrage. They drafted Sully to set the table after Patrick suggested that no one would be welcome in the kitchen, especially Jonas, for a while.

Just as Patrick brought Annabelle to her feet to lead her to the dining table, they heard a commotion at the side door and Edward stumbled in supporting the Conductor. Blood ran off his head. He collapsed.

Kang reached the Conductor at the same time the magician did. "What happened?"

"Someone coshed him as we left the stables and kicked me back inside," Edward held the Conductor steady as the automat examined his head.

"It is a mess, but he'll be all right," Kang told them.

"Stay here, everyone." Celwyn sent Bartholomew a direct look and bounded out the side door. The big man would make sure no one went outside.

Before Celwyn reached the end of the driveway, he flew more than a dozen feet above the ground and berated himself for not having everyone come inside sooner. As he soared higher, he added a strong block around the stables. Nothing would go in or out. Several passes by confirmed that the intruders had already run away.

What if Gaspard hadn't done this? Could it be someone he knew more intimately? The magician's face must have registered his turmoil because, as soon as he entered the house again, Nemo met him at the door asking, "Pelaez?"

"No."

"Your father?"

"Hell." The magician controlled the urge to punch something. Most of those at the dinner table could see them, including Zander and Otto. Kang must have taken the Conductor somewhere to rest.

"I don't know. Probably Gaspard."

"That would be just as bad." Nemo rubbed his chin. "If we were at sea, I would be very decisive about how to go forward."

The magician appreciated his sentiments. "How bad is the Conductor?"

"The Professor bandaged him and made him rest," Nemo said. "Edward is staying with him."

From the dining room, Patrick called out, "Ricardo is ready to serve the soup."

The magician took a deep breath. "I can't afford to upset Ricardo or Mrs. Thomas any further tonight." He bowed Nemo ahead of him into the dining room. He would visit the Conductor after the man had a chance to rest.

Once the pies had been served and admired, Mrs. Thomas assigned Jackson to monitor the table and marched out, still speechless over their indiscretions. This time Celwyn did not block what the porter could hear and decided the boys should hear it too.

"I checked the grounds and the stable. Whoever attacked the Conductor is gone. Beastie and horses are fine." He regarded the lads. "It is very important that Mr. Granger, Bartholomew, or I are with you when you go to the stables or anywhere outside. In fact, take two of us every time you leave Tellyhouse, for now."

Otto wrote fast and Zander read his tablet. "Otto says we understand. We will ask someone to go with us. We promise."

Celwyn waited until Jackson nodded. "Same here, sir, and I'll pass the word along to the others."

"Tomorrow, I'll ask for additional guards and station them between the house and the stables." Patrick's lips clamped shut, and he glared at the door leading outside.

When everyone had resumed eating, the magician sampled the shepherd's pie. He was pleasantly surprised at how good it tasted, thinking the touch of basil he had thrown in when Granger wasn't looking must be the reason.

"The sooner we find Gaspard, the better," Bartholomew said.

"I couldn't agree more," Tara said. "And if we need extra protection, I will arrange it."

Her words surprised Annabelle and Patrick a bit—they had forgotten how they had feared vampires—and when she could, Annabelle once again smiled like they discussed something simple, such as the weather.

Kang put his fork down and wouldn't look up again.

"Just say it," the magician told him.

After another long sigh, he did.

"All right. Despite the hints and clues, we do not know for certain it is Gaspard who attacked us tonight." He glanced at the boys and continued. "It could have been Pelaez or your father, just as easily."

Nemo said, "I totally agree."

"Who are they?" Zander asked.

After Celwyn told him, Otto seemed calm enough and wanted to hear more. And when the automat explained their relationship to Jonas, Annabelle's frown deepened. On her other side, Tara patted her hand, reminding her of the safety inside Tellyhouse.

The boys had graduated from childhood in the last few minutes. From Otto's serious expression, he would hold steady. In contrast, Zander's breath came fast, and his eyes remained huge.

"I am also armed." Tara winked at Annabelle.

That caused Annabelle to smile, until she asked, "But is it enough?"

Tara included the lads in her next statement.

"Your Uncle Celwyn has a protective block around the house, and the witches' spells are still in place." She gazed at Bartholomew and Granger, and back at Annabelle. "You have several people here who can more than take care of themselves if they must. Including your husband."

Annabelle tried to relax. "I hear you can be very, ah, supportive too."

"If the occasion requires it." Tara patted her hand. "I understand from Bartholomew that you expected to learn how to shoot before now, but there hasn't been time to learn. We can fix that."

Before Tara could offer to show her the pistol she carried in her boot, Zander demanded to know if Tara could wrestle.

"Yes."

Celwyn bit his tongue and told him, "She is a very good shot and will not let anything happen to you."

Otto had waited for a lull in the conversation before passing his tablet to the magician.

"Well..." Celwyn felt his digestion protesting, but he went ahead and answered the boy's question as to why witches watched the house.

In the thoughtful silence that followed, Jackson returned with bowls of ice cream and fruit. When he placed one in front of Granger, the Lieutenant whispered to Celwyn, "We forgot to make dessert."

Celwyn had just whispered back that they should consider this digression the least of what they didn't do, when Zander exclaimed, "I love ice cream!"

"Please tell Ricardo we are appreciative and hope we are forgiven soon," Celwyn requested of Jackson. The porter didn't look hopeful but said he would pass along the request.

Patrick regarded the Lieutenant and Celwyn with awe. "Those shepherd's pies were excellent." He checked the door. "But if it is that messy to cook, perhaps we should leave the kitchen to the professionals?"

"I can't agree more." Bartholomew sent a worried glance down the hall. "Things are much easier when Mrs. Thomas is not annoyed."

Chapter 23

K ANG WAITED TO BEGIN A SERIOUS conversation until the boys had headed upstairs and everyone settled in the parlor. "Many of the staff will not return until tomorrow. That could be viewed by Gaspard as an opportunity."

From his position by the fire, Nemo raised a brow. "Or as a trap."

"Did we create opportunity accidentally or on purpose?" Bartholomew asked.

"You can bet Jonas does not care and will enjoy the action," the automat said.

As Tara left him to sit with Annabelle, Celwyn instantly felt a loss. The mother-to-be did not appear particularly nervous about their conversation. If anything, it seemed the shepherd's pie did not agree with her.

"It is both at this point." The magician produced a tea service, and without asking dispatched a bottle of whiskey and glasses around the room. In a glass of milk, he added a pink and blue straw for Annabelle. "At first, we," he gestured at the others, "just wanted to do something nice for the staff. And Bartholomew insisted that I would be popular in green tights. Only after the offer for the staff to leave had been made and some of them had departed from Tellyhouse to enjoy the holiday did I realize what we'd done. The attack on the Conductor proved that."

Nemo said, "It is unfortunate, but the situation may still be to our advantage." He sipped. "If you think about it—our enemies don't know *why* we did it."

"We don't know either." Patrick chuckled.

But whatever the intent, in the next few seconds, it no longer mattered.

Anabelle made a strangulated, gurgling sound and gasped.

Tara swiveled and asked, "Professor, have you delivered a baby before?"

As the automat crossed the room to Annabelle, the big man headed toward the stairs saying, "I'll get your bag."

"No, I haven't," Kang said. "I would prefer a doctor came here who does this every day, and I could assist him." He patted Annabelle's shoulder as she cried out again. "But I will do so if needed."

Patrick stood and sweat had already decorated his forehead. "We had planned to bring Doctor Uttgart here." He knelt beside his wife. "Uttgart has been our doctor throughout the pregnancy and expects the call." He ran to the door and back, his panic growing until he again held Annabelle's hand. "How are you?"

She grimaced. "In pain."

The boys thundered down the stairs and pivoted at the calls to go find Mrs. Thomas. Celwyn addressed the others. "I will fly us to the doctor to speed things along."

"You aren't going to fly him back here again, are you?" Kang demanded.

"No. I'll make us something to ride in. Lieutenant, are you up for your first midnight flight through the streets of Prague?"

"I am happy to remain here on guard, and skip that pleasure," Bartholomew said.

Granger put his drink down and looked at Nemo. At his nod, Granger said, "Yes, I am."

"I imagine it will be a most interesting flight." Nemo said, "Meanwhile, I will guard everyone here, along with Mr. Swayne and Mr. Bartholomew, and, of course, Miss McFein."

"One thing. No one will see us depart if they're watching the house. And," Celwyn thought fast, "we'll be back here in a very short time." He took Annabelle's hand. "You and the baby will be fine."

Kang drew him aside where she couldn't hear him murmur, "If you don't scare the pants off the doctor first."

"You have so little faith in my methods." He brought Tara to her feet and kissed her. "I won't be long."

Bartholomew arrived with Kang's bag at the same time as Mrs. Thomas came up the hall on the run. The floor shook like a wild herd of buffaloes thundered toward them and a hallway vase crashed to the floor. The boys followed her into the room.

Patrick shouted, "It's time—"

"Calm down, Sir." Mrs. Thomas helped Annabelle to her feet and Tara took her other arm. "We will go to the sitting room as planned." She turned to Zander. "Tell Ricardo we're going to need plenty of hot water." Zander didn't argue and ran toward the kitchen.

Things seemed under control, and they would not dare to be in Mrs. Thomas's world. Celwyn asked Patrick, "What is the doctor's address?" When he had it, he looked at Granger. "Shall we?"

Verne said, "Mr. Granger, it will be an enjoyable experience flying high through the night sky."

"No, it won't." Bartholomew shuddered. "I suggest you close your eyes and hang on for dear life."

Kang asked in a whisper, "If either Wolfgang or Peleaz are out there, how will you leave the house? I assume you could avoid Gaspard if you cared to, but not those two."

"Anyone looking for me will be watching the entry doors. I'm going to wall off the fire in the grate and go up the flue." If he had a red suit like Bartholomew's and a fluffy white beard, he'd look fine when they emerged from the chimney.

As he spoke, the magician transformed into a small raven and miniaturized Granger onto his back. The boys had remained in the kitchen, so he did not have to explain. Celwyn soon recognized a tactical error on his part; even though he'd blocked the fire, as they went up the flue it still felt as hot as the blazes.

When he burst out of the chimney into the frigid air, the cold gripped him until he got his wings going and they swerved east toward Doctor Uttgart's address. He would be sure the carriage for the return trip stayed snug and the driver's cab enclosed.

Chapter 24

I T DIDN'T TAKE LONG TO GATHER UP Doctor Uttgart after they told him that Captain Patrick Swayne had sent them. Celwyn listened to the doctor dispatch his footman to alert the hospital in case of complications.

Granger kept the doctor company in the carriage, and appeared as calm as he could considering he'd watched the carriage suddenly appear. They'd agreed Celwyn would drive since he knew the city and could recognize anyone looking for them—such as Wolfgang, Pelaez, or Gaspard. The magician drove his "horses" as fast as possible, making what he considered record time in returning to Tellyhouse. He also promised himself to never use mice as horses again; they had no sense of direction.

As they traveled up the street, Celwyn frowned and silently sent Granger a message.

The front door of Tellyhouse stood open.

The magician propelled the carriage until it streaked up the street and stopped two houses away. He swung down from the cab and opened the carriage door. The small bald man squinted through his pince-nez and raised inquiring eyes to Celwyn.

"Doctor, there are hooligans in the neighborhood, and we will return to you in just a moment. We'll lock you in to keep you safe." As Granger climbed out with a studiously neutral face, Celwyn blocked windows of the carriage and secured the door. He pulled Granger aside and pointed at Tellyhouse.

"If this breach is my father, this won't work—but we can try." Celwyn transformed Granger onto his back again. As a fly, he flew close to the ground, skimming the top of the snow and through the front door of Tellyhouse. Sully lay just inside, unconscious, and his chest rose and fell like it should. The knot on his forehead looked as big as an egg.

Yelling and commotion came from the parlor.

When Celwyn arrived, he found Gaspard's automats in combat with Nemo and Bartholomew. Ricardo had just joined the fray, and the automats tossed him into the dining room. The magician and Granger transformed back and without any hesitation the Lieutenant slammed an automat against the wall. From atop the armoire, Qing screeched. Not surprisingly, Mrs. Thomas stood in the center of the room swinging an iron skillet like a bat. With satisfying cracks of the skillet, she swatted some of the automats into the hallway while Edward threw the one he had by the throat the other way down the hall. A pair of the automats jumped on Bartholomew's back.

Enough. Celwyn made a man-sized magnet and hurled it into the fray. One by one, the automats slammed into the magnet, collecting them into a pile. Two regular thugs still fought with Bartholomew and Nemo, but now things seemed more even. Celwyn ran for the sitting room.

He burst through the door in time to see Tara calmly turn away from Annabelle, reach in her pocket, and advance on a giant of a man who charged at her. She emptied her pistol between his eyes, each bullet on top of the other. As he fell, he crushed Gaspard who had been trying to drag Kang out the door.

"Ha—" Celwyn confronted Gaspard. In seconds, he'd wrapped the bastard in so many bonds he became unrecognizable. Bartholomew sprinted into the room out of breath, excited as could be—he loved a good fight.

The magician checked on Kang, received a nod, and turned back to the big man. "Please take Granger with you—two doors north of here. Doctor Utgartt is inside a carriage at the curb." Using his boot, he spung Gaspard like a top. "I'll clean up here."

Tara had rushed back to Annabelle. In a groan worthy of a sumo wrestler, Annabelle lifted herself on an elbow; alert and unafraid, and most definitely interested in the action at her feet. When she smiled, Celwyn knew she would be fine.

"Never fear, Uncle Celwyn, I expected an exciting delivery with everyone here."

"Not like this." Kang fussed with his torn jacket and kept an eye on Annabelle.

"One moment."

In seconds, the magician had moved the dead giant to the hallway along with the pile of automats and other intruders, all of them the worse for wear; Nemo had bashed his assailant silly and dragged him into the hall with the others. Celwyn swept his hands from side to side, spiriting the damaged furniture away.

Within seconds, the magician had collected the intruders in a second carriage out in front. The magician watched Patrick get to his feet again and sprint straight toward Annabelle. Tara nodded at Celwyn.

"Do what you need to do, we will be fine," Tara told him and began reloading her pistol from the lace bag in her pocket.

That's my woman, he thought. *She participates.*

Celwyn told Kang, "The doctor will be here any second." They heard a furious noise from Gaspard. "Would you and Bartholomew like to do the honors with," he kicked Gaspard and received a metallic clanging, "him?"

Kang stared at the man that had killed his wife. The fire of revenge overtook the melancholy in Kang's heart. His voice was choked, but clear. "Yes, we would be honored."

The front door slammed, and Doctor Utgartt's tenor and Bartholomew's baritone reached them. Tara finished stuffing pillows behind Annabelle as they walked in.

"Everything is under control here, Jonas," Kang said.

"All right." He took Kang's arm, and they trotted past a flustered Mrs. Thomas, whose hair stood on end like she had touched a live electricity wire. By the time they reached the parlor, silence reigned, and they found Nemo planted in the middle of the room, still alert and on guard. Granger stood beside him. They both brandished pistols.

"Sir, we have Gaspard and also need to dispose of the ruffians. Would you and the Lieutenant mind remaining on guard for a while longer?" Celwyn indicated the cabinet by the writing desk. "There are some excellent pistols in that cabinet if more are needed."

Nemo bowed. "Certainly." He spotted Kang's fierce and angry expression. "I take it the Professor has a chore to do?"

"Yes."

Celwyn had one more thing to do. His help for Ricardo consisted of pain relief and insisting he stay put until Kang returned. Sully already sat in the matching chair holding ice to his head.

"Excuse me—" Mrs. Thomas rushed by them and up the hall.

As he watched her go, Bartholomew said, "I suggest we give her a wide berth for a while."

"Agreed." The magician noted the blood dripping off Nemo's forehead, and Granger's long cut down his arm, "The Professor will be back in a few minutes, and he will blame me if you are not here so that he can look at your injuries."

Captain Nemo swiped at his face and shrugged his agreement. "As he wishes."

While they talked, Edward escorted the Conductor into the parlor. His bandage drooped over his brow, but he seemed alert enough if another round of mayhem erupted.

"The rear of the house is secure, and we'll head back there to be sure no one tries anything." Edward's anger caused his fists to vibrate at his side.

The boys had followed the Conductor into the room and saw bits of broken pottery, the leg from one of the smashed chairs, and the injuries. Otto gulped and faced the situation calmly, as if it had happened to him before. He and Zander crossed the room and stood ready beside Ricardo and Sully.

As they drove away with the carriage full of intruders, Bartholomew and Celwyn sat up top with Kang. On their return, Gaspard's power source resided in Kang's pocket. As they came through the front door, Qing flew up the hall to the magician and dived into his collar. They continued into the parlor with Celwyn patting the bird's back, walking around Kang as he examined the knot on Sully's forehead. "You'll have a headache, but you will recover," he said. "Perhaps you should go lie down."

"Will do, Gov. Same thing that Mrs. Thomas has told me." He grinned. "Pretty fondly too, for her. She called me a 'Stubborn old reprobate.'"

Before Kang could finish examining Ricardo's injury, from down the hall came a short cry before a louder one. Bartholomew bolted into the hallway with Celwyn and the automat on his heels. They halted outside the sitting room door.

Tara helped a harried-looking Mrs. Thomas gather towels and pans of water. While Doctor Utgartt talked with Patrick in front of the birthing bed, Annabelle handed the swaddled baby to Nemo, who appeared speechless. Like soldiers witnessing history, Granger, Edward, and the Conductor arrived outside the door.

"The baby is here!" Patrick announced.

A chorus of "Congratulations" met him, and Kang stepped into the room to approach the new mother. He kissed Annabelle's forehead and shook Patrick's hand. The act seemed to break the spell of the moment, and everyone began talking at the same time.

Nemo passed the baby to Bartholomew who had started to cry.

"Can I have your attention—" Mrs. Thomas moderated her usual voice, but everyone still froze in place. "Doctor Utgartt requests that you clear the room and let the Missus rest. Everyone out—" When they didn't move fast enough, she added, "*Now*, Sirs."

As they hurried out of the way, the magician stopped beside the baby. He, too, felt tears form as he gazed at the little one, thinking that this balanced the horror of Elizabeth's death and everything they'd gone through this evening.

"I said out, Sir. Miss McFein can stay."

As the magician obediently followed Kang out the door, he decorated the cradle with tiny bunnies and twinkling stars. He halted and turned. "What is the baby's name?"

Patrick smiled. "Elizabeth."

"We will call her Betty," Annabelle added.

Celwyn searched for Tara and sent her a silent and intimate message, and gentle kiss. From their observation point in the hall the boys watched open-mouthed. Otto handed the magician his tablet and Celwyn grinned. Zander read it aloud.

"He says he will call her "Sister," and I will too."

That brought tears to everyone's eyes, even Mrs. Thomas's as she finished shooing them out. The clock chimed the two o'clock hour as they trooped into the parlor. A crooked picture here and a broken vase there still reminded them of the attack. In seconds, the magician had cleaned away the remaining evidence of violence and straightened the room.

"Other than replacing a few things, I don't think Annabelle will be upset with the damage here." He scanned the hall. "I can't speak for Mrs. Thomas though." As he studied Bartholomew, he asked, "Where was she when the intruders arrived?"

"The kitchen. Sully answered the door, and they knocked him out and burst inside. The boys had already been sent upstairs to get ready for bed." He sighed. "The Conductor and Edward heard the commotion and came running along with Ricardo. Later they chased a bunch of the bastards outside."

"Thank God the boys were upstairs," Kang said.

"Yes. The Captain and Granger jumped into the fray with me. Most satisfactory." The big man looked at Kang. "What about you?"

"In the sitting room with Annabelle when I heard them." He growled, "Gaspard didn't hesitate. As he came in, he pointed a pistol at Annabelle, backed Patrick into a corner, and hit him with it."

"Patrick would have beat the daylights out of him if he could have." Bartholomew chuckled without humor. "The biggest surprise? Ricardo has a strong right hook."

"I agree," Nemo said. "Your chef is a brave man. He charged in here with one of his saucepans and bashed several of them until they piled on him."

Granger had been walking about the room and checking the hallway. He returned and asked, "You have protection spells from the witches on all the entrances except the front door?"

"Yes. Sully probably didn't check outside before he opened the door," Bartholomew sighed. "Even if he had, they could have battered down the door with the same result." He glanced at the Professor. "I didn't see Gaspard at all."

"After the bastard knocked Patrick out, he had the gall to introduce himself. Then he beat me with his pistol and started dragging me toward the door." Kang's expression darkened and the automat touched the leathery skin on his forehead.

"And the gunfire?" Nemo's brow went up.

Celwyn grinned at him. "Tara shot the gigantic one right between the eyes until she emptied her pistol. Annabelle was well protected."

"I should say so," Nemo nodded. "It has been quite an evening. And," like the others, he checked the hallway for Mrs. Thomas, "I enjoyed the altercation very much. Gaspard's automats turned out to be persistent and surprisingly strong."

Granger asked, "Please explain why they all crashed together. That clanking noise is louder than when the *Nautilus* slams her bay doors."

"It isn't the first time I've had to subdue them. They have a metal power disk right here." The magician tapped his chest. "A powerful magnet is the fastest way to overcome them. Wholesale, as it were."

The Professor reached into his pocket and held up a thin, hand-sized piece of metal. "This one belonged to Gaspard. After what he did to Elizabeth, he is no more."

From their position by the fire the boys perched like quiet little mice in pajamas, hoping not to be asked to go to bed. They had been listening to every word. Otto arose and handed Kang his tablet.

"Otto asks, 'Are we safe again? Is the man who hurt Miss Elizabeth gone?'"

Kang patted his shoulder and told the lads, "Yes." He swallowed hard. "I loved my wife very much. Now, we will have her funeral. She will rest in peace."

Chapter 25

BEFORE THE MAGICIAN WENT TO bed, he, Kang, Granger, Edward, and Bartholomew walked the perimeter of Tellyhouse. They could find no evidence of trouble. In the front yard, the snow revealed dozens of footprints. Even though Celwyn could have done this alone, he realized the importance of allowing the others to verify the conditions around them.

As they entered the house again, Celwyn said, "All the attackers, minus their power discs, now reside in the city trash dump with the ashes from the stoves and potato peelings. They'll look like rusty dressmakers' dummies if ever found. The other intruders, the kind who breathe, are in Major Jardin's jail cell. I put his guards to sleep, and we left a note on his desk informing him we discovered burglars on our property with ill intent." His voice lowered. "If it hadn't been Christmas, I would have killed them."

Verne held a whiskey bottle between his knees and couldn't stop trembling. "So, they'll stay in jail, and we won't have to explain how they got there?"

With a bark of laughter, the Professor said, "They won't contradict us by admitting to what they were really doing. Neither will Jardin's guards when they wake up."

"Even if they do, I doubt Jardin will let that go," Edward said. "Mr. Celwyn may have to explain how they got there." He gazed through the picture window as the snow fell once again in a million soft flakes. "Quite an exciting day. Thank God it is over."

Nemo looked at the author and asked, "Where were you during the attack?"

"Hiding under my bed upstairs."

Celwyn had never in all his nearly four hundred years slept in the same vicinity as a newborn babe. Those tiny bundles with a large lung capacity were usually kept in a nursery behind a closed door. All through the rest of the night, he thought he heard the baby even when he didn't—and there had to be more than fifty feet between the conservatory and the sitting room.

About dawn, the new parents announced all was well and Celwyn could go back to his tea with their thanks. When Patrick added that he would find Edward to drive the doctor home, the magician signaled to him from the hallway.

"Allow me to escort you, Doctor." Celwyn helped Uttgart with his coat and noticed a latent wisp of fear in his eye. "Everyone is still asleep and there shouldn't be any traffic across town." He wiped away any memory the doctor had of the attack last night.

When the magician returned, he found Jackson on duty at the front door. He handed him his coat. "Is Sully still recovering?"

"Yes, sir. He took quite a bashing last night." The porter frowned. "The boys were worried."

Celwyn figured out where Jackson had been during the attack. "You were putting them to bed when the thugs broke in?"

"I wouldn't let the boys come downstairs and believe me, they tried," he said as they walked into the parlor, keeping their voices low.

"We are fortunate you kept them up there. Thank you." The magician saw Jackson's glance toward the hall and said, "Please resume your normal duties and I will watch the door. Is Ricardo in the kitchen?" Celwyn waited until Jackson looked away before producing his tea. He could wait only so long.

The footman gave a start, averted his eyes, and continued as if nothing remarkable had occurred.

"Yes. Chef is there. He says he is sore, but well. The Professor said the same thing last night about him."

As Celwyn poured, he made a request. "Whenever you see Edward and the Conductor, please ask them to stop here. We need to coordinate how to retrieve the rest of the staff and get things back to normal."

Jackson touched his cap. "I will, sir. Mrs. Thomas said the missus and the baby will move upstairs when the missus is strong enough." He bowed. "I am very happy everything is well once more." His smile vanished. "But who were those men and what did they want?"

After Celwyn gave him the particulars and reassurances, along with pouring a second cup of tea, Jackson headed toward the kitchen. In the guise of a moth, the magician flitted down the hall and peeked into the sitting room.

Patrick slept in one of the armchairs with his hand still resting upon the cradle, where he had presumably been rocking the baby. Feet away, Annabelle lay on the settee and snored. That brought up the question; how did Patrick get any sleep? At the moment, the baby looked peaceful while the commotion from her mother sounded like a chorus of squirrels with stuffed-up noses. Nearby, Tara and Kang played checkers. *Bless her heart,* he thought. He hated checkers. The automat saw him and Celwyn beckoned to them.

Once again in the parlor, they conferred in undertones after Celwyn greeted Tara properly.

Kang said, "Thank you for taking the Doctor home safely."

"My pleasure." He asked Tara, "Can I assume between you, the Professor, and Doctor Utgartt, that the baby is healthy and there are no worries about Patrick's blood?"

"That is correct. We're staying close in case something happens, but as the hours go by, we think it will be fine." Tara pecked his cheek and turned to go. "One of us should be in there now."

Kang stood, ready to accompany her. "We are enjoying our checker games too. At least Miss McFein will play with me."

"Pfft." He grabbed the Professor's arm. "Another question. Wouldn't Annabelle and the baby be more comfortable upstairs?"

"Yes."

"When Mrs. Thomas is absent, find out if Annabelle would allow me to use magic to transport her and the baby upstairs. It will be quieter for them. The house staff will be returning soon."

"Uh-huh. At least you asked this time. I will inquire." He bowed to Tara. "After you."

Celwyn yawned and resumed communing with his Earl Grey. Outside the parlor window, a German Shepherd towed a pair of neighbors on skis past the house. On the way back, they stopped to stare at Tellyhouse and whisper behind their hands. Mrs. Thomas would not be amused. Idly, Celwyn wondered if they gossiped about the inmates of Tellyhouse or what happened last night. Or if they had seen Doctor Utgartt and speculated if the baby had arrived. Perhaps they had placed bets on the event as well.

With a yawn as big as his own, Edward walked in. Celwyn produced coffee for him and told him good morning.

Their head of security blinked in the bright light reflecting off the snow. "Good morning." He eyed the coffee cup hovering in front of him for only a second before drinking it down. "If it weren't for the neighbor's rooster, I'd still be asleep."

"You'll feel better after breakfast. What time do you make your first trip into town to pick up the staff?"

Edward eyed the wall clock. "In about an hour."

"You are always armed, I assume."

"After last night, always."

"Could you take either Granger or myself with you for each of your trips today?"

"Certainly, sir. Do you expect trouble?"

"Yes, and no. I don't want to worry the others, and above all, Mrs. Swayne. But yes, I am still concerned." The magician poured tea. "I want to be sure there are no other hooligans watching us, and I plan to check for them when we're out."

As he spoke, Nemo, Granger, and the big man walked into the room.

"That may not be all we have to worry about." Nemo included them all in a question. "Do you suspect Pelaez will try something?"

The magician felt his spirits deflate like a punctured balloon. "It is possible. But Wolfgang seems the more likely—if he is still following us."

"Oh, God," Bartholomew intoned. "I should have stayed in bed. Pelaez might only want to spy on us. Wolfgang is much worse."

Celwyn shrugged. "My suggestion is that the Lieutenant or I go with Edward for his trips into the city to retrieve the staff." With a yawn, the magician wondered if he could squeeze in a nap during the day. "Bartholomew and the Captain could remain here to guard the house. Of course, if the Conductor must go out, one of us would go with him in the other carriage."

"That would cover the situation." Captain Nemo nodded. "Mr. Swayne would also be wise to reinstate his hired guards until further notice."

"I'll pass that along to him. Tea or coffee?" He asked Nemo after floating coffee to Granger.

"Coffee." Nemo raised an amused brow. "You know I'm not fond of tea this early."

"I do." The magician grinned, but it never hurt to convert someone to the joys of tea leaves. "While we wait for the others to join us, there is news. The baby is healthy, per Tara and the Professor. Annabelle is doing well. Patrick looks like he had been hit by a speeding cart. Mrs. Thomas is still asleep in case you want to sneak a peek at the baby before she bars visitors again."

By noon, Edward had reclaimed all the staff, and Mrs. Thomas had declared Sully recovered enough to again assume his duties. She moderated her voice in deference to the baby, but everyone could hear her without any trouble when she told Sully what she would do if he ever opened the front door again without looking to see who stood there. On a positive note, Ricardo seemed invigorated by the previous evening's combat and fairly danced around the kitchen.

Over a hurried, but excellent luncheon, they talked about their plans.

First, Kang and the magician would visit the cooperative undertaker, Bosephus Crow, who had held Elizabeth's body in ice for the last several months. Tara didn't mind the luncheon subject matter, and Annabelle remained in the sitting room with the baby. Celwyn saw that Tara displayed no sign of being tired or worried; he could well believe her prediction that the baby would be healthy.

While they talked and ate, Celwyn noticed the Captain's twitchiness—or general appearance of being uncomfortable. It probably stemmed from being land-locked inside Tellyhouse, instead of sailing on the *Nautilus*. After Jackson had placed the platter of sandwiches in front of them and withdrew, the magician addressed Nemo.

"Sir, while we plan the funeral and help settle things here, could we assume that you have duties on the ship and would like to rejoin your crew on Findbar?"

"Yes. And look over the operations there."

"There is still our mission in Spain." Celwyn glanced at the others and saw nods. "We might be able to do something to speed this along." He noticed the sandwiches had frills of curly lettuce and what must have been greenhouse tomatoes. "I would go with you to the coast to make sure we're not followed, and that the *Nautilus* picks you up. You would be in disguise all the way."

Bartholomew said, "We respectively request that your Lieutenant," he nodded at Granger, "Stay at Tellyhouse a while longer if possible. We are not sure if Pelaez or Wolfgang are still lurking about. And we could use the extra help in case they are."

When Zander started to express his curiosity, the magician hesitated to tell him about his murderous grandfather and insane great-uncle. "I'll explain later, after your lessons."

Verne asked, "When will your crew check for telegrams?"

"Today is Saturday, and we'll look again Monday and on Thursday," Granger told them.

"It takes at least a day to get the train ready," Kang said as they munched. "This sandwich is exceptional … leftover goose from Christmas with spicy mustard. The only genius in this house is Ricardo."

"I certainly agree." Celwyn added up the time needed to prepare the train and the travel distance. "Assuming that your crew hears the news by Monday, we can have you to them Wednesday and on Thursday you'll be on Findbar."

"That is appreciated. Jules will be going with me. We'll also take the opportunity to fully stock the ship for our journey to Spain."

Patrick rushed into the room, wrapped two sandwiches in a napkin, begged their pardon, and rushed out again. The automat stretched his neck, trying to see down the hallway. The magician did the same and listened for Mrs. Thomas before he guided the platter out of the dining room and down the hall. After all, the new parents may wish for a second sandwich. He waited a moment and brought it back the same way.

Zander's eyes bulged, but he didn't say a word as they finished eating in silence. Otto snuck peeks down the hall, grinning, and hoping to see more.

They heard baby Betty crying.

"Aww. It will be interesting having a new baby in the house." Bartholomew elbowed Zander. "I understand I will be giving you your afternoon lessons."

Nemo asked, "Which ones?"

"Mathematics and history."

"Is geography part of their studies?" Nemo asked.

"It should be, but we haven't started it yet. Annabelle has been distracted lately and we must get all their lessons back to normal again."

"Perhaps I could teach them geography." Nemo shrugged. "I know something about it. Especially the oceans."

That brought several chuckles, and they continued when Bartholomew added in a confidential tone, "There is a reason we do not allow Jonas to teach mathematics."

Chapter 26

FOR THE REST OF THE AFTERNOON, they stayed in the parlor, writing birth announcements to friends, reading, or playing cards. The household seemed nearly normal again as the echo of Bartholomew's voice filtered down from the classroom upstairs. Nemo's lesson had occurred earlier. After the boys listened to colorful stories of the sea, they talked about it with unstoppable fascination all through luncheon.

When the magician returned to the parlor and made himself comfortable, he asked the Professor, "Is it Tara's turn with Annabelle and the baby?"

"That is correct." Kang refilled his pen and couldn't help a glance at the hall. "I just resolved one of the obstacles we would have encountered soon." He must not have been as sure of his success as he appeared, because he tiptoed to the door and listened before returning to the sofas. "As I said, I have talked with Patrick, Annabelle, and Mrs. Thomas. On Monday, Mrs. Thomas will begin a search for a teacher to give the boys their lessons. Without Elizabeth's help, and because Annabelle will be busy, it is for the best. We will continue to lead lessons as well as we can until the teacher arrives."

"So, why are you nervous about it?" The magician asked when Kang verified the door again.

"Mrs. Thomas doesn't know we are leaving Prague soon, and neither does Annabelle."

Celwyn grinned at him. "Don't try to dump that responsibility on me, or I'll do more than turn your ears blue."

"Fine. But it isn't urgent. It can wait a few days."

Nemo looked up from the book he held. "I do not wish for the ire of Mrs. Thomas upon my head, nor Mrs. Swayne's. I hope the blame does not follow me." His lips twitched, spoiling his deadpan effort. The automat stared, thinking how extraordinary it sounded for Nemo to try humor.

"There is something else," Kang said. "Annabelle's new nanny will arrive tomorrow, and we are all expected, I quote, 'to be on our best behavior.'" He paused and continued in a fair imitation of Annabelle's voice, "That means you, Uncle Celwyn. No magic in front of her. None."

By the time he finished, they were all laughing. The news of the nanny reminded the magician of something.

"Did you make the offer to Annabelle for me to transport them upstairs?"

"Yes," the automat said. "She says Patrick will escort her and the baby upstairs before dinner, but that she hopes you will be ready to supply unseen assistance as needed." He stood. "It nears the four o'clock hour and my turn to relieve Miss McFein with Betty. Thank God." He tilted his head at the magician. "You're smiling, Jonas. Leave my ears alone."

Celwyn told Granger, "He shouldn't give me ideas."

"Why change only one of his ears?" Granger rose in his seat to study the automat as he walked out. "That is a beautiful color, by the way."

"It will give the baby something to look at. Sort of like an animated toy hovering close."

Nemo asked, "Jonas, you have never been close to a newborn babe, have you?"

"Not for more than a few moments, no."

"It will be a while before the baby is old enough to see orange ears."

Tara arrived and greeted them. As she settled beside him, the magician handed her a glass of wine.

"How are the baby and her parents doing?"

Tara sipped and said, "Very well. She is a sweet baby." She gave them a look. "An exciting night for her birth."

"It certainly was," Bartholomew said as he joined them. "The boys will be down in a moment. Zander wants to play checkers with Miss McFein."

"He does?" Both Tara and the magician exclaimed.

"I told him she played with the Professor, and Zander insisted," he said with studious seriousness. "He also has a young man's fascination for her too."

Without batting an eye, she said, "I'll take care of it."

Celwyn imagined she would, with delicacy.

"What are our plans tomorrow?" Bartholomew patted a yawn.

"There are many. Early on we will go with Ricardo and Sully to the farmer's market, then the twins and the Conductor will visit the train yard to ready the *Elizabeth*." The magician paused to finish his cup. "About noon, we'll accompany the Professor to police headquarters to make a report on our intruders, and insist they incarcerate the hooligans that we left in their jail last night."

"That means I will stay with the baby since the Professor must deal with the police," Tara said.

"And the undertaker," Kang reminded them.

Nemo rubbed his chin before asking Celwyn, "Won't you have to explain to Jardin how you managed to put the attackers into their jail?"

"I'll figure it out." The magician had seen Bartholomew's yawn and felt one coming on. "Then we'll go to the undertakers to plan Elizabeth's services. You and the Lieutenant will be here on guard with the Conductor."

"That sounds good. Mr. Verne might be available for bridge, but we will need a fourth." He turned to Tara. "Do you—"

She shook her head. "No, but thank you for thinking of me. I am expected to begin embroidery lessons soon." Her expression did not reveal any hint of her opinion of embroidery.

"I am departing the city with the assumption that I am no longer needed here." Nemo gazed at the magician. "The general opinion seems to be that when the rest of you leave Prague, the danger will follow you and not annoy anyone here at Tellyhouse. True?"

"Gaspard has been dealt with… What are you expecting?" A frown crinkled Tara's perfect brow.

"We expect so, sir." Celwyn took her hand. "There is still the question whether Pelaez or my father are waiting for us." He nodded outside, where the rain had finished washing away the snow. "They have no interest in the other residents here. We need to explain that to Annabelle and Patrick so they'll understand why we must depart again." Celwyn felt like punching something.

"I have letters for Valentine and Simone." As she drank wine, Tara's eyes became thoughtful. "It would be prudent to send a much quicker telegram to let them know Gaspard exists no more, and that we will soon head toward Spain."

"Would you like to do so now?" Celwyn asked. "We have several hours until dinner." He glanced out the side windows and confirmed that the carriage had not been put away. "The telegraph office will be open for a while yet."

"Yes. It will be nice to get outside into the fresh air, even if it is a mite wet."

Otto and Zander arrived in time to hear the last of what she said.

"We get to see the ducks!" Zander declared. They pivoted and ran to change their clothes.

"We might as well bring Beastie along." Celwyn sighed. "I had rather hoped to be alone with you." She tweaked his nose. "Perhaps another time."

Chapter 27

JUST AFTER DAWN THE NEXT DAY, THE magician escorted Ricardo and his flock through the farmer's market and home again. He and Edward waited at the front door for the automat and Granger to come out and then set off for the police station.

It had turned into a fine, if cold, December day after the rain stopped. The automat seemed lost in his thoughts as they passed by the Alder district and onto a street with many policemen coming and going.

Celwyn asked, "Have you decided whether you will visit the police by yourself, or take us inside with you?" When the Professor said nothing, the magician prompted him. "Xiau?"

"What? Oh—" he frowned. "I think alone is best."

"We have a suggestion." The magician exited the carriage and held the cab door open. "Edward will go with you. The police know him, and he will be able to answer questions about our intruders."

Kang blinked for a moment and squared his shoulders. "All right. This also has the advantage of truth, and I doubt the attackers will mention anything else in case it earns them more time in jail.

Granger and Celwyn occupied their time watching the comings and goings into the Polizeiwache building. Most of the arrests appeared to be for drunkenness and brawling, usually vocalized in several languages. Prague's population included Slovaks and Germans, not to mention a Yiddish district, the Greeks, Turks, Italians, and Yugoslavs. No wonder the city boasted hundreds of churches.

A while later Professor Kang came stomping out again and Edward swung up top to grab the reins. The next stop would not surprise the automat; the discussion they planned would.

Bartholomew held the door of Ezekiel's Books open and the others followed Kang inside. Bartholomew addressed the automat in a tone of voice that should have warned him of the gravity of the upcoming conversation.

"We wanted to talk with you without interruptions. Or emotions," Batholomew answered him.

The automat swiveled to stare at them and then reverted back to the history section. "Ezekiel said they had received my history of the Greek tragedies."

He squatted to better see the books on the bottom shelf. "I hope it isn't gone already."

Bartholomew held up a hand to the magician, indicating he wanted to try.

"We know you are in pain, Xiau. We all mourn Elizabeth's death." The automat glanced at him and went back to searching for his book. Bartholomew soldiered on. "We are asking if you would like to stay in Prague to finish mourning. You should have time for yourself—you do not have to go with us to Spain."

Celwyn said, "And while you mourn, to not blame yourself. I would do something other than decorate your ears if that occurs."

"Jonas is right. This is not your fault." Bartholomew agreed. "This would have happened anyhow to bring you to heel when you returned. He would have used her no matter what."

In slow motion, Kang stood and faced them, his face contorted with emotion.

"Xiau, you could have quiet introspection ... and peace, if you stay here." Celwyn patted his shoulder. "Or you can jump back into danger. Only you know what you want to do."

"What about our supposition that there are other disciples of Talos? And that they are just like my dear dastardly brother and are more likely to follow us out of Prague?" Kang asked as his emotions faded to normal. "Is this still true?"

"That is still a strong assumption. If Wolfgang or Pelaez are monitoring us here, they will most definitely follow us," Bartholomew said.

Kang blew dust off a book and opened it. "So, logically, our best option is to remove ourselves from Prague, at least for now."

Celwyn inhaled a retort he planned to make; the automat seemed too serene. He grabbed him by the shoulders to face them.

"What do you want to do?" Bartholomew asked. "Tell us."

Kang almost smiled. "After all this time, you two don't know when I'm teasing?"

Celwyn elevated him until they were eye to eye. "Are you sure?"

"Yes. We will all go to help Nemo."

Bartholomew said, "Don't drop him."

The magician lifted Kang higher and planted him on top of the bookshelf.

"I'm going to visit the poetry section." Celwyn started off. "Perhaps they have something new."

Bartholomew laughed. "About friendship." He helped the automat down again.

"Let's go check the engineering section. There could be something we missed here last week."

"True." The big man led the way. "And we might need it when we go back to Findbar."

When they exited the bookstore, they found Granger leaning against the carriage while he talked with Edward. They made a pair, soldiers of the world with a strong sense of duty.

"To the undertakers next?" Granger asked.

"Yes." Celwyn eyed the automat, seeing a glower develop.

"Major Jardin is an oaf."

"We gathered that from Patrick's comments," Granger said. "Can you be more precise?"

The automat lifted his shoulders and let them drop. "The last time I saw him, the man suggested that Elizabeth's death could have been prevented if I had been here. No. She would have been killed by Gaspard for his purposes."

Keeping his face blank, Celwyn rejoiced; he had been trying for so long and hard to make the automat to see that it wasn't his fault. Finally, logic prevailed.

The automat looked at them. "If any of you had been present earlier, you would have done something to Jardin. Then the police would have remembered us so well afterward, we never could have gone anywhere without them following us." He lowered his voice, "But, it is true—she did die because of me."

Celwyn groaned. "Bartholomew would tell you that is rubbish. So would Nemo." The magician glared.

Granger grunted his opinion, probably afraid of overstepping.

"The Lieutenant agrees," Celwyn told Kang.

"Yes, I do," Granger spoke up. "Professor, evil will always find a way. We must be cleverer. Mrs. Kang struck me as someone who had confidence in you and not someone to run from trouble."

The automat managed a small smile. "That is true." He raised his eyes to theirs. "I'll save my guilt for now. We have much to do."

Bartholomew took a cab home, and the others climbed back inside the carriage to travel to Josefov, the Jewish part of town. Soon, they bumped across broken cobblestones, marveled at the old architecture, and continued into much narrower and ancient streets. They pulled to a stop in front of a freshly painted building with windows that sparkled in the drizzling rain.

An ornate sign over the door announced that they had reached:

Edward led the way into a too-warm room spiked with a chemical that caused the magician's nose to itch. Lace curtains framed windows surrounded by velvet wallpaper and quiet serenity. Celwyn couldn't name the spindly German furniture that crowded every inch of the room, but it certainly fit the atmosphere. Behind the counter, a quaint elderly man in a funeral suit and tails stared at them with quiet intensity, as if they had met before. The magician felt a flutter of apprehension as he returned the look, but not one of danger.

Although small in stature, the man had a deep baritone.

"May I help you?"

Kang stepped forward. "Good afternoon. Are you Mr. Bosephus Crow?"

"I am."

The automat bowed. "Professor Xiau Kang." He introduced the others. "We understand you have been holding my wife's body for us. Mrs. Elizabeth Kang."

Crow regarded them for a long moment, his scrutiny careful but not suspicious. Somewhere in the back of the building, a tenor began singing *Götterdämmerung*, from Siegfried. To the magician's ear, the singer sounded professionally trained.

"Pleased to be of service." Crow bowed. "Not interring the deceased is an unusual request."

"We are very grateful." Kang asked, "When could we schedule the funeral?"

"As soon as you wish."

While the automat discussed details, Crow's attention flickered to the window behind them, and he frowned. Something made the hair on the magician's arms rise and he pivoted just as the buzzing noise rattled the glass, and the window shattered.

"Guard the Professor!" he yelled at Granger as he started for the door, but it exploded, and a pack of automats burst inside.

Granger tackled Kang, pulling him behind a settee, and covered him with his body. The lead automat raised a pistol, and Celwyn dissolved it, but when he readied to remove the other automats, the nearest one turned to stone. Edward came in, swinging his rifle at the rest of them.

"Hold on to Xiau—" Celwyn called out to Granger as he magnetized a free-standing foot warmer and flung it into the middle of them. The expected clanking echoed in the small room as the intruders slammed together, making this the third time he'd had to magnetize these bastards.

"Hey—" Granger yelled as the same magnetization drew Kang toward the pile of automats only feet away.

"Allow me." Crow lifted a hand, and Kang flew across the room to land behind him. "I can hold on to him." And he proved it by sitting on the automat.

"Thank you," Celwyn panted as he enclosed the attackers in a metal cage. In the next second, he peeled back the roof of the building and sent them high into the sky and eastward toward the hills. Rain pattered into the shop as he closed the roof again and saw that Edward stood underneath it with enormous eyes. The magician grinned at him.

Kang wiggled out from under their host and peeked around the counter. As the undertaker helped him to his feet, from the back room a lad about Otto's age came running. Crow waved him back again. "Everything is fine, Daniel."

"Yes, sir." Daniel whirled and, as he retraced his steps, he switched to Wagner's Norse War song.

Crow bowed to Celwyn and Kang, and they returned the courtesy. "I'm pleased we survived that unpleasantness."

"Do I know you, sir?" the magician asked and lifted a hand. Another door with the same beveled glass appeared, replacing the one blown apart a minute ago.

"No, you do not." Bocephus Crow gestured and the debris from the attack disappeared. Curtains again fluttered in the windows and the room seemed just as it did before.

Edward and the others gazed at him. Kang voiced his curiosity.

"Thank you for your assistance, sir. Are you—"

Crow touched a finger to his head, and a pale cloud of glittery smoke enclosed him. It dissipated, revealing a much younger version of the man, his face unwrinkled and his eyes clear. He smiled at them.

"To answer your question, I am a simple mortician."

Celwyn found his voice. "And we are most grateful. We apologize for bringing our problem to your door."

"I've seen some of those men in the nearby shops over the last several months." Crow frowned. "Ever since the day they delivered Mrs. Kang's body. If they are after one of your party—then it couldn't be Mrs. Kang, could it?"

The automat said, "It appears so. You deserve an explanation." After Kang gave him some background on the automats, the undertaker had another question.

"Why did they slam together like that?"

After the magician told him, he mentally shrugged. Two attacks in two days? And an encounter from months ago fluttered at him in the back of his mind, something he should have questioned.

"Ah. Well." Again, the glittery smoke enveloped him as the undertaker aged and took his place behind the counter. "We better get on with the arrangements before something else happens."

Edward left them to watch the carriage, and Granger took up a position just outside the door with his hand on his pistol. Pedestrian traffic appeared brisk, and Granger checked each one as they bustled by.

The magician listened to the exchange of information and the strength in Kang's voice. Xiau faltered toward the end when he mentioned the birth of Betty and why they had to leave. "We are most proud that she has arrived, but you have just seen what can occur when we are around." Kang tried to make his voice stronger. "We will depart soon to draw these nefarious elements away from Tellyhouse. They are not safe when we're here, yet I worry they won't be if we leave."

"Such as what happened to Mrs. Kang," the undertaker surmised.

Celwyn said, "Yes."

"I cannot promise you anything today, but perhaps by the time you depart from Prague, I will be able to provide some assistance in defending those you hold dear."

The magician couldn't help it and entered the man's mind. He wanted to trust him but had to be sure. Once inside, Celwyn saw an orderly presentation of thoughts, concern for them, and moderate curiosity about Celwyn. The magician had a question for him.

"Mr. Crow." The magician lifted a hand and a thin image of Pelaez and Wolfgang stood in front of him, accurate in every detail, including his father's deranged eyes. "Do you recognize either of these men?"

Crow moved closer until he could have touched Pelaez's cheek. He explored the images and intently scrutinized Wolfgang. "Neither, however, I will be on the lookout for them."

Kang felt so relieved. He staggered to a chair and sat down.

"Thank you," the magician said. "We must caution you; both are most dangerous. They would not hesitate to harm you."

"I am used to danger, sir. In this neighborhood, I have been looked upon to protect the elderly and the weak. The neighbors thank me with smiles and gifts." He waved at the images still hovering in front of him. "Who are these gentlemen?"

Kang barked a short laugh. "They are Mr. Celwyn's father and brother. We don't know why his father would harm him—but he has been trying to. Pelaez, his brother, would do something obnoxious just for the entertainment of it."

"Pelaez is also a magician and cannot be trusted. I urge you to be careful, sir." The images vanished, and Celwyn felt a cold hand pressing on him... Just thinking about his father terrified him.

As they went out the door, Kang trailed an inscrutable look after Bosephus Crow.

Chapter 28

My house is small, but may heaven grant
that it is never too full of friends.

Jules Verne

Elizabeth's Funeral

A FEW DAYS AFTER CAPTAIN NEMO and Verne left for Szczecin, Tellyhouse prepared for a grim day.

From the parlor, Kang watched as Celwyn escorted the boys to the waiting carriage. The winter sun shone bright the morning of the funeral, and a moment later the sunlight dimmed, reminding Kang of their temporary and delusional existence in a temporal world. Long afterward, grief would remain.

Inside the carriage, the boys waited like statues, lost in their thoughts and adrift in the sadness surrounding them. When Bartholomew escorted the Professor to the carriage, the sun returned. It didn't take long until Patrick arrived wearing his grief and holding Annabelle's arm.

"Will the baby go with us too?" Zander bounced in his seat and pressed his face to the window.

"No. The nursemaid will keep an eye on her while we are gone. And Edward and Mr. Granger will help the Conductor watch over them and the house," Bartholomew said as he and the others climbed inside and Sully took the reins.

Tellyhouse would also have a few unseen elements of protection. The magician had told Kang about them; just a few surprises on the grounds to detour unwanted visitors. Some would growl, and the others slither. In case the neighbors should hear a loud clanging, any visiting automats might have encountered a magnet or two.

As the carriage rolled forward, Ricardo, Mrs. Thomas, and the rest of the staff, rode in the second carriage. Andy had worn his best suit, and with a morose expression, took the reins to follow them.

In front of the procession, an ornate black wagon led by twin white horses pulled into the street with Elizabeth's casket. Bosephus Crow himself drove the hearse.

Not a word passed between them as the carriages started forward, passing by shivering neighbors standing at the curb. They silently paid their respects as the coaches went by. Kang blinked and avoided Celwyn's sympathetic eyes, but he couldn't evade the boys' curiosity.

"Will we see Miss Elizabeth in her coffin?" Zander asked him.

Annabelle's eyes widened, but Kang answered.

"She will be in her coffin, and if you want to, you can say goodbye to her there. It is up to you and Otto." He regarded the other boy. "Whatever you are comfortable with."

When they did not answer, Bartholomew cleared his throat. "I brought a copy of Elizabeth's favorite poem, "The Eagle." He patted his breast pocket. "Do you remember the poem?"

Otto nodded and Zander tried to. "I think so."

Without taking the book from his pocket, Bartholomew recited Tennyson's, "The Eagle."

> "He clasps the crag with crooked hands;
> Close to the sun in lonely lands,
> Ring'd with the azure world, he stands.
>
> The wrinkled sea beneath him crawls;
> He watches from his mountain walls,
> And like a thunderbolt he falls."

"Thank you, my friend." To the boys, the Professor said, "Elizabeth loved you very much. I know you'll remember her forever." When the boys blinked away tears, Kang added, "We will get through today."

As he spoke, the hearse slowed between medieval statues and sympathetic trees, and the carriages moved sedately forward as if leading a royal procession. They wound their way to the far corner of the graveyard as small headstones progressed to larger, older ones. Zander nodded at a row of mausoleums decorated with carved cherubs and flowers, and one that resembled a small church with an angled steeple.

While Kang remembered Telly's funeral here, thinking how similar it felt, Otto grabbed his hand and pointed to an enormous moss-covered cross. The automat squinted, able to make out the dates 1723—1758, but unable to read the name before the hearse came to a stop before a block wall.

The grass appeared well-tended, and baskets of flowers adorned the end of each row. Elizabeth would love the flowers. Kang corrected himself; *she did love the flowers.* Here, there seemed to be a blending of the past and present in the ancient crosses and new tombstones.

Daniel, the young man from Crow's funeral parlor, hopped down from the hearse, straightened his top hat, bowed, and waited beside the rear of the hearse.

The boys escorted Kang and Annabelle toward the gravesite as Daniel, Ricardo, Patrick, Sully, Bartholomew, and Celwyn bore the casket to the platform by the freshly dug grave. Kang approached with an armload of white Helleborus roses from the Tellyhouse garden. He bent over the casket and picked up Elizabeth's hand, held it to his heart, and bowed his head.

Across the sea of graves and into the melancholy, floated the same dreamlike music that Elizabeth and the automat had danced to as the *Elizabeth* chugged her way over the gorge. That view of the Bay of Bengal had been memorable and seemed so long ago. At once, recognizing the music, Kang looked up and thanked Celwyn. Into the silence, thousands of rose petals fell from the sky, followed by tiny stars that showered them as, one by one, they approached the casket and paid their respects.

When Celwyn's turn came, he knelt beside Elizabeth and said, "Rest in peace. I will protect Xiau, no matter the price. I promise you." More petals fell as he gazed at the sky.

Bartholomew said, "This is most beautiful Jonas." He gestured to the tiny stars in the rose petals. "Especially these that melt in your hand."

"I caused the rose petals to fall, but not the stars." Celwyn frowned. "They are not of my doing."

"Oh..." Kang wondered how interesting this would become.

The magician jerked his chin at the undertaker. "I believe Mr. Crow provided them." As he spoke, the undertaker lifted his top hat and winked.

Chapter 29

OVER THE NEXT SEVERAL WEEKS, all appeared well.

At night, Granger and Celwyn investigated the various districts of Prague, scouting for more automats, and finding none. They verified the area near Crow's establishment, Kang's favorite pastry shop, and the many other haunts Bartholomew enjoyed. During the day, the magician checked the streets around abandoned buildings and any other places he could think of. Bartholomew went with him when he wasn't busy with the boys' lessons. After several months of school without science and mathematics, the Professor and Bartholomew made up for lost time.

Their new school mistress would arrive soon, and until then, everyone took turns teaching. Sometimes, the scientific displays drew the staff's attention or frightened them, and other times attracted the ire of Mrs. Thomas. After a particularly foul-smelling beaker exploded, Kang and Bartholomew decided to take the experiments outside. At night, the boys still worked on their mechanical frog, and by now they could control it, and cause it to swivel and back up.

Edward returned just before afternoon tea with a fistful of telegrams. Celwyn yawned and watched the baby waving her tiny arms. So did Patrick, with proud fascination.

"I believe she will command an army someday," he said.

"You wish it were so." Annabelle handed Betty back to the nursemaid. "She will own a big hotel and a string of theaters. What do you think, Olga?"

Miss Olga Ratzloff pursed her lips, deciding on a diplomatic answer with both parents staring at her for a biased opinion. Perhaps twenty-years old and pretty in a wholesome fashion, the nursemaid focused on the pins holding the baby's hat place.

"Both, I believe, Missus. We'll just have to wait and see, won't we?" She smiled at them. "It is time I took her upstairs for her nap." By the time she finished speaking, Bartholomew had hefted the cradle onto his shoulder.

"After you, Miss."

Because they still kept an eye on the baby twenty-four hours a day, Tara kissed Celwyn's cheek and followed them up the stairs.

The automat had been standing by the fireplace reading one of the telegrams. "Nemo sends his best wishes. He also says everything is fine on Findbar." The Professor glanced at them with a flare of excitement lighting his eyes. "He is asking when we will be ready to leave again."

Patrick must have been expecting this news and Annabelle's reaction to it. As she built up to an explosion, he gathered her into his arms and put his chin in her hair. "We wondered about this, my dear."

While Annabelle squirmed to get free, Bartholomew returned to the parlor in time to hear her blurt, "To where? Where are you going?"

Before anyone thought of something innocent and vague, Qing squawked one of his loudest cries and flew in loops just under the ceiling—a bird celebration party. When he reached Bartholomew, the bird bounced on top of the big man's head and kept up his calls. Annabelle threw up her hands.

"I believe Qing approves." Kang fished in his pocket and tossed a coin at the magician, who caught it with a smile. The automat told the others, "We had a wager as to whether or not Qing had evolved to understanding the finer points of conversation."

Bartholomew barked a laugh. "Beyond the annoyed 'stop that!' he usually hears? Like Jonas, I think he does understand, and I wish I had put money on it." The mechanical bird again circled the ceiling. "A celebration if I ever saw one." Qing landed on the magician's shoulder and scraped his beak across Celwyn's beard.

Annabelle snorted. "That damn bird is spoiled. Anyhow, where are you going?"

"The first stop will be Findbar," Celwyn said. "These two cannot tolerate being close by and not visiting the flying machine. Then—" He scanned the hallway for pint-size listeners. The hour or so before tea meant homework, but as he personally knew, listening to adults could be more interesting. He turned to Qing and asked in a low voice, "Since you understand, would you go see if there is anyone at the top of the stairs, please?" He pointed to the hall.

Everyone held their breath, even Annabelle with a less annoyed expression, as the mechanical bird tilted his head one way and then the other just as he did the first time Jonas had met him. He blinked glittering eyes at them and lifted off, flying lazily out the door and up the stairs. When he came back, he landed on Celwyn's shoulder again and fluffed his feathers.

"Have you been working with him?" Kang demanded.

"Yes, but he'd rather chew on Wye's scales if given a choice. Say, wouldn't it be interesting if we found Wye hovering at the top of the stairs?"

"Good grief, Jonas!" Bartholomew exclaimed. Other expressions of semi-amusement and shock followed.

Qing shook himself all over. Kang saw him and asked, "Does that mean he saw no one?"

Celwyn shrugged and went into the hallway. He gazed at the top of the stairs and said, "I think so."

"What do you plan to do after Findbar?" Patrick asked.

"That is harder to describe ... and most confidential." Bartholomew used his diplomatic voice. The three of them had discussed this very question and finally came to a compromise between the bare truth—that would unnecessarily worry the new parents—and something vague that would keep them informed. They also had an obligation to maintain Nemo's privacy about Spain. The big man had drawn the short straw to relay the news.

"Well, what is it?" Annabelle said, "I have to go up to the nursery in a few minutes and I swear I'll have you changing nappies if you don't tell us."

As quickly as he could, Bartholomew said, "Before I do, you need to know of a few things that should make our departure less stressful. First, would you agree that things are usually more dangerous when we are in town?"

Patrick said, "God, yes. When you told us of the attack at the undertaker's, I couldn't believe it. We had sent Edward there several times before without incident."

"Just so. We also can't ignore the murder of Elizabeth, the act designed to bring us back here."

Granger had been so quiet for so long that Celwyn had almost forgotten about him until he spoke. "We've been looking all over Prague for the rest of Gaspard's automats. It is likely the ones destroyed at the undertaker's were the last of them. I have also been introduced to Francesca and witches." He blushed. "She will continue providing protection spells."

"Did they take liberties with you?" Annabelle asked.

"They tried."

Patrick's look of relief he hadn't been the object of their desire brought a few smiles. He said, "I'll continue to employ the guards and disguise them as gardeners and footmen. According to Mrs. Thomas, we go through those roles at a regular pace anyhow."

"With what Bartholomew has reported, we feel that you will be safe, especially after we leave." The magician straightened his cuffs. "The Professor is sought after by villains much more than I am."

"Pfft. It's just that *lately* they seem to be after me." The automat's nose stayed in the air.

Annabelle tapped her foot and glanced at the clock. "It is nearly four and the boys will be here soon for tea. Finish it."

"Well." Bartholomew hesitated. "Part of what you heard yesterday regarding our last endeavor carries over to our new problem."

Patrick studied Annabelle. "Things are still a bit confused here, what with the attack and birth of Betty. Could you explain what you mean?"

Just then, Celwyn caught a whiff of Tara's perfume, and she arrived in time to hear Patrick's request. As she took a seat, she shot a quick look at the others and said, "The paintings that Nemo retrieved from Dearing's vault provided clues to the location of where his wife died." Her voice grew serious. "The Captain intends to retrieve her body."

That certainly let the cat out of the bag, Celwyn thought. At least she did not mention Doctor Lazlo or his experiments. He checked the new parents for expressions of acceptance and saw them in their whispered nods to each other. He breathed again.

Patrick asked, "And then you'll stop at Findbar to work on the flying machine before coming back here?"

"Yes. We would again continue to mail the lads' science lessons." Kang addressed Annabelle, "I understand the new teacher does not have a scientific background and can't provide that education. What do you plan to do?"

"You understand correctly. She thinks science is the devil's work."

"Oh, how quaint." The magician laughed.

"When does she arrive?" Bartholomew asked.

"Two weeks." Annabelle smirked. "I want to be present when she sees a mess from one of your experiments."

"We have no idea what you mean, do we?" the big man asked Kang. "Anyhow, we will buy baby presents wherever we go." Bartholomew changed the subject as his frown developed. "What size is she?"

Annabelle said, "Choose clothes at least large enough for a one-year-old baby. She might be twice as big by the time you see her again."

"Have you noticed the wooden poles that are being erected around the city?" Patrick asked, displaying his adeptness at subject changing. "They are about twenty-feet tall and have wires on them."

"Yes, I did. Xiau and I spotted them on Trojika Street and wondered." The big man wore a confused expression.

Tara laughed and jabbed the magician in the ribs. "I bet I know who is going to be very happy when everything is done." The magician frowned until he figured it out.

"That new invention—" Bartholomew slapped his thigh, and exclaimed, "The telephone?"

"Yes," Patrick said. "They are building the service for it in the commercial district first, but soon they'll offer it elsewhere, including residences."

Granger said, "I've heard of the telephone. It will replace the telegraph?"

"Not at first—it is too expensive to install those poles, and the other machinery between cities." Patrick thought more. "Or over rivers and oceans."

"I want one."

"Of course, you do." Tara patted the magician's hand.

They all enjoyed his undisguised lust for the new contraption until Xiau said, "Knowing you, why don't you just make yourself one?"

Before he finished his question, one of the square shiny black boxes sat before them.

"I have no clue what to put inside it." The thing emitted a shrill ringing sound. "I do remember the way it sounded."

"We could drill a hole on top and use it for a flower vase." The automat grinned at him.

"Funny, Xiau." Celwyn turned to Patrick. "When will they become common?"

"A year or two? I will find out."

Kang said, "It will eventually help us keep in touch with everyone here while we're with Nemo. We can still use telegrams for long distances. Or maybe the telephone could be used between cities— perhaps from a big hotel to another big hotel."

"On a practical note, we added additional security to Tellyhouse for while we are away." Celwyn asked, "You'll recall the undertaker, Mr. Crow? He is also a magician. And he will stop by periodically to check that all is well."

"But—"

"How? It has been arranged for you to message him if you need his help. He would be an unexpected asset if you have any further unwanted visitors."

Annabelle asked, "What could he do?"

"From what we can tell," Kang pursed his lips, "his magic is limited, but he can at least provide suitable distractions. He is an agreeable fellow. Mr. Crow also saved me during the attack at his establishment a few weeks ago. Not as flamboyantly as Jonas would have, but he gets the job done."

"Mrs. Thomas tells me Crow was the only undertaker in the city willing to hold Elizabeth's body until we returned," Bartholomew said.

"Yes, it is true." Patrick nodded.

"If you could arrange some of Ricardo's snacks for his visits, Mr. Crow would appreciate it." Kang told them, "No other payment would be required. He is a widower and from what he says, he is not a good cook."

Chapter 30

L ESS THAN A WEEK LATER, THE
Conductor and his helpers readied the *Elizabeth*
for the journey to Szczecin. After an extended discussion, Annabelle announced that no one from
Tellyhouse would go with them; either they were
needed to guard Annabelle and the baby, or they
were needed for other chores as dictated by Mrs.
Thomas. Patrick insisted the baby was too young
to travel.

On the day before their departure, both Tara
and Kang went with the new parents to visit the
baby's doctor. Valentine had sent a recommenda-
tion for Doctor Gadola, saying Gadola knew a great
deal about the physiology of vampires. Before they
settled into the carriage for the ride downtown, the
magician mentioned what his fertile imagination
had thought of; what if the baby had much more
vampire blood than Betty ... and all of a sudden, its

teeth made their first appearance? It might be an exciting visit to Doctor Gadola. Annabelle shook her head and shooed him into the carriage.

With Betty's examination finished and everyone back in the carriage, Annabelle fussed over the baby with the nursemaid's help.

Kang, indicating the carriage park, asked Celwyn, "Is everything quiet out there?"

The magician packed his pipe and caught a frown from Annabelle, slowly putting it away again. "Yes. Edward kept an eye out while you were gone." He aimed a hand at the driver's seat overhead. "And I also made a short flight while I waited." When Kang saw the nursemaid's head jerk up, the magician added, "Flight of fancy. Then I took a nap."

"Of course you did," Kang murmured with a smirk.

"Uncle Celwyn," Annabelle said, "The doctor says Betty is healthy. She is perfect too."

Patrick kissed her. "She certainly is. And she has your nose."

"She is doing fine," Tara smiled at the baby.

Their carriage turned down Parizka Street, and they headed toward Tellyhouse. "What do you think the boys are doing?" Annabelle asked the magician.

"Before we left, Granger reported they'd planned a field trip to the north corner of the property." He grinned. "To look for snakes."

Bartholomew said, "This time of year snakes would be hibernating because of the cold."

"I bet Zander insisted he could wake them up,'" Kang predicted.

Minutes later, Patrick held onto the strap as they made the turn and could see the top of Tellyhouse above the trees. "Has Annabelle told you of my plans?"

"No—" Kang perked up. "Tell us, please."

"Well. If there are no scandals—"

Annabelle interjected, "Specifically from you three."

"Then I plan to run for city government this summer," Patrick said. "I would have plenty of work to do before then." He waited while Annabelle kissed his cheek. "We're excited about this."

"Congratulations." Celwyn shook his hand, and the others did the same. "I promise that Xiau won't embarrass you."

"Pfft." The automat made a face. "Patrick doesn't need your flamboyant antics making news."

As they turned into the driveway, Patrick touched the baby's chin. "My campaign will concentrate on the importance of building a modern, strong city while preserving its history. Of all things," he raised a brow at the magician, "I see the telephone becoming common here as part of that."

A discussion ensued about how a telephone worked, and it ended with the automat having the last word. "Somewhere in the center of each city, they will build an office where all the connections will eventually meet. There will be frameworks for the wiring, and perhaps employees to route the calls to specific places. It is a massive endeavor."

Tara snuggled into Celwyn's side. "And even if it takes years, you will acquire one."

"Also, a great deal of money is needed." Kang nodded at her. "If I had time before we leave the city, I'd invest funds with whoever is building this project. Eventually, there will be a nice return on investments."

Patrick stared into the distance. "That isn't a bad idea. Leave me the information for what you want to invest, and I'll see to it that it is done."

<hr>

Before noon, the *Elizabeth* sounded her horn as she pulled into the trainyard in Szczecin. A pouring rain greeted them, and as Bartholomew peered through the window and shrugged into his coat, he remarked that it felt cold enough for snow.

Celwyn sent Kang and Granger to the front of the train to entertain the Conductor and the twins, Abe, and Andy, so that he could move all their luggage at one time to the waiting area by the road. By the time the *Elizabeth* chugged forward and circled back for her return trip to Prague, everything had been loaded into their 'carts,' along with Tara.

"That saved a great deal of effort."

"Xiau prefers it that way—he'd hate to haul all his books around by himself." Celwyn teased the automat. "I hear the word for what you might get from that is a hernia."

"Pfft. But we still need a better way of doing this every time we're here." Kang yawned.

After Bartholomew's comment about snow, the magician added awnings over their luggage carts. "How many books did you two bring this time?"

Bartholomew sat on top of the boxes and chuckled. "You should have asked how many we wanted to bring but thought better of. The cabins on the ship aren't that big, and we'll see many book-shops between here and Spain."

"Is that so?" The magician shivered and pulled his coat closer around Tara, knowing she didn't feel the cold, but he enjoyed embracing her during the half-hour to ride out to the bluffs north of town where the *Nautilus* would surface. Thick, soft snowflakes began falling as they reached the road that paralleled the coastline. Initially, they passed several wagons and carriages traveling west, but soon had the road to themselves. Celwyn enjoyed the eerie quiet of the snow and the way the waves glinted like silver underneath the falling flakes. With a shiver, he pro-duced a cloud of warmth and handed over cups of hot chocolate.

"Thank you," Granger said. "It's awfully cold."

Celwyn nodded. "You are most welcome."

Kang passed one to the big man, who sipped and handed it back so he could hold the reins.

That wouldn't do. Celwyn began steering the horses—also known as the yard rats he'd conscripted as horses. As soon as Bartholomew realized the change, he retrieved his cup from the automat. For the rest of the time, they said nothing but enjoyed their journey with its promise of the unknown and the mystery of the sea. For the first time, Tara's per-fume accompanied them along with the smoke from Granger's pipe.

Chapter 31

Early February 1878

AFTER THEY BOARDED THE SHIP, the scientists unloaded boxes like busy bees. Kang asked for, and received, a separate cabin for the books he and Bartholomew had accumulated. As the magician surveyed the over-stuffed room, he said, "Oh, really Xiau?"

The automat stopped rooting around like a happy rat in the books and lifted his chin. "We're going to call it our Library of Flight."

"Excuse me." Bartholomew moved around Celwyn and deposited another box on the floor. "These are about lift and wind speeds. I assume you are arranging things by subject?" he asked and received a nod from the automat.

From over the magician's shoulder, Verne scanned the small room.

"Where is Miss McFein?"

"Napping. You may not be aware that she sat up all last night with the baby."

"Why?"

"It would be her last chance to do so for a while." The magician passed books between the automat and Bartholomew. "Like us, she is rather attached to the child."

"Betty is a charming baby." Bartholomew handed Kang a volume. "That is Pickler's ideas on propulsion. Are we going to have enough room in here for everything?"

Kang could see the big man actually wondered.

"I'm not sure, and no comment from you, Jonas."

Under their feet, a familiar gong sounded and repeated.

"Lunch is served." Celwyn brushed off his coat and headed down the corridor to the study.

"As usual, an excellent meal." Bartholomew patted his lips with his napkin.

They had just sampled the wine and tasted a lobster bisque, when Nemo said, "In a few hours, we'll stop in the Havre for supplies, and of course for anything you need before heading to Findbar." Captain Nemo appeared in good spirits; his eyes alive with the excitement of finally heading to Spain. Kang squinted—detecting a touch of apprehension behind his expression too.

Qing joined them, ready to greet "his" fish. The water outside seemed darker than usual as they traveled through it at a moderate speed. It took a minute until the automat realized why—the snowstorm and heavy clouds still accompanied them. Poor Qing. It would take many hours to reach the Havre, and he would not be amused if he couldn't see fish.

"The only thing they need is more books, sir." Celwyn grinned at the automat.

From beside him, Verne said, "They do? I saw boxes full of them."

"Droll, Jonas." Kang turned to the author. "We have what we need for now. How is your writing going? It has been three weeks since we last saw you."

"Very well, thank you. Before I left Prague, Jonas took me to the Castle for my research." He blinked rapidly. "We saw strange things."

"I bet you did." The automat asked Celwyn, "How much of that came from you?"

"Not too many. I may have added a few details to a painting, but nothing that lived and breathed."

"I'm sure it was a memorable visit, Jules." Nemo's tolerant mood showed he had missed them. "At last, we are on our way to Spain."

"Yes." Now that they were on their way, Kang felt a frission of doubt about what they'd find there. Would it be plain evil or worse?

Nemo said, "I understand Miss McFein is resting." At Celwyn's nod, he continued, "Do you know if she contacted Mr. Soriano to tell him we are on our way?"

"Yes. He will be waiting for us in Gibraltar by the tenth of the month," Celwyn said. "Before we left

Singapore, I remember that you planned additional research about Lazlo's fortress."

"I did. Perhaps later this afternoon we can go over it all and bring Miss McFein into the discussion. Last week, Jules found some newspaper articles about Lazlo." Nemo's face registered disgust like he'd stumbled upon a field of camel dung. "It makes curious reading."

Chapter 32

BY FIVE O'CLOCK THAT AFTERNOON, Celwyn had to agree; Doctor Lazlo seemed more than "interesting." His story sounded like a nightmare.

When Bartholomew leaned back and knocked Qing off the back of the sofa, the bird flew to Celwyn for comfort. He also tried to snag one of Tara's curls. She felt it and patted his back. The bird stopped—he considered it fun only if accompanied by outrage and cursing.

Bartholomew read aloud from one of the articles the Captain had provided.

"This is dated from twenty years ago in the United States. Both Doctor Lazlo and his sister are Americans. The doctor graduated from the University of Pennsylvania School of Medicine before leaving for Vienna." Bartholomew hesitated and caught a neutral nod from Nemo. "His sister did not arrive in Vienna until much later. As part of his research team … she had a specialty. Genetic testing."

Qing waddled over and hopped onto the arm of the other sofa. The Captain leaned closer, and they blinked at each other before Nemo sighed and took over the narrative.

"Marie and I were married in 1856." Nemo shut his eyes for a moment and went on. "She continued to work with her brother. When I realized what he was doing, I asked her to stop. She," Nemo waited until he could go on, "she said that if I cared for her, I would not interfere. Then she asked me to leave."

"Sir," Kang said. "If this is too painful—"

Nemo shouted, "It is damn painful!" He lowered his voice. "Excuse me. But if you are going to put yourself in jeopardy, you deserve to hear everything." He looked up to see a glass of whiskey hovering in front of him and downed it in one gulp.

"You will not have to repeat any of this," Tara said. "I will tell my uncle when he joins us."

"Thank you, my dear." Nemo had developed a fatherly stance with her over the last few months. "Like I said, Marie asked me to leave, and I did, traveling to a remote location where I built the *Nautilus*." He waited for questions but saw stunned curiosity instead. "I kept up with the medical periodicals, and when the scandal drove Lazlo and Marie out of Vienna, I heard of it. Once they left for Spain, I again knew of it." He got to his feet and turned his back on the room before speaking again.

"When Marie first arrived at the clinic in Vienna, we spoke continually of her work. I visited her there as often as I could." His frown faded. "At the time, my activities were clandestine—there is no need to say more about them. One day, I returned from a mission and discovered my wife in a state..." He opened and closed a fist. "...screaming at her brother about his work and calling him a devil."

"What did he say?" Bartholomew asked.

Instead of answering, Nemo came back to the sofas and collapsed beside Kang. "Later she told me he wanted to design a race of perfect babies; removing any genetic material from nationalities with what he considered substandard attributes. That left only one race."

"Let me guess, only a Caucasian Aryan one," Kang said.

"Yes. My brother-in-law wanted a 'pure' race, in his opinion. To maintain it, the men and women chosen for the project would be put under scrutiny for each detail about their lives; the fanatics who employed him would make sure the pure race only mated within itself." Nemo's voice grew colder. "The worst part? Lazlo insisted they kill any un-pure offspring."

"Oh, my God," Bartholomew whispered.

Verne heard them. "It gets worse." The author had quietly waddled into the room without his notebook. The man couldn't help rubbing his stomach and staring down the corridor leading to the galley.

"Let's finish this," the Captain said. "Over a period of weeks, my wife changed her horrified reaction to one of tolerance, and then evolved to defending her brother. About this time, the local Vienna populace demanded that they leave." He barked a gallows laugh. "The racist politicians defended Lazlo, even praising him."

"I had thought Vienna a human and tolerant city. But it seems not," Tara said.

"At that time, it had more subversive forces compared to today." Nemo shrugged. "To go on; a dozen years passed as I traveled and explored, all the while hoping Marie would realize what her brother represented. Through channels, I heard they had moved to the Moorish fortress. I sent letters, but they were not answered. No one had seen her for an extended time before that." He remained quiet for so long that Kang made ready to say something when Nemo took up the narrative again.

"All my sources reported that Marie is most likely dead. She," he stopped and tried again, "last wrote a note to her nephew many years ago, simply saying 'the end is soon.'"

Celwyn would agree that on the face of it, Marie Nemo's fate might already have been decided. But... "Sir, this is all circumstantial. You do not know for certain."

"At the same time, I cannot hope that she is alive either. Lazlo has made a point of telling various people that she died."

"And hoping that you would hear of that," Kang said. "Why else would he lure you back with the messages in those paintings?"

Nemo's expression held a grim kind of satisfaction. "Over the last few years, I've made a point of cutting off his external funding to bring him out into the open. A few of my methods were direct, others not as much." A hard smile arrived. "He has finally deduced what I did."

"Isn't this too simple?" Kang asked. "You could simply crush him upon your arrival."

"And then find your wife, or her remains, afterward," Bartholomew suggested.

"I agree, but there is more to the story." Tara raised a beautiful brow. "He must be threatening you on another front."

"Correct," Nemo said. "Some of this is assumption, some guesses; Lazlo is rumored to have become adept at the dark arts. Especially the factions that originate in the Sicilian mountains."

Bartholomew groaned. "I know what you are leading up to, and I wish we were sailing up an underground river in the opposite direction right now."

"What is it?" Tara asked.

"In those mountains are the origins of the Mafioso," Nemo said. "They may want revenge for what we did to them in Turkey last year, or they remember my association with the flying machine. They could still want it and are drawing us into a trap." He looked at the magician with his usual confidence. "A rather dangerous choice, I suppose."

"Like Bartholomew, we all enjoy a good fight. If Lazlo is a part of that, perhaps it is a deception. Or he is seeking revenge of his own volition." The magician wondered which.

"Oh, Lord." Kang stood and stomped his foot. "This deranged madman isn't satisfied his work is an affront to humankind. Using the occult will only ignite his insanity."

"Not to mention that Mrs. Nemo could be alive and possibly a prisoner there," Tara said. "Or pretending to be bait." She walked to the window and back. "I don't think time is a part of the equation, otherwise the lure would have been more direct or urgent."

"All this time, he waited to use her to get to you?" Verne asked.

"A good question, but it is complicated." The Captain studied them. "The Mafioso has been at war with the Church—consider that Lazlo's experiments may be part of a campaign to demonstrate that the Church's tenants have no meaning. That is also one of King Gregory's fanciful ideas. If so, there could be all kinds of skullduggery lurking about in the Spanish fortress."

"The situation with the church is recent and the Santa Alleanza's spies may be a part of this." Tara frowned. "There are good and bad factions at play within that group."

"I know who they are." The magician regarded the room with a growing sense of dread.

"For hundreds of years, the Vatican has employed them as spies." Nemo nodded to himself. "It isn't farfetched to assume there are a few rogue factions within them."

The magician gazed at Tara and spotted an odd expression on her face. She covered it with a sudden cough. *Has Tara worked as a spy for the Church?* Celwyn growled under his breath. *Did he want to know?* After that debacle about Keats, he stopped himself from checking.

"Would the Church become our ally if needed?" Kang asked.

Nemo stared back at him like he'd grown another face. "They have a certain relationship to the black arts also, but not with the same nefarious purposes." He tapped the sofa arm. "Possibly … it is an advantage, but initially we won't know."

Kang asked, "You've waited a long time for this, but shouldn't we check with the Church before confronting Lazlo?"

"We could." Nemo rubbed his face in exasperation. "My men, as you know, are highly trained and can acquit themselves in a fight. However, they are not prepared to engage with supernatural foes or whatever Lazlo could dredge up. I would consider this a personal affront if any of my men died in this endeavor and have told them so. They've been given the option to step aside. I could hire mercenaries if I had to…" For the first time, Nemo appeared to seriously consider it.

Bartholomew said, "In my estimation, your crew would wish to assist you, even if they encounter something unexplainable."

"That is true." Verne hesitated in saying anything else—which didn't give any weight to his statement.

"Sir, tell us about Lazlo's lair, please," Tara asked. "I have some experience in scaling fortifications and handling explosives."

Oh, my. The magician was still worried about the Vatican's spies, but her request somehow calmed him down. *And explosives?* He grinned. *Of course, she would use them.* He could just picture her scaling the side of the castle in riding trousers.

"I will remember." Nemo removed a flat package from his pocket and unwrapped it. "We have a bit of help; one of my lieutenants, Doctor Tuttle, has taken up photography. The methods are still rather haphazard, but he produced this." The Captain passed around a small print depicting an ancient fortress clinging to a cliff over a churning sea. Judging from the angle of the picture, it had been taken from the surface of the ocean, and the magician could imagine the rolling waves and the submarine's crew holding the equipment while several others held onto Doctor Tuttle.

After everyone had viewed the picture, Nemo said, "The Moors built the fortress in 1492 to defend the nearby Castle of Leon."

"The castle is not close by in this picture." Verne squinted at it.

"It is not there at all," Nemo said. "The Ottomans sacked it in the early 1600s. They also blasted the fortress to pieces, as you can see."

"Doctor Lazlo lives within what is left of it?" Celwyn asked.

"Possibly, or in the warren of caves inside the cliffs."

"I refuse to call that man a doctor." Kang cursed. "Lazlo might set up almost any kind of reception for us." He saw Nemo nod assent. "Does he know of this ship?"

"A very good question," the big man murmured.

Tara said, "That certainly would change the way he defends his castle, so to speak."

The magician agreed.

"The day we took that picture, a storm sat on top of us, which made visibility difficult for anyone watching the water." Nemo tapped a finger on the sofa arm. "We surfaced for only a few minutes."

In a gentle voice, Tara asked, "Sir, at any point did you talk to your wife about building this ship—even just as a whim?"

Nemo regarded her as she sat next to the magician. "You are illustrating why having a diverse set of viewpoints on board is so valuable. This time from a woman's perspective." He shook his head. "No, I never mentioned it, and at the time considered it just an idea. Perhaps inside some marriages, secrets are exchanged but not in ours."

"That is encouraging news," the automat said. "Anyhow, we must assume your wife is alive until it is proved differently. And that willingly or not, she would have told her brother something about you that could hurt us." Kang glanced at another of the pictures Nemo provided. "We would have the advantage of this ship, plus your divers who could approach the caves from underwater. Of course, from above there would be Jonas and his fondness for birds." He sent the magician an expectant look. Celwyn produced a plate of cookies.

"Thank you." The automat selected one and passed the plate around.

"It won't be long until we pick up Valentine in Gibraltar." Nemo asked Celwyn, "Do we need the person you mentioned before that? I believe you described him as an old friend?"

The magician remembered the last time he had encountered Swango, feeling some amusement, a bit of terror, and awe all competing for prominence. That time, they had been trapped together in a rather ferocious fire in the Pyrenees. If the magician hadn't been unconscious when things became rather extreme, it wouldn't have happened. And he wouldn't have let Swango save them. For something like that, the man always extracted a price.

"I can't say 'friend' describes him, but I certainly know him. Do we need Swango? It really depends on the reception at the fortress," Celwyn said. "I could send a telegram to Taormina where Swango lives, letting him know we're arriving soon." As he talked, Nemo nodded at the idea. "We'd also ask Valentine to meet the *Nautilus* in Taormina instead of Gibraltar."

"Tell us about Swango?" Bartholomew asked.

Usually, Celwyn had no problem filling such requests, but he wondered where to start.

"He is, at times, treacherous, or virtuous, and always full of surprises." The magician twisted his mustache as he talked, recalling some of their encounters. Especially the one at Victoria Falls and the surprise that General Awaitti had uncovered there.

In his most sarcastic drawl, Kang asked, "Let me guess, he is a magician?"

"No. Not exactly."

Chapter 33

THE WINE, THE SHRIMP IN GARLIC sauce, and the soup had all been served and admired before they returned to the subject of their impending adventure.

"We will be near the Hague in about a half hour, and need to dispatch someone ashore if we plan to send telegraphs." Nemo raised a brow at them.

"The idea of asking my uncle to meet us in Taormino won't work," Tara said. "It's too late for a telegram to reach him; he thinks we're on our way to Gibraltar."

"I've been considering Swango," the magician said. "I suggest we interview him—but not aboard this ship—he can be capricious. Otherwise, we'd have to await him near the Castell."

"Oh? A capricious magician ... how surprising." Kang yawned.

Nemo rubbed his face in exasperation.

"He isn't a magician." Celwyn glued the automat's fork to the table. "He isn't immortal, at least in the classic sense, either."

Everyone at the table frowned in confusion or raised a brow, including Verne, who voiced it. "I've never heard a description such as that."

Celwyn ate sparingly. For some reason, his appetite dimmed with the mention of Swango. "The reason I'm suggesting Swango is that he is one of the most highly educated people that I know of in the black arts. It would not be surprising to discover he practices the occult upon himself."

Their recently consumed shrimp seemed to be rebelling in Bartholomew's stomach. He noted aloud that Annabelle would be most vocal if she sat at the table with them.

"An example, please." The automat stared at Celwyn.

"I'll reserve my answer for now, but I will tell it, eventually. The point is that he could help us, and finding his kind of help would be most difficult otherwise." Celwyn tried to use the right words that wouldn't set off more questioning. His audience grew suspicious and restless, as evidenced by Tara's attempt to pin his gaze down and the big man's lowering brows. Like a beleaguered ship, he plowed forward through the waves. "Just for the entertainment of it, Swango appeared as the Pope and incited some parishioners to the point they almost burned down Westminster Abbey—I got us out of there."

"What happened afterward?" Bartholomew asked.

The magician shrugged. "He loved it. He even won a purse off me at the gaming table that evening."

"Would you say the main advantage of using him would be protecting us from any black magic we encounter?" Nemo asked.

"Yes, but I can't predict his mental state or actions."

"Can you control Swango if things become serious?" Kang asked.

Celwyn pushed a clump of potato around his plate. "Based on my previous encounters with him, yes. However, I have not seen him in ages."

"What is he doing in Taormino?" Tara eyed him. Celwyn had not lied to her yet during their relationship. The way she looked at him, she suspected he might be about to.

"He has a conclave there, filled with a group of followers. They pay him handsomely for the privilege of learning at his feet about shamanism, high magic, low magic, white magic, black magic." The magician smiled. "They haven't discovered it does them no good if they do not have his innate talents."

"What motivates Swango?" Tara asked. "Money? Ideology?"

Bartholomew nodded at her. "Knowing that would go toward how much we should trust him."

The conversation halted while the crew served the coffee and fruit in creme. A wonderful intermission in the magician's opinion. It didn't last long.

"When the Moors built the Castell de Ferro fortress, they used stone. The Castell was intended as a defense against the Turks," Verne said. Things worsened for them militarily by the time the last battlements had been put in place. Soon, the Turks raised their flag over it."

"I thought the Moors won?" Celwyn asked.

"It is a good thing you are not teaching history to Otto and Zander. They ask questions like that." Bartholomew grinned. "Their war lasted until 1492. The Moors abandoned the fortress in 1490, and it sat empty until the war ended. Then the Prince of Alleah took it over. By 1842, no one claimed it because of the amount of damage."

"Why did the doctor pick that location?" Verne asked.

"Unknown, but I hear one of his clients had something to do with it. General Maximilian Hess." Nemo made a face of distaste. "From all accounts, he is especially fascinated with the idea of a superior race."

"And he is the source of Lazlo's funding that you cut off?" The big man asked.

Nemo held his glass to the light and admired the golden color. "Yes."

"Do we have a map of the grounds of the fortress? Perhaps local stories of the underground chambers?" Bartholomew asked. "Even suppositions would help."

"Nothing definitive." Captain Nemo tilted his head to the side. "You should know, there will be a slight delay before Findbar. We'll spend the night offshore and tomorrow Jules will go into the old part of the Hague and see what else he can find about the Castell."

"The Royal Library of the Netherlands has been there since the late 1700s. It is called Koninklijke

Bibliotheek." Verne consulted his notebook. "They are known for their medieval literature. The Koninklijke began with the collection of William Birman."

"While everyone else hunts through old records tomorrow," Celwyn began, "I suggest that the Lieutenant and I go to the museum. I'll visit the thoughts of the employees who might have seen those paintings when they were tampered with. Or who allowed Lazlo to do so."

Tara asked. "How could they guarantee the tampered paintings would be viewed by the Captain?"

That brought the conversation to a stop; no one had an answer.

"That is something we need to discuss," Kang said. "For now, the rest of us will continue our tasks. Of course, with a bit of caution—some librarians are quite territorial."

"Now that we have tomorrow settled, I wish to be the Professor's partner for bridge tonight," Verne announced.

Celwyn snickered into his sleeve and winked at the automat. While they played cards, he planned a romantic moonlit interlude topside with Tara. It might include a few dancing fish, shooting stars, and of course an atmospheric opera, just for her. He hummed the opening chorus as the others adjourned to the game table.

The following evening, everyone seemed satisfied after returning from the Hague.

"Please pass the butter, Xiau," Bartholomew requested. "Yes, we did rather well today. I searched until I found a detailed drawing of the fortress—from 1487. However, we can't verify any differences that have occurred in the years since."

"Yet, it will be very helpful. Did you make a copy of it?" Celwyn asked.

"We did not have time," the big man controlled his amusement. "So … we borrowed it and brought it here so you could make one."

The magician stopped a bite of fish before it reached his lips. "You're serious? The two of you have never come close to doing anything risky or illegal." He turned to the automat. "If I stole a map, I'd hear about it from you for months."

"As you should." Kang tried not to laugh. "You need training. Anyhow, Bartholomew and I decided that after you made a copy for us, you could return the original later tonight." Kang covered a broad smile with his hand and added, "We know how much you enjoy a nighttime flight."

Bartholomew grinned at him.

"Oh, for God's sake. All right. What else did you steal?"

When they just blinked innocently at him, Verne spoke up. "I had success with the newspaper archives. My Dutch is not that good, but I can understand keywords." He shuffled his notes. "Unlike the others, I concentrated on the purported underground chambers and their proximity to the coast. For instance, is there access from the beach into them?"

Bartholomew said, "Did you check the articles about wrecks in the area? There may have been pictures or drawings of the coastline and eyewitness accounts."

"I did and discovered some." Verne nodded at them. "The rumors of underground chambers had been mentioned by an imprisoned monk held there between 1398 and 1402. He described the corridors and cells in detail." Verne handed over a drawing to Bartholomew. "These drawings are rudimentary but have enough detail we can consider them accurate. Twenty-four cells are mentioned, along with two offices and some luxurious quarters located closer to the surface."

"I wonder if our quarry sleeps in there?" Kang mused.

With a nod of understanding, Verne held up a crude drawing from his notes. "The cells shared a wall with the cliffs over the sea. Small windows let in air, and the elements."

Celwyn smiled. "I'm sure they would be big enough to allow a handsome gull entry."

"A green-eyed one?" Tara asked and received a silent kiss.

"What is the underground compound shaped like?" Nemo asked. "One chamber, or?"

"It is a long rectangle with the nicer quarters at the most northern point next to a staircase leading to the sea. The staircase also ascends to the surface," Verne said. "If it's still there."

"Did they imprison only political and religious people?" Bartholomew picked up Verne's drawing. "It seems like a curious place to incarcerate someone."

"To your question, I do not know." Verne tapped the papers. "From what I can tell, the Moors added at least one other staircase that ends in the caves below." He handed a document to Nemo. "They also had a docking area for their boats in those caves." He stopped talking to watch as the crew entered the room with the dessert dishes. "Of course, this information is from three hundred years ago, so there is no way of knowing what the cliffs are really like, or the stairs. Were they made of stone or wood that is rotted by now? We don't know."

"Thank you. This adds to our information," Nemo said.

The magician asked, "Would there be another entrance above the cliffs?"

Again, the author shrugged. "I saw no evidence of it. We may try more research in the local area."

"There is the library in Salou near Barcelona," Kang said.

"It is time for something of a more pleasant nature." Nemo tried a bite of his dessert. "Let us talk of Findbar, the flying machine, and the books you brought along."

"We'll have a lot to talk about," the magician grinned at Kang.

Chapter 34

Findbar

"IT IS ONLY NOON." PROFESSOR XIAU Kang faced Bartholomew. "Shall we?"

The automat sprinted across the *Nautilus's* floating pier and up the stairs with the big man in close pursuit. Celwyn noticed that in the months since they had left Findbar, the crew had installed a handrail and more lights in the grotto in case the vibration from a racing Bartholomew bounced the automat into the water.

Nemo and the others followed, with Verne bringing up the rear of the parade. As they walked, Nemo played the gracious host to Tara, the only newcomer to the island.

"This cavern has been used by smugglers and others since the Middle Ages. In the 1600s, Lord Adolphe Spencer owned the island. The Queen had

258

gifted the island to him for his financial contributions to the Crown. To thank her, and display his ingenuity, Spencer began his own smuggling operation. It consisted of running rum from the Colonies, rare birds, and exotic animals."

"That is interesting. What are those?" Tara pointed to the life-size carvings on the slick walls above the pool of water the *Nautilus* rested in. "They remind me of something from the Scots ... or Eire."

"The Professor thinks they are Celtic devils," the magician told her.

"I see."

They followed Nemo out of the cave and down the paneled hallway with its gallery of portraits and macabre subjects.

Nemo made a point of ignoring the paintings but politely awaited Tara's inspection of them. When she finished, he asked, "Would you prefer the unique experience of exiting through this door," he indicated the older one that spanned the width of the hall, "or a more normal one?" He gestured at the door beside her.

"That unique one please."

The magician had expected no less from her. As Nemo held the heavy oak door open, Celwyn escorted her into the back of a carriage-sized fireplace tall enough for Bartholomew. The remembered aroma of burned wood accompanied them. The magician scanned the floor; thankfully the crew had removed the skull they had found here on their last visit. Meanwhile, Verne had selected the other door and trotted around the corner of the mansion's ballroom to rejoin them.

"I must say," she ran a hand along the carved mantle running the length of the fireplace, "this is just amazing. I have stayed in majestic hotels with fireplaces much smaller than this."

Celwyn checked with Nemo, saw his nod, and said, "There is an interesting history surrounding the Spencer mansion." He took her elbow and led her across the Harlequin floor toward circular stairs leading upward. "The Spencers lived here until catastrophe struck, then in 1822, a sanatorium for the criminally insane operated here. Once again, tragedy visited Findbar."

When the Captain and Verne joined them at the bottom of the stairs, Verne edged away from Nemo until he stood nearly on top of Celwyn's boots and trembled. The author's half-hearted grin bellied the fear dancing in his eyes and his words. "We discovered a big chess set there—huge pieces taller than me." He pointed to the middle square on the floor. "The queen ... she ... she cut off the bishop's head ... it rolled across the floor." By the time he finished speaking, his voice had risen to a squeak.

Celwyn patted his shoulder.

"Who was it?" Tara asked.

Nemo and Celwyn exchanged a glance, and the Captain said, "Since then, we determined it was Mrs. Spencer."

"I see. The woman who must have died over one hundred years ago." Tara tilted her head at them. "Why do all of you still seem uncomfortable?"

"Because she has appeared to us again, several times, and that is why the Captain has asked that we don't venture anywhere here without an escort or two." Celwyn noted that Tara did not appear frightened. In fact, he wondered if she believed them. He cleared his throat. As that American, Farragut, said, "Full speed ahead." He continued the story. "Weeks later, Jules asked Xiau and Bartholomew to accompany him upstairs and up to the tower."

This time the author scurried away, putting his hands over his ears while intoning, "Excuse me, excuse me," until he had reached the ballroom where Nemo's guards awaited them.

"Xiau and Bartholomew agreed to go with him, and nothing occurred until they ascended to the tower room." Celwyn waved at the automat. "You should tell this part."

"As you wish. We explored the tower, and then I opened an old trunk. It appeared empty. Bartholomew continued to talk and ... as I glanced back, I saw a ghostly vapor drifting out of the trunk. It took form as the beheaded bishop that Jonas had seen on the floor here."

Tara still studied them without fear but with a bit less skepticism.

"When I saw the bishop, I shoved Verne out of the way." The automat licked his lips.

Celwyn tried not to laugh—this had not happened to him, and the others still seemed traumatized. Kang continued, "I pushed Verne out of the way because I had spotted something worse hovering in the air outside the tower window."

"They saw the same woman again with her broadsword," Nemo said. "She used it to smash through the window. Whether she wanted the ghostly bishop or our friends—we do not know."

"Why did she attack?" Tara asked.

The magician couldn't help laughing. "No one knows. But Bartholomew and the others ran like hell, down the stairs, and back to the submarine. I hear the Professor can run very fast."

"Jonas, they tell me you fled from her first." Nemo's eyes twinkled.

"Why, my dear?" Tara asked innocently. The magician stuck his nose in the air.

By now they arrived in the yard and had rejoined Verne. Celwyn could hear Verne's teeth chattering.

Full sunlight warmed the courtyard, dispelling the unsettling effects of their story. In the distance, the North Sea sparkled under the sun's rays, and to the south, the flags of the landing field fluttered from a mile or more away. Celwyn glanced into the shadows of the forested area before the cliffs.

"Err—" Celwyn hesitated. "You might want to avoid that area." He indicated the trees. "Unless we go with you."

Tara tried to smile. "Do I want to know why?"

The magician took her elbow, and they started toward the hangar halfway down the runway. "I will tell you later." He pecked her cheek. The experience he'd had in those trees sand what happened there to the patients from the sanitarium would not make a pretty story. It could wait.

When they entered the hangar, frantic activity met them. The fever surrounding their endeavor had been bottled up for months, and the sight brought satisfaction to Nemo's usually stoic face. Bartholomew and the others looked like two-legged beavers at work with shiny metal instead of wood.

The big man had donned his overalls, as had Kang, and they jogged back and forth between their invention and the specifications tacked to a nearby wall. Bartholomew waved a greeting as he helped the automat down from the cockpit. As he watched them, the magician felt his spirits dive low; grief had an insidious way of sneaking into one's thoughts. Elizabeth would no longer worry about the automat and the flying machine. She wouldn't plead with Celwyn to keep Kang safe. The magician inhaled and waited until his tears stopped. He would honor her wishes and keep the automat safe.

Thankfully, the flying machine made an excellent distraction. The new version had quite a few improvements; from the size of the engine to the addition of brakes. Like the original, it had been painted a blindingly bright yellow.

"As per your instructions, this model is six feet longer and three feet wider," Nemo said. "Bartholomew reports the new braking system has been installed, but not tested yet. I also understand that work is about to begin on an improved exhaust system for the engine."

Kang trotted by, lugging what looked like a five-foot wide ring with strips of metal crisscrossing it. Judging from the noise when he dropped it, the thing must have been made of steel. Bartholomew retrieved it with the effort most people expended on picking up a dropped pencil.

"When we return, we will finish revamping the new engine. Captain, in our conversations, you were torn between staying here a while and what you must do in Spain. Is that still true?" Kang handed Bartholomew a screwdriver nearly as long as his forearm.

As one of the assistants passed by them, Celwyn recognized the man from their last visit to Findbar. The assistant's attention lay not with the scientists; instead, it rested on top of Miss Tara McFein's pretty head.

"I still am of two minds about this, but we will go to Spain first." As they closed the door to the hangar, Nemo gazed at the scientists clustered below the undercarriage of the flying machine. "They are in their world, aren't they?"

"Yes, one could even say on their own planet." Celwyn snapped his fingers. "I might have to cause another rainstorm to retrieve them for dinner."

Tara raised a brow.

Nemo grunted. "Just make sure they are outside when it occurs. And don't mention I know about it."

Celwyn asked, "On a more serious note, will we need to stop at the museum in Barcelona before we approach Doctor Lazlo?"

The amusement in Nemo's eyes evaporated like water in a puddle on fire. "Yes. We will depart in two days' time."

Miss Tara McFein had planted bombs in royal palaces, came face to face with the notorious Tyryl, the sorcerer in the Black Tower in Brussels, and survived. She had also fought and won a battle of wits with Peter the Great's son Alexis, who employed devils—although she didn't see any, only felt their dry hands upon her. No matter the well-intentioned patronizing from Jonas and the others about Spencer Mansion, it couldn't be all that bad here. Tara laughed to herself. If they knew of some of the other things she had survived, they wouldn't worry so much about this place.

In an hour, the dinner gong would sound. Thinking this a prime opportunity, she slipped away from the study, let herself out of the *Nautilus*'s hatch, and trotted across the floating pier. She nodded calmly to the guards on duty and climbed the stairs to the paneled hallway.

Because the Captain, Jonas, and the others had stood beside her trying, and failing, to be patient, she had not had enough time to study these paintings, nor go up to the tower. The view up there must be amazing, and she half-doubted parts of the story of a resident ghost terrorizing them. She didn't have any inklings of anything unusual anywhere here. Perhaps a few unsettled spirits, but nothing else.

Another guard passed by before she finished studying the paintings, especially the last one that had been left behind the end partition. As she brushed the cobwebs off, she couldn't see any fingerprints on it from unusual entities. Tara held the canvas under the strongest light in the hallway.

Perhaps two feet square including the frame, the miniature scene clearly represented the Harlequin floor in the next room. Candles had been painted in the vintage candelabras and highlighted the fine details in the picture. Although the artist had painted a man in courtly clothes on the right side of the room, a faint, see-through collection of chess pieces had been intricately added. Each figure wore ancient finery, just as described by the terrorized author and Jonas.

Tara blew off the remaining dust and held up the picture for more light. "Good grief," she muttered to herself. She saw exactly what Jonas had described. A rather homely woman in a queen's vestments stood behind the bishop wearing a deadly sneer.

Without warning, a cold hand gripped Tara's neck, and another seized the painting from her.

Tara's scream died as she shrieked and ran for the door. Thank god vampires could run fast. By the time she re-entered the submarine and found Jonas, she had stopped screaming and practically jumped into his arms.

"I believe you! I just met Mrs. Spencer!"

PART II

*The Journey to
Spain Begins*

Chapter 35

EVIDENCE OF SPRING DOTTED THE verdant hills of Huelva province as the *Nautilus* cruised by. Dusk arrived in a palette of golds and pinks. As they neared Cadiz, darkness fell, and the automat and the others left the platform to descend into the ship again. Kang waited while the magician handed Tara off the last step and escorted her down the hall. Ever since they left Findbar, she seemed much more like herself and not whatsoever interested in talking about Mrs. Spencer. Kang didn't want to think about that insane woman either.

All seemed well. As the automat sat at the chess table, Qing tracked him from his perch under the aquatic window. Xiau patted the mechanical bird's head; Qing considered the chess pieces, especially the pawns, his property. With the bird still watching him, the automat reached into his pocket and produced a foot-long wooden board with rows of peg holes. He raised a challenging brow at the magician.

"Join him. I have several letters to write." Tara kissed his cheek. "You don't need to be distracted by me."

The automat suspected Celwyn *wanted* to be distracted by her.

"Noddy is not my favorite game," the magician told the automat as she left the room.

"Do you know how to play, Jonas?" The big man asked as he settled on the sofa with a map book.

"But of course."

"The Americans call it cribbage," Kang said. "No matter what we call it, you will probably complain when I win. You can have the red pegs." After he dealt the cards, he added, "Don't get fanciful; you can't distract me."

"Ha." The magician picked up his cards and asked Bartholomew, "Will we stop at the museum tomorrow, or do you already have the information we need?"

Kang studied his cards. "Yes, and no."

"It would be helpful to know exactly what area of black magic Doctor Lazlo is interested in," Bartholomew said. "'Black magic' by itself is like saying one likes to study world maps—but for which country?"

"A long time ago, before I met Elizabeth, I spent some time in Ibaraki." Kang fussed with his cards. "It is located in the rural countryside of Japan, near Tottori."

"Let me find it here." Bartholomew flipped pages of the atlas. He squinted. "Very well. That is near Matsue city. Why were you there?"

"To see the Shunan Gardens, mostly." The automat laid down his cards and took the points he had earned. With a superior grin at the magician, he said, "Anyhow, I spent a few months there getting to know the people and history. I met an elder named Nara who told me a story."

By the time Celwyn dealt the next hand, Nemo came in and pulled up a chair. The automat made the proper greetings and said, "I am relating something we might want to consider, sir." At his nod, the automat continued. "You are aware of the Japanese city of Matsue? Near there, in Ibaraki, I heard a story about Japanese jiāngshī. They are a type of reanimated corpses in Chinese legends and folklore."

Celwyn stopped frowning at his cards and transferred his confusion to the automat. "A Japanese zombie?"

Bartholomew joined them, leaning against the bookcases. He didn't say a word, but the automat detected the sheen of perspiration across his brow.

"Japanese zombies have been the subject of their lore for centuries, complete with the terror they brought to the villagers." Kang stopped looking at his cards and visualized their fear, once again feeling fortunate he never dreamt about these things.

Bartholomew asked, "What did they do?"

"Keep in mind this is a verbal record passed down person-to-person," the automat said.

"We will." Nemo nodded.

"The story mentioned a bit of cannibalism, some supposed witchcraft, and something that doesn't go with either of those." Kang watched Celwyn play out his cards. "You're taking advantage of my distraction."

"Of course." The magician produced a tea tray at his elbow.

"Pfft." Kang tossed the rest of his hand on the table. "It is not logical, because the final conclusion from the story is that he had already died."

Bartholomew cocked his head to the side. "How?"

Nemo growled, "Doctor Lazlo is not connected to cannibalism if that is where this is headed."

"Not exactly." Kang shook his head. "The storyteller described how this jiāngshī had made a deal with the devil, allowing the devil to occupy his body if the zombie could have one last visit with his family. That theme is not unusual. The Irish and others have a similar version."

"And the connection to us?" Bartholomew's expression hoped there wouldn't be one.

"Well ... when we visited the archives of Malaga's museum, we went a touch further than swiping that drawing. Bartholomew and I appropriating something else." Kang pulled a book out of his inner pocket.

"You stole that too?" The magician demanded. Kang ignored him.

"That looks old ... perhaps from the 1500s?" Tara had reentered the room and peered at it.

"Ah, I remember now, Xiau insisted we take it." Bartholomew shrugged virtuously to a chorus of giggles and smiles. "The curator appeared even more curious when we asked about Castell de Ferro."

"How?" Nemo asked.

"Far away expression, and just plain strange." The big man blinked at them. "So, I asked him if he knew Doctor Lazlo."

Nemo reared back in amazement. "What did he say?"

"The curator glared at me and walked off." Then Bartholomew surprised everyone. "So, we took his book and left."

"Close your mouth, Jonas." When Nemo and the others stopped laughing, Kang continued, "It is an elaborate volume on genetics; exactly like something Lazlo would be interested in. Did you know zombies were mentioned in the Bible?"

"Jorgeson, that curator, is one of Lazlo's benefactors." Nemo developed a frown.

While they talked, the magician had flipped through the book, stopped, asked Bartholomew for a translation, and read again. "If anyone wants my opinion, I have one."

"Oh, you do?" Kang loved to tease the magician and with the passing of each day, he felt more like doing so once again.

Celwyn read another page before adding another comment.

"We should still check the museum in town tomorrow. Also, I've never encountered a Japanese zombie before, and do not know how it would affect my magic—if we encounter one."

A discussion ensued. Tara added a witch's point of view to the list of questions, and the lack of answers increased.

Finally, Nemo held up a hand. "If Lazlo is experimenting on people or torturing them, or anything else untoward, our first objective is to make him stop. I also fervently wish to discover what happened to my wife."

Chapter 36

LATE THAT NIGHT, CELWYN HANDED Tara off the last few steps of the spiral staircase and onto the open-air platform above them. They were alone except for the crewmen on duty at the matching platform on the prow. The man dutifully turned away, understanding how romantic the night could be.

The *Nautilus* lay in the shadow of the Diego headlands and would spend the night performing maintenance. About twenty miles east of them, the harbor lights of Estepona provided a suggestion of illumination, a smudge in the inky night. Celwyn shivered. In early February, it could have been even colder.

He smiled to himself and then at Tara. When this operation concluded, perhaps they could stay warm together in one of the chalets in the French Alps.

"What is so amusing?" Tara grasped his lapels and pulled him close for a kiss. "Is your plan to continue to tease the Professor? So that he forgets his sorrow? He has been much less melancholy lately."

Celwyn embraced her again. "Yes. He is coming out of it, slowly. Years ago, he helped me with my grief, and I should do the same."

"Suzanne?"

"Yes. You have also made me realize that the past is gone." He ran a finger across her jaw. "The future can be most beautiful."

She chuckled. "You sweet talker, you." She tucked herself into this coat. "What has been bothering you? And do not say, 'nothing.'"

The magician shut his mouth and blew her a kiss, buying time. Somehow, she knew he had something to tell her. With a sigh, he kissed her brow. "Hypothetically, I have been worried about aspects of the future. The Professor has also. As usual, he expects me to fix it, and then be the one to deliver the news."

"You poor thing. Of course, he does." She thought for a moment. "It isn't about Bartholomew's superstitions ... is it?"

"No, although they are connected. Hypothetically ... eventually the Captain and Bartholomew will both grow old and die. I don't want them to." He felt Tara stiffen as he spoke, and her intuitiveness came alive. "The obvious answer would be if they could somehow..."

"Become immortal, and the easiest, most common way is by very close association with a vampire."

"I know a beautiful one who has captured my heart."

Tara stopped what she intended to say, and her eyes softened.

"But if you are still irritated with me—"

She kissed him thoroughly. "I am good and irritated."

When the subject resumed, he said, "There could be other ways to accomplish this. Perhaps a blood transfusion from a different entity—it would do no good to use mine. And cause too many complications." He sighed. "There may not be an answer."

"That won't help Bartholomew and Nemo."

"There is one person who might know of an alternative. Perhaps even be able to do the deed." Celwyn raised a brow at her. "Thales."

"Ah. And how would that be arranged?"

Celwyn wondered. Only weeks ago, they had unexpectedly encountered Thales. How long would it be until he saw the demi-god again? Or at all?

"Even if you could arrange something, are either one of them willing to change their futures?" she asked.

"You sound like Xiau."

"The Professor is more intelligent than I, but my bustle is full of common sense."

He had noticed that. They gazed across the water. "If faced with the certainty of death, I do not know which they would choose."

"And if you had to guess?" she asked.

Celwyn shrugged. "The Captain would eventually be agreeable to the idea, but if he couldn't control things, or felt rushed, he would not agree."

"And Bartholomew?"

"I want Xiau to deal with it. He is not any closer to Bartholomew than he is to me, but they speak the same language of logic. Bartholomew would find much of it distasteful ... but in the end—"

"He would decline."

"Perhaps. Unless he would miss something or someone too much to leave them forever." The magician said, "I need to consult Xiau again. What if the situation became urgent and suddenly my decision? And Bartholomew hated me for what I decided?"

A forlorn whale breeched in the distance.

⌣

Two days later, the *Nautilus* cruised into the bay of Roquetas de Mar.

Everyone crowded onto the ship's platform for their first look at Castell de Ferro as they neared the coast. Dry air from the rocky dunes wafted over the *Nautilus* and the gulls cried out, their racket extremely loud in the stark silence. To enhance their observations, Lieutenant Tuttle set up his photography apparatus and took a picture, which reminded the magician of security. He surrounded the ship in invisibility.

"There is very little left of the previous settlements. Look just above the rocks. And I see no evidence of a town for miles." Verne pointed with the spyglass he held. "Not too much is left; just that wall, two turrets, and a pile of bricks. I wish we could have seen the entire fortress back then."

"I agree. Zapillo is the closest village, about a dozen miles away," Kang said. "It probably has 500 people, no more. The only thing nearby is the highway that runs parallel to the entire Espania coastline."

"Is that where Doctor Lazlo gets his supplies?" Bartholomew asked.

"We'll have to question Nemo about that when we go below." Kang squinted across the water. "He is undoubtedly studying every aspect of the beach, the ruins, and the structures around it. Also, any underground features."

"He is using the documents we obtained on the way here," Tara glanced at Kang with a twist of her lips, "no matter how they were obtained."

The automat blinked his innocence and asked Bartholomew, "Whatever could she be talking about?"

"I'm sure I do not know." The big man always had trouble restraining his giggles while prevaricating.

Celwyn put a tiny policeman, in every detail, on Bartholomew's shoulder and went back to examining the coast, and then the skyline, detecting little except the sunset as it built into full, glorious color. Bartholomew gasped at his shoulder and the magician pretended he didn't hear anything. "Do you see the birds above the castle's right turret?"

"No." Verne squinted and brought up the spyglass again.

Celwyn said, "Look to the north, above the cliff face."

"Ah, now I do."

"Those are not birds." The magician said, "I must be a bit closer to know exactly what they are."

"The herd of daemons we saw in Hong Kong are starting to seem fairly benign about now." Bartholomew sighed. "At least we know what to expect from them."

Minutes went by while the *Nautilus* hovered in the water behind Celwyn's magical shroud and directly across from the Castell de Ferro.

"As I understand it, today we're just making a preliminary survey of Doctor Lazlo's compound, and picking up Valentine tomorrow," Tara said. "Unless our plans have changed?"

"They have not. After retrieving your uncle, we meet Swango in Taormino if all goes well." Kang studied the magician. "Did you tell him we are coming?"

"Just the telegram the other day." Celwyn realized his weeks of avoidance were about to run out. "Otherwise, I've verified he is teaching one of his classes and will be at home for a few more weeks."

"Hmm." Kang pursed his lips. "Have you decided to tell us more about him?"

Celwyn's attention stayed on the middle turret of the castle ruins that overlooked the water. The small windows, designed to protect the turret-keepers from cannon balls and flaming arrows, appeared every ten feet or so all around the keep. The magician thought he saw movement behind one of the windows on the upper level. That reminded him of what happened at Findbar, and he bet Bartholomew still shuddered at how that turned out. Perhaps he should give Lazlo a few ghosts for something to do.

The big man must have thought so too. "Which window are you looking at?" He brought a spyglass up to his eye.

"Second from the right, very top."

They could hear each other breathing until Bartholomew said, "I see nothing."

The automat had watched with them, and before he could repeat his question, Tara nudged the magician and raised a brow.

"I think we should wait and talk with the Captain. The most important thing everyone must know is," he gave Tara a peck on the cheek, "not to trust Swango under any circumstances." He made sure they were all listening. "He is also a notorious womanizer, thief, and scoundrel."

Chapter 37

FOR SOME REASON, THE AUTHOR HAD a dab of butter on his nose. When Kang raised a sarcastic brow at him, Celwyn shook his head; he had not decorated Verne. This time.

Dinner had nearly ended when the subject of Swango came up again.

"We will be in Gibraltar to pick up Mr. Soriano late tomorrow, and then travel to Taormino to your acquaintance." Nemo addressed Celwyn. "Now is a good time to hear what we should know about him before he comes aboard my ship."

The magician sighed. He hadn't really been avoiding this conversation as much as deciding what he would actually say about Swango and trying to understand the aspects around the situation that none of those present knew about. God knows he would not tell Verne so he could gossip about it.

The magician eyed the author until Verne looked at him with a nervous smile. No, a guilty one. Perhaps he should block what the man could hear? Nemo caught his glance and shook his head slightly. Celwyn sighed again—Nemo was right. He couldn't block Verne forever. It could be dangerous to anyone aboard the ship if they didn't know everything. If Swango became offended over something, he might react. That caused the magician to grin as he remembered the incident in the Black Forest.

"Jonas, I can see you are amused, and our desserts are beginning to melt." Kang asked, "What is it?"

"All right." His regret over this conversation went all the way to his toes. "Swango's background should come first, since I know how all your orderly minds work."

"I bet you don't." The big man laughed.

Celwyn would have to agree. "Anyhow, Swango is not an immortal. He was born in Pania, near Milan, and spent most of his life there, or in Bern. I don't know much about his education or early life. As a young man, he began collecting followers."

"Why?" Verne asked.

"Because of his stage performances as a clairvoyant. He appeared in most of the major cities."

"A clairvoyant, eh?" Nemo rubbed his chin. "I personally cannot understand the attraction; we make our own futures and can change them."

Tara thought about that and asked, "How accurate is he?"

"Very." Celwyn finished his fruit ice, even licking the spoon to delay what else he must say. "Well … I happen to know why he made such accurate predictions, and it is not just because I witnessed several of his stage performances."

It may have been a change in his voice, but Tara and Kang both stared at the magician with concern.

"I attended some of his acts early in the century. But I knew of how he obtained his information much earlier that … by 1759, I had my first encounter with Swango's talents. It is a memory I try to ignore." He smiled at them to defuse their suspicions. "This would be easier if I had some Earl Grey, and we were in a more relaxed setting."

"Of course." Nemo threw his napkin on the table. "Let us adjourn."

After everyone had settled on the sofas and the author perched at the chess table, Celwyn made his tea and inhaled the steam from it. He considered this a most pleasant sensation, one similar to when Tara sat beside him. When the author opened his notebook and uncapped a pen, the magician didn't hesitate and dissolved them both—Verne would find them in his cabin later.

As Celwyn sipped his tea, the others lit their cigars and pipes, everyone politely waiting, except for the automat, who studied him with an impatient expression. The tension continued to build like a pot of boiling water until the magician sighed and spoke.

"Around 1752, I met Swango in Paris at a séance hosted by Mme. Muriel Smithback. Seconds into the session, I recognized it as a farce and heard Swango muttering the same under his breath. He caught my chuckle and our comments increased until the hostess threw us out. Before we left, Swango related in detail how Mme. Smithback perpetrated her swindle. To show my appreciation, I bought the first round at the bar, where we spent the rest of the night singing and telling tall tales."

"*You?* You can't sing—" Kang roared with laughter, which caused Tara to join in along with the others. When the hilarity died down, Celwyn continued.

"For the next several weeks, we met again over meals until I had to leave for Seville and Swango for his first professional show—at the Globe in London." The magician had reached the point in the story where things would become noisy. He glanced at Nemo, whose eyes twinkled; he had noticed Celwyn's nervousness increasing. Nemo probably thought embarrassment caused it. Jonas wished it were that simple.

"Spit it out," Bartholomew advised.

"It is not that what I'm saying could be upsetting to you. But, well—" He knew how they would react. "What occurred in 1759 did have some dangerous aspects. Some things were frightening also. Through it all, I realized Swango's point of view matched mine; he is not a bad person, and he has little patience for evil. You should know that, at times, his reactions can be colorful."

"Good God, just tell us," the automat blurted. "His antics can't be worse than yours."

Celwyn cursed silently as the Swango memories came back. "It happened during one of our drinking sprees—which contributed to my preference since then for tea—and because I happened to be much younger at the time and not afraid of much ... or cautious whatsoever." He glared at Kang to stop his sarcastic agreement. "It happened during one of our outings that I bet Swango I could influence a war."

"Oh? I've noticed your and your brother's opinion of armed conflict." The fire in Nemo's eyes indicated he again relived Pelaez's crimes.

"Even then, I hated needless bloodshed and insisted that a well-placed confidant could sway royal decisions. They could save the lives of soldiers and villagers victimized by it."

"They can," Tara murmured with what the magician assumed was first-hand knowledge.

Celwyn shrugged. "My brother is just more extreme in his actions concerning it."

Bartholomew's frown darkened as he thought about Pelaez.

"Has anyone seen my notebook?" The author sidled closer. "I had it a moment ago."

Tara had watched the notebook dissolve. "I'm sure it will turn up after our discussion is over." She checked with Celwyn. "Won't it?"

"But of course."

Nemo prompted him. "So, you made a bet—"

"Yes. I wish I hadn't. Yet, if I hadn't, I never would have met several most interesting individuals, and discovered many things, both good and evil." To the magician, life should be romantic, not technical, or bloody, and he had witnessed much more of that than he wanted to.

He relaxed and began talking.

As vividly as if it happened yesterday, Celwyn again sat beside Swango in the bow of a toy-sized punter called *Sweet Dreams*. Celwyn rowed. Today had become a red wine afternoon, and Celwyn predicted that Swango would be snoring by the time they passed under the Folly Bridge of Oxford.

As they floated by the bucolic country landscape, birds twittered overhead, gossiping about the intruders on the lazy river. His companion's wan complexion did not appreciate the warm sun, and he refused to wear a hat. If Swango had been female, his gentle, deceptive features and mischievous pale eyes would have been thought attractive along with his curls the color of an Irish setter.

"What are you going to do in Swindon?" Celwyn rested a moment, letting the boat drift downstream. Insects buzzed across the river in a tiny storm and settled on the water.

"Search for some cocaine." Swango finished his bottle and yawned, causing the magician to hide a smile; Swango would be asleep before the next bridge. "And an antique shop that is supposed to have many curiosities. My main purpose is a visit to the Westrogothian war memorial."

"Why?" The magician began rowing again.

"I have a great-grandfather buried there."

"I am sorry."

Swango uncorked another bottle. "Don't be."

"If properly motivated, I could stop a war."

His companion dropped his bottle and sat up with a most interested expression.

"How?"

"I'm not sure, but I'm certain I could."

After he tossed the empty bottle as far as he could, Swango asked, "Care to place a wager on that? You wouldn't be able to change the main facts of history—that is the premise of the wager."

"I won't." The magician's smile promised it would be a lively contest.

As Swango watched the bottle traveling upriver against the current, it sailed into the air and multiplied. Dozens of bottles fell from the sky and splashed back into the river. Soon, an army of bottles covered the water—the first example of magic that Celwyn had allowed himself in front of Swango. He couldn't afford indiscriminate talk and gossip floating like a drunken swan all over Oxford. Someone else might challenge him magically, which would attract other unseemly characters.

Also, his new acquaintance, who lounged only a few feet away, might be squeamish or the superstitious type. Little did he know.

"Is that all you can do?" Swango drawled.

Celwyn raised a brow, and a salivating monkey sat on Swango's stomach. When it licked his nose, his companion growled, "All right, all right." He wiped his face, and the monkey faded away.

Swango eyed Celwyn with speculation. To appear as daft as possible, the magician gave him a silly look and dropped his oar.

"Well now. Since our acquaintance, you've been rather shy, haven't you? But you should know you are not the only one with special talents." His stare at the magician grew uncomfortable, and it felt as if a line of ants marched up Celwyn's arms and clustered around his neck. After another moment, Swango said, "I've noticed you are a betting man."

"That I am."

Swango started to chuckle and then smirked at Celwyn offensively. Just as the magician readied to give him something tangible to be amused about, the man continued.

"Here it is formally; I wager that you cannot influence or stop a war. And I will provide an opportunity for you to prove it."

Celwyn stopped propelling their punter forward and tipped his hat at a boat of young ladies with a burly gentleman at the oars.

"Tell me how."

"Do you accept the challenge?"

"What are we wagering?"

Swango pursed his lips. "If you win, which is doubtful, I will show you how to manipulate history safely. You won't be able to now, therefore I'll win the bet."

"Ha—" While Celwyn waved at the comely girls, especially the one in ribbons and lace with a sunburned nose, he played with a small silver mouse in his pocket, a gift from a vendor in London last week. The mechanics inside it must be fascinating. When he twisted the head, the feet wiggled. If he moved the tail, it stuck its tongue out.

"That is a worthy prize."

"The girl or my offer?" Swango asked.

The magician grinned. "Both."

"If I win, you'll teach me magic of my choosing."

The wager sounded like a trap. Celwyn had enough confidence he would prevail and wouldn't have to pay off this smirking drunk. "I will not be responsible if you cannot perform what I teach you. However, if that occurs—I will provide something else of value."

"It is a deal."

"Which war will be the test for our wager? The Seven Years War?"

Swango yawned. "You will have no problem finding it."

The last thing Celwyn remembered was the sunlight on the river as it dissolved into thick blackness. He didn't panic, but it felt like he swam in a vast unending tunnel where the darkness competed with the air that rushed by at an extraordinarily high speed. It brought a world of scents, from pungent manure to fresh oranges, then sweet roses. Everything swirled around him all at once.

Without warning, Celwyn's world exploded into light as bright as if an enormous match had been struck. Everything seemed so very different from the sun-drenched landscape of only a moment ago. Not only had the Isis River disappeared, but the rolling green hills had vanished too, along with Swango and their little boat. In their place, he saw frozen terrain.

A dead horse lay across Celwyn's leg. The animal shuddered its last breath and became still.

Celwyn gulped, instinctively repulsed by the wide gash exposing the horse's chest and revealing its rib cage. As its intestines fell into the dirt, a foul odor blossomed into the air, and steam escaped from the beast's nostrils, a signal that its soul departed, too.

What had Swango gotten him into?

The magician's wits returned. On high alert, he pushed the corpse off his leg and realized that whatever violence had killed the animal had missed his knee by mere inches. He shook his head at his own silliness; instead of hesitating to use magic in front of Swango, he should have established his superiority before the man did the same. Swango had just done something remarkable, perhaps astonishing; Celwyn wasn't in Oxford anymore. Far from it.

He studied the road in front of him, then the surrounding mountains and trees. None of them looked like anything from England. And the huge drifts of snow... Perhaps what he saw displayed Swango's idea of an elaborate and realistic scene, just to make a point? The smell of the dead horse caused him to discard the idea. That didn't fit any scenario he could think of ... yet the magician felt more curious than afraid.

For as far as he could see in any direction, cold air blew over snow piled higher than a carriage. He shivered at the desolation he found himself in. No, not a staged play, nothing like that could instill the fear he suddenly knew.

Yet, with a small smile, reality and the present combined, calming him, as he remembered something that had nothing to do with Swango and his clairvoyant performances, womanizing, or his irritating habits—the magician pictured a rather short mechanical man with elfin ears, too long hair, and leathery skin teasing him about being reckless. Professor Xiau Kang.

Celwyn stood, brushing off the dirt, blood, and snow from a fine woolen suit, not the wrinkled sack suit that he'd been rowing in. These clothes had been designed strangely; not only did they appear snug and formfitting, but the vest had strange buttons—much different from those used on ladies' clothing. They were not made of horsehair or bone. He bent over to look at the trousers. No buttons here. A metal strip meshed with another metal strip. He pulled on the tab at the top. The strips separated and his trousers fell down. Celwyn had to use magic to pull the metal strips together. *Damn Swango.*

Where in the world was he?

From far away came the rumble of a motor, and it seemed to be getting louder. Using magic, he held up his trousers and scrambled off the road. Before he elevated himself into the trees, he made sure the saddlebags under the dead horse followed him.

It seemed odd—he couldn't hear chattering birds, growling wolves, or anything in any direction across the landscape, except that motor. He seemed to be the only breathing entity in this forest. The eeriness increased his nervous cursing.

The noise from the engine grew louder, coming from the south. He opened the first satchel and found clothes and toiletries. Then he held up some very odd footwear. In the other saddlebag, he discovered more of the same, plus a small leather fold, a box, and several sealed envelopes. Perhaps they contained clues as to what he had fallen into?

Celwyn opened the leather fold first and nearly dropped it; his own face stared back at him from a tiny picture. He had never seen a photograph in color before. How wonderful! Although blurry, his expression seemed grim, but the brilliance of his eyes looked as marvelous as usual. His expression bothered him … in the few pictures he'd ever seen of himself, he had looked so serious, but not as deadly as this one. The name of "Monsieur Jean Tremaine" appeared on the matching papers. Celwyn looked at the other wallet, finding another picture. When he pawed through the envelope, he discovered a dossier for a second person adorned with his picture again; a certain Elmo Linnsen. That Swango sure was a jokester.

As he reread the captioned name under his chin, the once faraway sound of a motor became many engines. *Damnation!* He whispered to himself, seeing something unbelievable.

Five vehicles stopped behind the dead horse. Celwyn had never encountered anything like them, but it made sense. If an enterprising person took a carriage, lowered it to the ground, eliminated the horses, and put the coachman inside the carriage— that described what he saw. Another difference? The wheels looked fat, not spindly, with their rims black and slick looking.

Uniformed men clambered out of the first vehicle and the cart-like transport behind it. The man with the most medals on his uniform ordered them to move the dead horse. Celwyn had no trouble hearing them, but they spoke in heavily accented Bavarian, which he didn't understand very well.

The man with the medals gestured at the woods. "Suchen sie hier!" *Search here!* "Der flüchtling hat nerven aus stahl. *Who shot the horse?*"

"We don't know, Herr General." The soldier turned and barked the order to the others. As they began stumbling through the snow, Celwyn became invisible and congratulated himself on retreating to the trees without leaving footprints in the snow. Soon, the soldiers would give up, and they'd assume their quarry had continued along the graveled road.

A chill blew over Celwyn; if these soldiers hadn't shot his horse, who had?

While the men combed the woods, as a moth, he rose into the air and hovered at the treetops. Perhaps a mile away, scores of quaint buildings with peaked roofs ringed a frozen lake. In the far distance, a range of snow-covered peaks reached for the sky. The landscape reminded him of Austria ... and the Bavarian accents he'd heard so far fit that conclusion. To the east, the forests took over as less and less snow carpeted the land. The soldiers continued their search.

He took a moment to reflect.

Where was he? Probably the Black Forest. How did he get here? That God-damned Swango. A glance at his clothes brought up something harder to answer.

During the brief visits he had made into Swango's thoughts, he had seen so many unrecognizable things. It astounded him. And the magician couldn't very well have asked the man about them without explaining how and where he saw them. Swango might block him from another unauthorized visit or shoot him. One thing he had noticed before seemed familiar now; those same motorized carriages, in different colors and sizes, traveled like grotesque monsters throughout Swango's memory.

A series of barked orders from below interrupted the magician's reflections. He descended until he once again sat on a branch, invisible and curious.

"Curses!"

"Ja, General Heidal."

The general stomped off the road and into the snow, relieved himself, and returned as another soldier ran up to them and made a report. The general's face grew redder with each word.

"No one?" The general stomped his feet. "Then who killed the fucking horse?" By now, Heidal's face matched the red stripe running down the leg of his uniform.

"We—" Sweat beaded on his underling's face. "We do not know. The nearest village is more than a mile away through heavy snow." He checked the rifle that the soldier nearest to him cradled, and with a fingertip pointed it away from the general. "We saw no footprints or evidence of anyone here at all."

It did not take long for the inference to settle on General Heidal. He stopped talking and gazed into the trees. Not just a peek, but a serious, probing look.

"Captain, we should leave. Now." Heidal Heidal licked his lips. "We'll find Herr Tremaine another way."

So that is how you pronounce my new name, Celwyn thought. Heidal marched back to the first vehicle and the rest of the soldiers scrambled into the other contraptions without being urged to do so. Their glances at the woods verified their growing nervousness. Old folk tales about Bavarian kobolds in the forests, perhaps? *Or because they feared who-ever had killed the horse?*

As the motors grew louder and rolled away, the magician also wondered why he had been on a horse in the middle of nowhere. He felt the weight of coins in his pocket—and he should have been able to obtain one of these new fancy vehicles—they appeared to be faster than a horse. Unless ... it could be that he had wanted to travel on something qui-eter. Celwyn grinned to himself. Perhaps he didn't know how to operate one. Normally, he would hire a driver, but the magician suspected things might be far from normal in this cold and lonely countryside.

Which brought up the question: *how would he travel?* He could make another horse, but it may be blown out from underneath him again. It would also be best to keep the satchels with him. With a critical eye on the other bag, he thought it a shame to not wear the finery in it.

All the while, he wondered about the General's interest in a man called Tremaine.

In seconds, he had miniaturized both saddlebags to his back and, as a gorgeous owl, flew toward the village by the frozen lake. As he circled the trees surrounding it, the magician read the sign on the rough track announcing the village of Wolfach.

Perhaps three dozen houses framed the lake in front of dozens of buildings that sold supplies and services. A small sign had announced Doctor Zelig's surgery, and another hung in front of the Hotel Ibis Mainz.

Something he had never seen before caught his eye; The Ehrliche Garage. Below it, another sign advertised; "For Hire" *How interesting,* he thought as he peered through the oversized doors. Although he could learn to maneuver the horseless contraptions, Celwyn didn't relish the idea of it any more than steering the flying machine when Bartholomew had offered to teach him. In the last few seconds, he'd remembered something from the 1870s—long after Swango sent him here, and recognized his memory of Swango and Oxford as just that, a memory. Everything around him he suspected lay in the future.

Once again, he wore the odd-looking hat and shouldered the satchels as he walked down the main street to the hotel. For his debut, the magician had threaded his hair with plenty of silver and added a thick beard. He passed by a boy and an old man, both of whom stared at him for a few seconds, and in the boy's thoughts he heard, "...another verdammt tourist."

Inside the warmth of the hotel, it only took a few minutes to determine if he could either order a whiskey in the hotel bar or must do without. Wolfach did not have any other drinking establishments. Celwyn frowned. Probably the fastest and easiest way to answer his questions would be to obtain a newspaper. Swango wasn't here to complain about his methods or answer his questions.

"Zeitung?" He asked the man behind the bar, who appeared barely tall enough to work the counter. He did speak English.

"Yes, sir." He reached under the countertop and slapped a newspaper with big headlines in front of him. "That will be a saar mark for this and your drink."

Celwyn searched his pockets for a coin and picked up the paper. *Oh my,* he thought as he read the large titles that screamed at him.

Celwyn read for several minutes, thinking. So, 193 years after his wager, Germany waged war and called itself the Third Reich. A fission of dread traveled down his back on cold feet; things here seemed so somber and dark, and the pictures in the newspaper depressing. As he read more, his fear didn't dissipate, instead, rising until he shuddered and wondered what he'd gotten himself into.

By the time he finished the next few pages of the newspaper, he decided everything had been written by the same hand that perpetuated a one-sided view of battles and conquests. Glorious victories depicted German superiority, no matter how bloody. On the second page, he read an editorial railing against the Jews and the Romani. The fear he had felt turned even colder.

Chapter 38

In the study of the *Nautilus*

THE GONGS IN THE BELLY OF THE *Nautilus* echoed under their feet. Celwyn stopped speaking and waited.

"What!" Professor Xiau Kang jumped to his feet. "This is incredible!! The future ... I suppose it would be too much to hope you have a copy of the newspaper?"

At least Xiau had gotten over most of his despondency. The magician wouldn't call the mood in the study jovial, but it certainly seemed expectant and alert. As he met each of their expressions, he felt the submarine descending and enjoyed a measure of normalcy in the cloud of bubbles outside the aquatic window.

Qing squawked with excitement; Over what, the magician didn't know, but he took it as proof that he most definitely had arrived back to the present time just fine. Ever since the Swango adventure, he had worried that the bastard would drag him back to the Black Forrest. Even worse; his mind played tricks on him at times—the future seemed intense and enticing, as if wanting to sink claws into his flesh and hold on to him. Celwyn shook himself; another good reason to get this over with.

Verne told him, "This is all so fantastic. I wish I'd known of it before so I could have used it in my books."

Celwyn reared back. He didn't remember the author sitting beside him, nor had he really paid attention to the room after he began recounting Swango's episode. Nemo puffed on his pipe and regarded him through slitted eyes, while Bartholomew gazed at him as if the magician would sprout horns and spit fire out of them.

"I am used to the danger you face, Jonas. The way this story has begun is ... concerning," Tara said.

Nemo said, "I suspect the rest of it will be much worse."

It certainly felt like it. The magician patted Tara's hand. "I am here. I survived." He turned to Kang. "To answer your question, no, I do not have any of the newspapers from that time. I can barely remember some of the nonessential details, but I will do my best to reconstruct what I read and saw."

"That will suffice," the automat said.

Nemo stood and stretched. "Let's hear it after our luncheon," he gestured to where the crew had begun setting the dining table. "Perhaps what comes next will help us understand this."

"I hope so." The magician leaned back again, and, as he began his recanting of the story, he tried not to think about what he had yet to tell them.

Chapter 39

OVER SEVERAL WHISKEYS IN THE hotel bar, Celwyn read some, and thought. *There must be a reason Swango brought me here.* For a long time, the magician tried to figure out Swango's intentions in this beautiful land where a precise and horrible evil existed. Could it be this exercise meant more than a bet to him?

Celwyn found Hitler both interesting and wicked. And he needed other newspapers to know what actually happened in this world.

"Is this the only newspaper you have?"

A flash of fear crossed the barman's eyes before it retreated to where the Nazis couldn't see it. "Yes, sir. Perhaps there are others in Freudenstadt. It isn't that far away."

Instead of asking how far, the magician entered the man's thoughts to find an answer. First, he discovered a fleeting picture of hundreds of soldiers marching along before scores of strange vehicles, and then another scene of parading soldiers in different uniforms holding out their right arms, palms up toward a bandstand full of more men in military uniforms. In the barman's mind, they had been labeled as "Luftwaffe." Nearly on top of the image, a man screamed in the barman's face and twisted his arm. The words sounded like a threat and concerned his family. They repeated over and over again; a worry the barman couldn't shake.

"What is your name, sir?" Celwyn asked.

Surprise or fear of the Nazis stopped the man from answering until the magician nodded at him. "It is all right."

"I am called Henry."

Celwyn thought it best not to mention the name Tremaine because of the Nazi's interest. After reading the newspaper, he now knew what that symbol, a funny backward-looking cross, meant. As the magician observed the other patrons in the bar, he re-entered Henry's mind. None of the customers stood out to the barman. How could they? Every one of them stared at their drinks, spoke little, and never smiled. Perhaps the Nazis frowned upon happiness.

Foremost in Henry's thoughts, he found a wish to see someone called Guenther again. They had been separated years ago when the SS arrested Guenther and he had not been heard from him in months. *Who is this SS?* Celwyn retrieved the newspaper and flipped pages until he discovered information about them. When he finished, he decided the newspapers had been produced by typeset puppets, written in fear instead of truth, and dangled on deceitful strings.

A glass slammed onto the bar by Celwyn's elbow, effectively dissipating his curiosity.

"Schnaps!"

Celwyn gazed into a set of eyes that flashed with both electricity and irritation. He saw a woman, young and wearing a smart black uniform and tie— just like those in the pictures of the Gestapo. Her hair had been piled on her head and, from under a cap, blonde ringlets surrounded her face, like a halo over a questionable angel. The magician admired her profile, thinking it one of the finest he had seen in a while.

In the shadowy corner of the bar, two men, not in uniform, studied him and the woman. Again, Celwyn felt thankful for the silver he'd added to his hair and the fluffy beard.

"Here you are, Fräulein." Henry deposited a glass in front of her. As he turned away, she grabbed his wrist.

"Address me as Lieutenant Dosher." Her melodic voice belied the hard command, and she waved away Henry's feeble attempt to respond. "Go back to work—"

When she focused on the magician, he sensed he could discover something useful here. The fierce and delectable Lieutenant Dosher might provide information the newspapers did not and possibly transportation out of the village. In the newspaper stories, it appeared the Gestapo worked for the

Hitler fellow, and if Celwyn expected to derail this war, the Gestapo could be valuable.

The magician swallowed revulsion and used all his charm as he took her hand to kiss it. She did not pull away.

"Please honor me," the magician said, "by accepting an invitation to dinner later. I hear the food at this hotel is quite acceptable."

Her pale eyes regarded him over the top of her glass. Celwyn entered her thoughts, finding only curiosity about him, nothing more. He maintained his adoring gaze.

She switched to accent-less English. "How delightfully old-fashioned you sound. If I knew your name, perhaps I would." Her voice played with him, and he recognized seduction; one false step and he would drown. Or she could shoot him. From the intensity in her eyes, she knew it too.

The magician made his reaction appropriately smitten. "I'm Elmo Linnsen, from the Hague. Originally from the United States."

Sparks of interest danced in her eyes like a tiny rocket exploding. She leaned closer. "Lieutenant Millicent Dosher of the Gestapo." She ran a fingernail along his collar.

That act represented extraordinary confidence; just mentioning the Gestapo while trying seduction. Celwyn held his breath and did not react. It appeared that in 1943 women were not shy either. He refrained from looking at her exposed legs below her skirt... He'd always wondered how a woman's dress would look without dozens of petticoats. While covering a yawn, he glanced downward and didn't see any petticoats at all. Her skirt seemed much too tight for any.

Celwyn raised his eyes to hers.

"I am pleased to meet you." Once again, he entered her thoughts, and this time discovered her attention lay not on him, but on the fatter of the two grey-suited men in the corner. She had a nickname for him: Porky. Most interesting; he worked for her as a bodyguard and helped with her work. Celwyn searched until he learned more. His customary good luck held; the blonde warrior had a most useful occupation—she gathered information for Herr Hitler, and by his request, regularly met with him about it. A coincidence courtesy of Swango?

The magician finished his drink and got to his feet. He also needed to collect facts. With charm seeping from his voice, he said, "I look forward to this evening. Would dinner at eight o'clock be acceptable?"

Instead of answering, she stood and smoothed down her skirt. The top of her head came up to his chin, making her statuesque and enhancing her attractiveness. He had never completely backed out of her mind, and with surprise, listened to her worry about checking into the hotel and reading dispatches from Berlin.

"Will you be staying in Wolfach long?"

In this light, her eyes reminded him of shadowed snow. "It depends, Herr Linnsen. I am part of a team hunting a traitor to the Reich. I may be here hours or days." With a glance at Porky and his friend, she jerked her chin at the door. "If you should happen to see another man with the same brilliant green eyes such as yours, it could be who we seek. His name is Tremaine." In her thoughts, she added, *he looks very much like you, and at dinner, I will find out more.*

Celwyn kissed her hand, thinking, *No, you won't.*

"Au Revoir, Miss Dosher." He tried to appear so smitten he forgot to address her as a soldier, not a woman.

After Celwyn watched her pass through the glass doors with her two escorts, he climbed thirty-five steep steps to the second floor. Vases of lilies perfumed hallways leading to both the east and west wings.

When he opened the door to room 215, the magician stopped still; enjoying his intuition. His smile broadened, remembering Xiau hated it. The tiniest hint of Lieutenant Dosher's perfume lingered in the air where it should never have been. Before he innocently invited her to join him at dinner, she must have found his hotel room interesting. Theirs had not been a chance meeting.

The magician checked his bag and toured the room, not seeing anything amiss. He had taken care to hide the fold with Tremaine's picture and the envelopes in a protected area of the hotel roof. Again, thinking like a thief and blackguard had proved useful.

Celwyn lay on the bed and considered his situation. Yes, he wanted to win the wager with Swango. And now, he admitted he desired victory so that the prankster would have to show him how to visit the future on his own terms. The possibilities seemed exciting and endless. A growl escaped from his throat. When he read about the Nazis, he wanted to stop this war, wager or not. Lieutenant Dosher would be dealt with separately.

On a fascinating note, he'd read how the enemies of the Nazis included the English, Russians, and Americans—quite an alliance, and he doubted they trusted each other any more today than they did in 1870.

When he crossed to the suite's windows, he felt the chill from the snow coming through. It would be very useful to know what the Gestapo planned. A minute later, the window opened a fraction of an inch to allow a most handsome fly to escape and head down the street.

He made his first stop at the village surgery, a place likely to have several visitors. In listening to the conversations, Celwyn noticed their discussions did not appear to be guarded here, and one especially, stood out. A dowager's voice supplied gossip and a strong opinion at the same time. Celwyn got comfortable on top of the bookcase above her head.

"... she sent him money."

"That is not true, Truda," a young matron protested.

Another woman with unnaturally red hair whispered, "Why?"

"She expects him to marry her," Truda said. "But if he is stationed in Normandy or any place where the Englanders will invade us, he might be too dead to be a husband. Think about it, Marta," she told the young matron.

"Do you know for certain he is on the coast? Lila should look for a different man. Preferably one who can work when this stupidity is over."

"How much longer is Doctor Zelig going to be?" Truda craned her neck and stretched both of her double chins to see over the receptionist's shoulder.

"Who knows? I hear he is required to treat the Gestapo when they come here," Marta said.

"Humph. We will be waiting forever then. Two men went in right before you arrived."

The woman with the red hair asked, "Are you done with the French paper? I haven't seen it yet."

"No, I'll drop it off tonight." Truda opened the satchel at her feet and withdrew yarn and needles.

The magician considered needlework of any kind akin to watching an ant crawl up a wall. He flew past the receptionist and into the surgery.

When he slipped under the second door, he found the good doctor and his opinions about the Nazis. As Celwyn settled down to listen, he studied Doctor Zelig's visitors. Close up, Dosher's helpers appeared disposable and not very interesting. The thinner one yawned as the doctor lectured them about military strategy.

"Listen to me! Make Admiral Gottwold understand. You must stop the Americans from landing on French beaches. Stop them!" He shoved a book into Porky's arms. "Herr Fendor writes of winning at sea. It is priceless!"

"We appreciate your interest," Porky's partner said. "We will take that with us. Again, about our question; have you seen this man?" He waved the picture of Tremaine under Zelig's bulbous nose. By the time the doctor focused, the magician made sure the man in the picture looked like someone Celwyn had seen in a story about Goebbels. That caused the doctor to stop and carefully study his visitors from under lowered brows. The magician planted a strong suggestion into the good doctor's mind, even adding a few details to make him believe it too.

"I hear that the man you seek hitched a ride east, toward Berlin," Doctor Zelig said. "One of the farmers on Weizen Road saw him late yesterday. He is wearing a brown woolen suit and is clean-shaven."

Porky and the thin man traded a glance and excused themselves. As the Gestapo left the office, Celwyn rode on Porky's coat collar and listened to his companion complain about the doctor's fantastic ideas. When they started up the street, the magician spied something that drew his admiration. This village must be rich and important; on the street corner, one of those new telephones had been nailed into a glass box taller than a man. The thin man put coins into it. Celwyn's envy grew; *anyone* could use the contraption who had money. A woman had already walked up to the glass box and waited while the Gestapo talked.

Porky's friend identified himself as Corporal Frackler and asked the person he talked to about the weather in Berlin. Snow fell as he listened to the answer. "Fine. Thank you." Frackler clicked his heels together even though the person on the telephone couldn't see him. "My report; the subject Tremaine was last seen riding a horse toward Wolfach. We are there now and can find no one who saw him before, or after, they found the horse about five miles out of town. There is an unverified sighting of him on Weizen Road." He listened and straightened his shoulders. "Yes, sir. I understand. I do." He waved Porky closer. "Here is the Corporal."

Celwyn entered Porky's mind and explored, searching until he located what he needed; the Nazis suspected Tremaine of being employed by the Americans to assassinate Hitler. What a promising idea! The magician thanked his luck—he couldn't have asked for a better opportunity.

But his good spirits did not last. Seconds later, Porky's thoughts turned to images of a torture session that he and Frackler had conducted on a French sympathizer. *Such nasty men,* Celwyn thought and controlled the urge to bite his ear off—at least until he drained him of information. Whatever plans he made, these two would not survive. Meanwhile, Porky's chubby cheeks began to sweat as he listened to his instructions.

Chapter 40

I T NEARED FIVE IN THE AFTERNOON as Celwyn strolled along, marveling at the bright lights on the street and inside the village shops. He walked in a slow start-and-stop pattern, punctuated with glances to the rear to confirm that Porky still followed him. Frackler had headed in the other direction.

Celwyn side-stepped into an alley between a two-story building and a Lutheran Church. The alley only extended to the end of the building and ended at a wooden fence covered in snow. Nearby, someone had stacked crates and a decrepit bicycle against one wall. *How convenient.* The magician made himself into a rat, nested into the spokes of the bicycle, and waited.

Porky walked by the alley with his hat low and his interest casual. On his second pass by, he slipped inside. As the Nazi toured the alley, he held a sleek pistol at his side. When he reached the end of the alley, he peered over the fence and searched; seeing no footprints in the snow, nor the man he had trailed here. Still confused, he extended the pistol in front of him as he moved back up the empty alley.

Celwyn dissolved the gun and Porky barked a curse and dropped onto his knees. He started to look for it in the snow. When he moved to the bicycle, the magician blew a manure-scented cloud over him and caused the rat to speak in a proper English baritone.

"Why are you following that man?" The magician hummed the first few bars of *Hail Britannia.*

Porky tried to back up but slipped and fell flat. Celwyn scampered onto his chest and repeated the question inches from his face. When the Nazi tried to swat him off, he discovered his arms wouldn't move.

The magician caressed his plump cheek and explored Porky's thoughts, discovering additional background to add to his growing knowledge. Among other things, he learned that the Gestapo suspected the pastor of the church next door of anti-Nazi activities, including hiding Jews sought by the SS.

Whoever discovered Porky first would find his clothes folded neatly on top of the bicycle. Of course, the corpulent Nazi would need some entertainment until then. A lively waltz began filling the alley, and the last thing Porky saw would be a playful rat dancing from side to side as it scampered out of the alley.

When he reached the sidewalk, Celwyn glanced at the tower of the church where a collection of birds sat like holy statues, silent and unmoving. Another bird would be appropriate. From the shadows, a bluebird emerged flying upward, beating his wings lazily, and circling the tower to gauge distances and study the houses lining the quaint streets. Wolbach appeared twice as large as he first thought. There must be a thousand residents, perhaps more.

As he settled into an alcove in the tower, one by one, the other birds departed with speed. Humph; Celwyn never suspected birds could be so superstitious.

From the open floor below, a spiral staircase snaked upward beyond an altar. Now, the magician flew a moth, traveling down corridors until he located the pastor in the kitchen. While the pastor ate, the magician settled into the cupboard next to him and explored his thoughts. It took a while before he discovered exactly what he needed.

An hour later, Pastor Theodore snored in his chair with an empty wine bottle cradled in his arms. He wouldn't miss what the magician took with him.

Chapter 41

Surprises come in many flavors. They can be horrible or spicy and sweet. Tonight, Celwyn believed the confusing ones to be the most fascinating.

The Ibid Mainz Hotel's clock chimed eight bells as the maître'd ushered Lieutenant Dosher to the table where Celwyn waited. He experienced several facets of surprise: from her distinctly non-military dress (and how immodest it appeared) to her unpinned hair cascading over her shoulders and, finally, the look in her eye. Lieutenant Dosher planned something. So did he. Celwyn smiled a greeting as she neared the table.

They said nothing until the maître'd pulled out her chair and she sat.

"Good evening, Mr. Linnsen." It sounded more like a purr than an order. "The food here remains very good, even during war."

The magician had entered her mind as soon as she drew close enough, finding her attention wandering down many alleyways. In one, he glimpsed her standing in front of a mirror while she applied cosmetics, which he found intriguing. She made a variety of faces as she worked, especially when darkening her eyelashes. While she applied powder, he discovered her opinions of many people; including the concierge of the hotel and several military men whose images she regularly reviewed.

The newspapers that he'd just obtained contained excellent photographs, and he recognized some famous men taking up much of her recent memory. Several times, the Lieutenant relived a telephone call about Tremaine; in it, she heard clear instructions to bring the fugitive to Gestapo headquarters, not shoot him.

The blonde warrior had no problem expressing her opinion to Herr Himler and others. Idly, the magician wondered if she traded on—or hid behind—her beauty. In contrast, her rather bloodthirsty point of view that anyone unfriendly to the Reich should be disposed of probably distracted a few people she met and attracted others. If her methods did not produce results, then she advocated a few bullets in their ears.

Celwyn gave her a look of appreciation.

"I'm honored you joined me this evening."

She regarded him for several moments—not as a woman studies a man. Her eyes calculated his weight, his wealth, and anything she could superficially gather. Perhaps to compare to the research she had gathered about him? The magician compared the perfection of her features to what wallowed in her soul.

"Where is that music coming from?" she turned in several directions. "It is beautiful, but I do not see an orchestra or anyone playing a piano—" she started to rise to investigate. The magician put a hand on her arm.

"Please, let's enjoy our evening and not worry."

The sommelier approached.

She gently removed her arm and softened the action with liquid eyes. "Yes, you are correct." She waited while Celwyn ordered and then continued. "Before the claret arrives, perhaps you can tell me more about yourself?"

He had been expecting the question. Prior to answering, he scanned her thoughts, conveniently discovering the Gestapo official dossier about Elmo Linnsen up front. To display his cooperation and humor, he answered her—listing the facts she knew in reverse order. When he purposely switched the ages listed for his parents, she frowned but said nothing.

They sampled the claret. While the magician sipped, he talked, and she silently compared what he said to what she had read. She seemed to be convinced, somewhat. To her, he sounded harmless, but not completely. *Would it matter?* The real Elmo Linnsen, of Celwyn's height and build, had probably reached safety in England by now, according to the papers in the saddlebags. At least Celwyn hoped so. It would be difficult to explain two of them.

"The steak sounds good." She studied the menu. "Why are you not married? Perhaps you have a paramour?" She asked with greater warmth than anything she had said so far.

With matching intimacy, Celwyn said, "Not at the moment."

"I see." Her eyes flickered at him like a playful cub with a piece of meat.

After a sigh, he said, "I regret I cannot spend any more days here to explore new possibilities. I must catch a train for Berlin tomorrow."

She put a hand on his. "But that is wunderbar! I must return there in the morning, also. Would you care to travel with me?"

The magician had expected the invitation. "A marvelous idea." He wondered if Porky and Frackler would be going with them. By now, Frackler should have found Porky and given him back his trousers. "What time do we depart?"

"At eight." Again, she subjected him to impersonal scrutiny. "Is it business that takes you to Berlin?"

"Yes, and no. I must meet with a buyer, and then I plan to see the Pergamon Museum. I enjoy architecture. Do you?"

"Oh yes."

A swift array of battle scenes painted in blood and terror marched by in her memory. Celwyn stifled a laugh; he had discovered a Valkyrie. Hopefully, one so blinded by her ambitions that she would not detect inconsistencies in his planning.

As their dinner progressed, he tried repeatedly to elicit personal information from her, but she side-stepped all questions except two, which she inferred but didn't confirm. Although nearing her

30th birthday, she had never married. Two, she hated children and Jews. At that news, Celwyn strengthened his resolve; no matter how repulsive she became, the more charm he applied.

Hours later, they left the dining room and Celwyn spied Frackler sitting behind a newspaper beside the street exit. He pretended to read while he watched anyone entering or leaving. Before he could make eye contact with the lieutenant, Celwyn caused an exact effigy of Tremaine, the beardless one, to brush by Frackler and out the door. The Gestapo man couldn't get to his feet fast enough as a frigid blast of air rushed in and Frackler ran after him. If Xiau were here, he'd sputter in surprise at the effigy of Tremaine, and Bartholomew would faint.

The magician made sure the Tremaine imitation gave Frackler a merry chase and several close-up views of his face; the Gestapo needed to believe he chased Tremaine and that the handsome magician concurrently seducing the lieutenant—could not be him. Tomorrow, while he and the Nazis traveled to Berlin, he'd make sure a few citizens reported Tremaine getting on a train for the coast.

When they parted ways by the staircase, the magician implanted a delightful idea in Dosher's mind as he kissed her hand. She would ask herself if she should introduce Elmo Linnsen to Goring, or even Herr Hitler. Or should she try to recruit him to gather information for the Nazis as he went about his business across Europe?

As he walked away, the magician blew her a kiss goodbye.

Chapter 42

THE NEXT MORNING, CELWYN awaited the Nazis in front of the hotel, occasionally tipping his hat to nearby shopkeepers and stepping aside for pedestrians.

He had spent hours the previous evening pouring over the items in Tremaine's envelopes and growing more curious with each discovery: a list of "special friends of Mrs. Goebbels," a train schedule between Berlin and other cities for Tuesdays and Thursdays (with particular stops circled), pictures of various people, a bank receipt with an illegible signature, and a copy of one of Hitler's speeches.

In the collection of papers he had borrowed from the pastor, he found lists of dates and people who had nothing to do with Tremaine or Linnsen. Did the pastor keep them because Tremaine was actually a spy, or a trick by Swango to waste Celwyn's time?

At least as Elmo Linnsen, the magician had a reason to visit various people on his buying expeditions.

"Gutentag." The magician tipped his hat to a wholesome fräulein with dimples and a milk-fed complexion. Although she bustled by in a hurry, she trailed an appreciative eye after the magician.

He added a bouquet of roses to the packages she carried and as he debated whether to add a card also, a throaty voice at his elbow said, "She is but a child, not a woman." Lieutenant Dosher drew a finger across his wrist. "Are you ready?"

"Yes, Ma'am."

She winced at the formal title reserved for matrons. As Frackler and Porky approached, she recovered and introduced them, even though the two probably thought they already knew everything about Herr Linnsen.

Porky's handshake came and went quickly as if he suspected the magician had dirty fingernails. In contrast, Frackler tried to crush his knuckles. Celwyn returned the handshake in kind and as he backed away and left a whisper in his ear, "Herr Hitler sleeps with sheep. *Bahh bahh bahh.*" As the whisper intensified, Frackler swiveled and bumped into an angular man in a splendid suit. The stranger retrieved his hat with a glare and continued on his way.

"What is wrong with you?" Lieutenant Dosher demanded.

Frackler looked like he'd swallowed a sheep. "Nothing, nothing. Shall we?" He opened the driver's door while Porky hopped forward to hand the

Lieutenant inside. The magician settled beside her, leaving Porky to load their luggage into the boot. It took so long, Celwyn assumed he tried to search some of it. Celwyn made sure the metal strips keeping his case closed did not open. He also congratulated himself on mastering the set of them on his trousers. When Porky finally climbed into the front seat, he appeared a tad grumpy.

During the drive, the Lieutenant and Frackler pointed out sights of interest, usually ones attributed to the success of the Nazis. The bridge at Hannover seemed to inspire the most pride. As they drove over it, Porky explained, "We used the dirty Jews to build this. They are inferior people." He opened his window and spat. After a few minutes of silence, Frackler asked a question.

"What do you do for a living, Herr Linnsen?"

You know damn well what I do from your investigation. Celwyn wondered where they trained these sadistic imbeciles but answered.

"I own my own business and travel extensively. This is also a pleasure trip for me." The magician favored the Lieutenant with a secret smile, and although surprised, she returned it. "Could you please recommend a good hotel in Berlin?" He asked. "It must be near the museum and theater district if possible."

As Porky slowed for a turn, he held on tight to the wheel and they slid a bit on the ice. When he had control again, he said, "The Whitebriar. They are loyal to the Reich. Are you loyal too, Herr Linnsen?"

Porky thinks he is a smooth talker.

"For what I know of them, I am. I also admire your Fuhrer. It would be an honor to meet him someday."

"He is busy," Frackler snapped.

Celwyn checked the man's thoughts and asked, "Is he involved in the battle near Riga?"

Frackler clamped his lips shut and ignored him. Mile after mile of snow had become simply boring, so the magician added a few items to the landscape as they drove by. The Lieutenant gasped and pointed. Porky put his reaction into words.

"Fuck!" He gaped at hundreds of small gnomes. They had Hitler faces and twitchy mustaches. A few waved at the automobiles driving by.

"Stop the car!" Lieutenant Dosher yelled as more and more gnomes joined the others, covering rolling hills of snow that disappeared into the distance. Travelers passing the other way honked and their passengers laughed.

"This will be investigated!" Her voice did not sound seductive at all; it shrilled. "*Where* are we?"

"About fifteen miles from Brunswick." Frackler gazed at the river that followed the road. "There are fields to the south of here, but most of it is wasteland and rocks."

"The Underground did this. Those hoodlums." She bestowed a hard eye on the magician. "The man I asked you about, Tremaine, is supposed to be their leader. But nobody knows where he is!"

"Not at all?"

Her grim smile promised something unpleasant. "We have sources of information."

"I see." Celwyn checked the statues. "I am curious, but it is none of my business to ask questions. Even about that."

She threw up her hands. "There are no secrets about him. Tremaine taunts us."

Porky growled. "Last week he put an advertisement in the newspaper falsely claiming the Englanders killed the Fuhrer."

"That's horrible!" The magician fanned himself. As the Nazis nodded their agreement, the British anthem began to play, softly at first, but it grew stronger as it came through the closed windows, following the car no matter how fast Porky drove.

"What *is* that?" Frackler demanded. He rolled down his window and Celwyn increased the volume. Porky had already started braking when Frackler yelled at him to stop the car. The Mercedes bumped onto the side of the road as the final chorus of "God Save the King" reached its climax. While the music swelled, both of Dosher's minions exited the car, stomping through snow drifts to find the source of the horns and enthusiastic drumming. Immediately, the American "Star-Spangled Banner" began echoing around them. When it came to the "rocket's red glare" the magician made sure a few rockets exploded overhead.

"Get in! Beeil dich! This is some kind of trick—" Lieutenant Dosher pounded on the seat in front of her.

They ignored her and continued searching for the rockets and under the car. When the American music stopped, the Russian anthem took over. She cursed and screeched. "*Get in*!!"

Porky jumped backward with a shriek. In front of him, one of the gnomes sat in the driver's seat with its mouth opening and shutting as it sang to the music. It kept time by waving its Hitler arms until Porky flung it into the snow.

"That is quite odd." Celwyn filled his voice with wonder. "Have you seen anything like this before?"

"Yes…" The Lieutenant stared at the gnome and the others that had sprouted in the drifts beside it.

The magician's expression of confusion urged her to say what it was, although he already knew, and had seen her reaction to it.

"It's a damn trick. Just like the—"

Frackler blurted, "What?"

"You weren't with us." With a glance at the magician, she said, "Yesterday morning, we went by where Tremaine had been seen when he arrived in Wolfach."

"I remember…" Porky cocked his head at her, not understanding, and went back to looking for the Hitler gnomes as the Mercedes once again sped along the frozen landscape.

Celwyn decided not to add anything else to their journey; they might think things only occurred when he happened to be with them.

"Listen to me." She slapped the back of Frackler's head and cursed. "Do not mention any of this in your reports."

"Yes, Ma'am."

"You mean about what we just saw?" Porky asked.

"No." She growled. "We will investigate that. I am talking about yesterday when we examined the dead horse. You'll remember we wanted to know what kind of ammunition had killed the beast."

Celwyn blinked innocent curiosity at her even though when she had left the hotel bar yesterday, he'd followed the Nazi's car to the dead horse and knew exactly what she meant.

He said, "Please, if this is unpleasant…"

The most feminine Nazi cursed again, and her annoyance clipped her voice into bite-size pieces. "We found the horse in complete rigor or simply frozen. I managed to push a branch underneath it. Then I crawled as close as I could to examine the wound. Just as I touched it—" Her face grew redder. "I heard something." The Nazi warrior patted her perfect hair. "Of course, I wasn't frightened."

"What did you hear, Ma'am?" Frackler asked.

Celwyn itched to imitate exactly what she had heard but refrained.

"It is not possible—that is why it can't be reported. But the horse appeared to speak. It … it commented on my rear end." She slammed a fist into the car door. "Just drive!"

Chapter 43

Berlin

OVER THE NEXT FEW DAYS, THE magician made a point of investigating the new inventions he saw, especially the horseless carriages, as he detoured around bomb craters and avoided soldiers on street corners. Every few blocks, he would pass by a building leveled by the Allies. Sadly, he would step over a shoe or a scarf from a civilian who had been unlucky enough to be on this spot when their world exploded.

Some of the city seemed normal and untouched, including the Whitebriar Hotel. His accommodations looked older than he preferred but comfortable, and the bathtub was long enough to accommodate all of him; he didn't have to bathe with his knees in the air.

Pastor Theodore thought that the Gestapo used clandestine listening devices. The first evening in the city, the magician did not find any of them in his room, just a few spiders. When he returned from lunch the next day, he stopped searching after locating three of them. Since his magic caused no noise, Celwyn doubted they would learn much; however, he would use their tools to entertain the Nazis in a most artistic way ... something to display his fine sense of color and irony.

For several days, he compared 1944 Berlin to 1851 Berlin and decided that if someone chased him, or if he chased someone, he could navigate the streets without getting lost. He even discovered an excellent observation post above the Jungfräulichkeit Bridge.

That morning, the magician had spent time in the main square until he found what he needed; a pair of youths who hated the Nazis and who spent time deep in the workings of the Underground. One of the boys, a pimply one named Herman, must have been addicted to sweets for all his sixteen years, judging by his missing teeth.

Herman talked in a low voice and enunciated with care as he leaned close to the second boy, who appeared a bit older, although not as presentable with his mismatched dirty clothes, and the jittery movements of an opium habit. Herman would do well to watch what he said to Will. In Celwyn's experience, opium addicts would sell any, and all, their secrets for more of the drug.

"That one could use a new brassiere." Will nodded at the girl stationed behind barrels of flowers. "She might be pretty if she did."

Herman lowered his voice. "I'd rather talk about what I heard. The Nazis are reducing the age for when they drag you into the Army."

"To what?"

"Fifteen."

"No!" Will shrank back into the shadows between the booths. "You—you … you look younger. But me? They will take me away!"

The girl with the old brassiere walked by him smirking, likely having heard his exclamation and smelled his fear.

"Shut up, you fool." Herman elbowed him.

"We need to go to Barcelona. It is safer there. We should ask One."

The magician checked his thoughts and instantly located One—a man called Paul Smeltz, the local leader of the Underground. Celwyn planted an open question in Herman's thoughts: *Shouldn't they ask One to hide them?*

"Let's visit One tonight. After dinner. Five should be there too."

Will asked, "Why not now?"

"My mother found some pork. I want some."

With a snort, Will grabbed his stomach with both hands. "The last time I ate her 'found' pork, I was so sick." He pointed toward the river. "Meet me at the bridge at seven."

"All right. And don't be messed up."

The clock in the bell tower chimed, and its comical wooden figures moved through the quaint door at the top. If Celwyn remembered correctly, this building dated from King Rudolf's time. With a sigh, he realized he would have to take an early dinner to accompany the boys to the Underground meeting. It would not be pork.

"Hopefully, he knows about the Englanders," Herman said. "They plan to attack the armory by the park tonight."

"Sure, he does." Will lit a cigarette and blew smoke into the breezeway between them. The magician detected the musky aroma of Londermichung cigarettes that he'd seen in a pipe shop. How could the boys afford such expensive tobacco—unless they pinched them?

Will ground out his stub. "If the Allies win, the Nazis will lose everything. You know that, don't you?"

"I do." Herman demanded, "Give me a cigarette." The sound of a match striking sounded loud. "Those fags came from that fat vice marshal last night."

Will giggled. "He was so drunk they carried him out of the bar."

"Where did you hear about the Allies winning?"

Will laughed. "At a much more entertaining place. My sister is the chambermaid for Magdalene. You know who she is?"

"Of course, I do. An actress." Herman waved a hand. "She has been living here for a long time. So?"

"When I bribe my sister well enough, she lets me hide in the armoire while Magdalene is entertaining." Will laughed again, a dirty laugh. "She says it is easier than teaching me about 'intimate relations.'"

"Does she know you are gathering information for the Underground?" Herman asked.

"Yes."

"Whatever. I don't understand what this has to do with us."

"Magdalene's new boyfriend is Field Marshall Adalhard."

"Oh." Herman whistled. "He is high up with those sick bastards."

How convenient, Celwyn thought. He sent Herman a question to ask that Will should have thought of on his own.

Herman wiggled his head and made a face. "When are you going to be in the armoire again?"

"Friday night, if I am lucky. Usually, it is interesting. Very interesting."

Chapter 44

HOURS LATER, CELWYN ACCOMPA-
nied the boys—who were full of pork and
whatever drug Will preferred—as they blended into
the shadows of the early evening. As an adorable fly,
the magician clung to the back of Herman's collar,
which seemed the cleaner of the two.

The city teamed with brave citizens, the crowd
bustling along, well aware of the war as if it had
always been with them, threaded through their lives.
That showed in the speed that they walked, and in
furtive glances over their shoulders. It could be they
expected soldiers, or the Gestapo. If a vehicle back-
fired, they ran or scampered behind anything they
could find.

As the boys passed by a middle-aged woman—
and there were many more women than men
remaining in the city—she tugged on the elbow of

an older woman, urging her forward. "Faster Hilda. Faster. Almost dark."

The crone moaned. "Bombs! We will all die—"

"No." The other woman yanked on her arm. "We will be safe. You know where we must go." But her words faded to a whisper as she gazed at the sky. From far away, the echo of the bombing reached them.

As the women scurried down a flight of steps, Celwyn hoped Paul Schultz and his merry band intended to meet in a basement, or similar. When Will waved a greeting to another boy they had caught up with, Celwyn amended his earlier wish to that *all* of them bathed.

An hour later, they joined a group inside a cave located at the foot of a rocky hill somewhere north of the city. The entrance could not be seen from the road. They must have been late, stepping inside in time for Herr Schultz to intone the rules of order. Interestingly, the first rule stated that smoking was not permitted—which would have greatly improved things while the restless audience of ten listened to their leader.

"Sit down so we can start." Schultz squatted on a milk stool. The others settled on the dirt floor in front of him.

If Celwyn had encountered the Underground leader in the city, he would not have associated Schultz with clandestine activities. The magician had never met a more guileless set of blue eyes in the baby face of a middle-aged man. Most of his left leg and left hand were missing—which accounted for why he hadn't become part of the Nazi army by now. It took all the magician could do to interpret Schultz's heavy accent and that of the others.

"Good evening. I did not bring our beer tonight because we will not be here long." He handed out slips of paper to each of the seven men and two women in front of him. "Elsa," he addressed the older woman on his left. "Please, go first."

The magician listened to each of the reports, noting the activity attempted and the result. He heard an organized approach and, in nearly every case, their patriotism to Germany to stand against the Nazis. The exception was Celwyn's pal Will, who seemed to be involved purely for self-preservation. The magician grinned. He liked that new word, "pal" he'd heard earlier and pictured the automat's face when he had a chance to call him his pal. Bartholomew would love it. Some of the curse words this evening seemed unfamiliar, but the derogatory names and phrases assigned to the Nazis had been simple to understand, colorful, and usually involved farm animals.

Schultz's own report described the American assault expected soon at the Leyte Gulf. He had details only a high-ranking officer could have imparted, such as the exact number of troops, precise landing time, and date.

As Celwyn listened, he felt a tiny germ of an idea and when it brushed by him, it winked. On its second pass by, the magician grabbed it and examined it from all sides. *Oh yes, it would do nicely*. Swango would lose their bet. And many people would not die.

The Underground's meeting continued with a treasurer's report. It seemed the Americans regularly sent them money for explosives and beer. As he listened, Celwyn tried to decide what he could do to help without frightening them.

When it came time for the boys to speak, Herman and Will listed their ideas, including blowing up a recruiting station. The tension in the group shifted when Will detailed his plan to eavesdrop on Magdalene.

Schultz interrupted, "What is the purpose of that?" Will blushed, and Schultz swore at him. "Why are you still doing this? Is an unnecessary risk for nothing." He pointed at Will. "You haven't found out anything important yet."

Herman listened to a silent suggestion from Celwyn as if he'd thought of it himself. "Sir, there might be an opportunity to do something useful. Do you have a small camera we can borrow? Will here," he nodded at him, "could take pictures of papers in the general's coat."

Schultz stared as if he'd just heard the first good idea Herman had ever had. "It will take a few days to get a camera small enough. For tomorrow, leave the coat alone and just listen to anything he says."

All the way back to town, the magician again bounced along on the collar of Herman's coat. He reviewed what he'd seen and heard, and considered how it would be a shame if something befell the boys before Will could gain entrance to Miss Magdalane's boudoir.

Celwyn miniaturized the lads and put them to sleep on his back. As a sleek blackbird, he flew into the city, swooped low over the marketplace, and dumped them in the fountain to wake them up. After they shrieked and splashed their way out, the magician followed Will home. From an upper-story window, a baby wailed and then stopped. The magician did not want to dwell on the conditions inside, instead listening to Will's thoughts until he discovered when they would leave for tomorrow's assignation.

By the time he returned to his suite, the magician felt much more confident in what he must do. He whispered a love poem to the Nazi listening device and got ready for bed. For the first time since this adventure began, he had time to realize how much he missed Tara and everyone on the *Nautilus* and Qing. Perhaps the shock of the time change had worn off and allowed his memory to return. He very much wanted to win this wager. Doing so in the future brought complications he only now had begun to understand.

What if he inadvertently changed more than just the Nazi's war?

The next morning, when the magician walked into the hotel's dining room, he saw Lieutenant Dosher at a table in the corner, gaily waving at him. As he crossed the room, he decided if it weren't for the starched black uniform and the un-romantic speculation in her eyes, she could have been mistaken for a wholesome young woman of character. Celwyn knew better. Especially after he spent part of yesterday wandering around her thoughts. It seemed the delectable Nazi specialized in torture to extract information from prisoners.

The faint aroma of sweet rolls reached him as he sat down and listened to her silent approval of the way his jacket fit his shoulders. She even described him as "dishy" while deciding on what tools to use for the interrogation of an elderly man later in the morning.

"Gutentag, Elmo Linnsen. Did you sleep well?"

"Yes, I did." In the wee hours of the night, Celwyn serenaded the listening devices with a few love songs for the Lieutenant. And from the triumphant gleam in her eye, she had already heard them. He blinked innocently at her but wondered; something else must have occurred because underneath the satisfaction, she still appeared leery of him.

"How often do you see Herr Hitler?" Celwyn shrugged with shyness. "I would like to meet him."

Nazi furor replaced the suspicion. "We might be able to arrange that." She regarded him. "He is not fond of beards."

As Celwyn decided what to say, he let himself appear confused. If he shaved his beard, he'd have to expend energy to maintain a different face. Or make a copy of the real Elmo Linnsen's face...

Their waitress arrived in a cloud of sweet perfume made stronger by her profuse sweating. Her harassed look worsened when she recognized the Gestapo, and before stuttering a good morning and asking what they would have, she dropped her pencil twice. The Lieutenant found the waitress's distress amusing.

Throughout breakfast, Dosher batted her eyes at the magician and put her hand over his. His skin crawled as if a snake had kissed him. He soldiered on and sent her another besotted glance.

"Yes, I visit the Fuhrer on Wednesdays, sometimes other days too." She chewed a piece of ham and added, "I will arrange for us to see him together. It would be advisable if I coached you on what to expect." The secret smile came and went. "And what not to say."

"My German is not as good as it should be."

Lieutenant Dosher waved it away and poured cream into her coffee.

"He keeps translators around. It is not a problem."

The magician maintained a neutral expression and proceeded to flirt with the Nazi warrior. He had learned the word "flirt" from Herman's musings while the boy hungered after the girls in the marketplace. The Lieutenant met Celwyn's adoring gaze with surprise and then purred, "Why have you never married?"

The magician allowed tears to fill his eyes and shook his head with regret.

"Oh, I see." She patted his hand and her expression hardened; that did not match her research.

Whoops, another expression learned from Herman. "I'm sorry for the confusion. As a very young man, I *was* married. It occurred so many years ago, I pretend it never happened." He hesitated while the Lieutenant again reviewed what she knew. "Her name was Emilia, but she died during the 1920 influenza in Madrid." He'd read of the disaster only last night and knuckled away a real tear. "It has been so long … I try to forget the pain."

She relaxed again.

Chapter 45

Nazi Headquarters, Berlin

THE BASEMENT OF NAZI HEADQUARTERS consisted of two dozen dank cells, interrogation rooms, and a large open area where the special interrogations occurred. The Nazi officers had arranged their desks in a ring around the room to view the proceedings. To new officers, they explained that the suffering of others usually softened the remaining prisoners to their fate, so they often left the door leading to the cells open for these performances.

"The moaning from the prisoners bothers me more at dinnertime," Porky said aloud to no one. "You'd think they'd be quiet so that they won't be shot or win a ride to Auschwitz." His pinball eyes bounced around the near-empty room. The rest of the Gestapo staff, except for himself and the

Lieutenant, had either left for the evening or had gone upstairs for dinner.

For Porky, it had been an interesting day. Especially after Gestapo Captain Lenz had described the destruction of the bridge at Sonheim, only a score of miles away. Despite strict security, somehow a bomb had been put there. Worse, it would take months to replace the bridge while they heard repeatedly about the situation from Captain Lenz. That could be ignorable, but not the shiver of unease Porky relived when he recalled the picture of the bridge debris that Lenz had waved in his face. It had a peculiar feature.

"Well?"

Porky gazed at his superior officer, judging her mood. Sometimes honesty should be ignored. Then again, this didn't seem like something that could be blamed on him.

"Certainly. What happened at Sonheim is an affront to the Reich. It is also—" he licked his lips, "It is also too fantastic to be believed."

She snorted. "Really? What does it remind you of?"

Porky didn't want to, but answered, "Our car ride back here from the country. It, too, seemed odd."

She cursed and threw the report on her desk.

"Perhaps it will stop," he suggested.

"Of course it will. And fat little pigs will fly?"

"No—"

She tapped the picture in the report. "We saw those same statues sitting in the snow. Miles and miles of them!" She punched the wall. "How did they get into the debris from the bridge? How?"

The music from a playful flute seeped into the room, filling the air until it seemed to vibrate the walls as it increased in complexity and volume. Then a line of drums arrived, and the music of *Yankee Doodle Dandy* began, preceding something most entertaining in the magician's opinion.

The two Nazis shot to their feet and ran to the windows, then around the room, searching for the source amid Lieutenant Dosher's shouts of outrage. When the music called for more, the magician caused a parade of ghostly images to climb over the furniture and anything in it. Porky dove under his desk. The bloody images would remind them of the prisoners that had passed through their hands.

The Lieutenant demanded the corporal stand up, and then stopped... Porky saw her expression, which revealed that she also felt the atmosphere change. She pivoted in time to see why Porky shrieked and scrambled back under the desk.

An enormous mastiff, black as the night, hovered just under the ceiling. Saliva dripped from its jaws and a low growl escaped its throat. As Dosher backed up, its translucent wings fluttered like a delicate butterfly, and the dog descended toward her.

"Help—" she croaked, "Help *me!*"

Porky crawled out from under a desk with his service revolver extended like a man encountering a vampire would brandish a cross. When the dog flew over his head, he sidled closer to Dosher.

"Don't shoot!" She batted at his hand. "The bullets would go through the ceiling— General Hausser is up there."

Porky froze. "Goring has an office up there too." He didn't take his eyes off the dog who had landed on the desk next to them. When it barked, they both hurried under the desks.

"How did it fly—" Dosher stopped and turned pale.

The dog had begun singing, the song sultry and slow as if Marlena Dietrich serenaded them in her rich contralto. When Porky inched his way out, the dog landed on his back, and he fainted.

Dosher dared to look again; now two dogs leaned together crooning *Es zittern die morschen Knochen*. The Rotten Bones Are Trembling. They certainly seemed to be. She hated that song. The Lieutenant crawled toward the door. When the second dog saw her, it leapt high and pounced on top of the delectable Nazi warrior. She yelped and screamed.

From the holding area there came the clattering of locks and clanging of metal as one by one the cell doors swung open—much to the surprise of the prisoners inside. Like newborn calves, a few ventured forth on tiptoes, walking stiffly, amazed, and afraid of their good fortune. Some of the able prisoners helped the more severely injured to stand and move into the main room. At the doorway, the prisoners hesitated—seeing the dogs and hearing the serenade.

An emancipated man cradling a broken arm surveyed the cowering Nazis and barked a laugh before addressing the other prisoners.

"We need to get out of here, and we can't use the door—there are guards out there."

The others rumbled in agreement. Some of them seemed more interested in the dogs than their immediate problem. The youngest of the prisoners, a shy-looking lad, asked in a soft French accent, "What are we going to do?"

Before anyone could answer, the dogs did.

"What to do? What to do? Use the stairs, we say!" they cooed in a singsong duet.

The wall beneath the windows shimmered and dissolved into a set of shadowy stairs leading upward.

The emancipated man charged up the stairs. Several prisoners followed him. The others went more slowly but made it to the top.

Foul-smelling saliva dripped on Porky, and when the dog growled in its throat, the Nazi stirred and then squealed, realizing the dog sat on him. From feet away, Lieutenant Dosher yelled curses. The second dog had rolled over on top of her again.

"Help me, you fool!" She screamed louder. "Now!"

When the hallway door opened and the guards burst into the room, the dogs dissipated into the air. The stairway dissolved as if they had ever been there. Behind the guards, a blackbird flew by the window, slowly, as the music faded to nothing.

Chapter 46

AFTER HIS VISIT TO GESTAPO HEAD-quarters, Celwyn spent the rest of the day in pursuit of a good cup of tea.

He never really found it but enjoyed sampling a variety of German pastries and gathering information. In between stops at the cafés, he monitored the thoughts of the everyday patrons. Among worries about Heinie's bunions and Gertrude's choice of men, Celwyn learned that many of the citizens of the city either feared the Nazis, or felt deathly tired of the war, or both. It neared dusk when luck favored him. He had discovered Herr Maxim Schiller, a man who actively worked against Hitler. The magician got comfortable at a petite table in the Osterglocke Café and listened.

"...had so many more dead than they reported for the battle," Maxim said. "The Nazis will lose in

Russia because of the new weapons the Americans are providing."

"This sounds promising."

Next to the darkly handsome Schiller, his companion resembled a bleached porcelain figurine in both skin and hair. His long ears did not make him lovelier.

Schiller said, "It is, David. And our efforts need momentum to rid us of the Nazi filth."

"Shush! Keep your voice down." David lost color, if possible. "Good grief!"

Celwyn listened to Schiller's unspoken worries. It seemed he knew many of the resistance groups and spent his time funneling money to them. He also provided advice on a tactical level. His usefulness came from being a trusted darling of the Nazis.

After Celwyn listened to the man's random thoughts, he finalized his plans for his upcoming audience with Hitler. Anything else he discovered tonight would be icing on the cake.

The magician grunted. Swango was about to lose a bet.

Berlin seemed so different and yet the same since Celwyn last visited in 1852. The motorized taxis and armed men on every corner had been added of course, and the quaint unhurried way the local people traveled between streets and shops no longer existed, along with the friendliness they once displayed. One difference; without the voluminous skirts, female citizens seemed able to go anywhere. He wiggled, reminded again of the new type of masculine trousers—without suspenders—deucedly uncomfortable.

The bell tower on the square struck the eight o'clock hour, and from the distance came the bombing, faintly, as more vibration than noise. Most evenings, it flowed across the city without rhythm, just the irregular beating of the heart of war. Tonight, it seemed different. The low hum from dozens of engines filled the sky, disconcerting and unstoppable, before the bombs exploded. Celwyn had a first-hand idea of how they got into the air, but he could not get used to how they could fly something so fast or big. He didn't want to know. These thoughts led to remembering his, and Pelaez's, abhorrence of war.

Under the nightly blackout conditions, Berlin's streets appeared cave-like, with their streetlights extinguished and windows curtained to block even pinpricks of light. The few citizens who ventured forth dressed in dark colors and carried muffled torchlights that barely illuminated the sidewalk underfoot. A few of them bumped into walls or trash bins but did so quietly. Celwyn sniffed, detecting a coal fire and a sour cabbage boiling. The light mist that covered everything seemed to be alive with tendrils that waved long arms. A rather unsettling evening all around, he decided.

Although the magician arrived early for the rendezvous, he spied Herman already wedged into the shadows under the bridge, and his nervousness was obvious. His hands twitched; first to his cap, then his cuffs, before retying his shoe. When the ground shook and the screams began, the lad didn't react except to retrieve the cigarette he had tried to light. The bomb did not land close to them but still merited respectful attention—making the magician wonder if sheltering under a bridge was a wise decision.

Will appeared, slithering under the bridge like a walking rat. Tonight, he must've found a new source of opium; no rat would have eyes that opaque.

Herman frowned at him. By the time they began whispering, the magician had joined them again as a moth and nested in the curls around Will's dirty ears. Celwyn detected the sweet scent of cannabis, but even that could not compete with the boy's body odor. It had been at least three days since Will's last encounter with a bar of soap.

After they complained to each other about their unexplained nocturnal dunking in the fountain, the boys exchanged opinions about the camera that Herman had brought along. Before it disappeared into Will's pants pocket, Celwyn noted the camera seemed incredibly small compared to the ones he had known of before now. Even the name painted on it, RCA, he hadn't heard of. Also, this contraption did not require an enormous case or a cape to cover the mechanics and block light, nor a tripod or special gauge to judge the light.

⁓——⌣——⌐

Celwyn wondered about Will's ability to operate the camera as they headed north up Wilhelmstrase

Street toward the affluent district of Ebertstrasse. Soon, they stood in front of the Engelshaus apartments with their beautiful rococo façade. Although only a few stories high, they exuded the olde-world charm of money and privacy.

They entered the lobby and the aroma from massive vases of roses overpowered the lingering stench of Herman. The occupant of the concierge desk, a gloomy frau in a long black dress and a dour expression, ignored them.

As they walked by her, a hiss came from a corridor off to the side. Will whirled and saw a young woman smoking a cigarette and waiting beside the elevator. The magician noted the resemblance between the siblings; both had the same hawk-like nose planted in a face of delicate features.

"Nadia, dear sister," Will said. "I am on time."

She blew smoke in his face and held out her hand. Only a small amount of money needed to be exchanged before she sent more smoke into his face. "Come on."

They took a short and luxurious ride to the next floor while surrounded by the deep velvet walls of the elevator car. Celwyn resisted the urge to explore how this moving box lifted people off the ground. After the doors opened, they moved down two doors and waited while Nadia hunted for her keys. "They are due back from dinner in a half-hour." She grabbed Will's arm so hard she almost knocked Celwyn off his ear. "And no stealing!"

"I wouldn't—"

"Yes, you would." She gave his arm a twist. "It will cost me this job. So don't."

With a furtive look up and down the hallway, Nadia unlocked the door and waved him inside. "You and your politics. Be careful—" she whispered and trotted away on high heels.

Herman took up a position in one of the alcoves nearby. After Will slipped inside, Celwyn peeked out of his hair and saw the entryway had been decorated with life-size pictures of a beautiful woman. He had never seen so many photographs before.

His unwitting host perused them too, muttering, "Ah, a new one," when they stopped in front of the last frame.

In the magician's opinion, Magdalene's most striking feature stared out at him in a direct gaze from a pair of silvery eyes. Long, dark lashes brushed her cheeks and cascading black hair framed a perfect face. She did not appear Aryan, or at least not classically so. The curve of her lips promised many secrets.

A wall of awards and framed scripts from various theatres came next. Many originated in Norway and Denmark. When Will heard a scratching of the lock in the door behind them, he squeaked a curse at Herman under his breath and bolted for an armoire in the corner. Dinner must have ended early, or the lovers had become anxious. Celwyn flew to the top of the valance above the window just as the door opened. One of the newcomers touched the wall. More lamps suddenly came alive. Many wonderful things seemed possible in the future. This one the magician approved of.

As she drew closer, Celwyn decided the picture gallery did not go far enough.

The actress stood close to six feet tall, and the magician considered it adorably scandalous that her toes had been allowed to peek out of the top of her fancy shoes. Something winked at him in the lamplight, causing another pleasant surprise; her toenails had been painted a bright red, matching the crimson of her full lips.

The much smaller man at her side kept a hand on her elbow until she shook him off. Celwyn wondered … *this* was Field Marshal Adalhard? His face glistened with sweat and the magician bet the delicious Magdaline thought that off-putting. Celwyn entered her mind and nearly laughed out loud. She likened his sweating to a rutting donkey.

As the actress gazed dotingly at her companion, she pictured him on a summer's day rowing a boat across the middle of a lake with the bluest water that glimmered like molten glass in the sun. Once the surface of the water became agitated, the undulating water rocked the boat and Adalhard lost his oars. He clung to the side of the craft. When the boat began rotating, Magdaline's smile gained wattage, and she patted him on the hand.

"What is so amusing, my dear?" he asked as he threw his coat on the settee.

Her thoughts kept the boat spinning until it tipped toward starboard, and water flooded in.

The general hadn't a clue. Celwyn hoped his shoes were waterproof. When she didn't respond, he reached into his pocket and handed her his offering.

"Thank you, darling."

As she opened the small box, the boat started to bounce, throwing the portly Nazi into the air like a toy.

Magdaline removed her prize from the box. Seconds ticked by as she held a wristwatch high and regarded it with a critical eye, causing the image of the boat to dip low at the stern. If the Nazi could have looked behind him, he would have seen the sharks circling in the water and their teeth reflected in the sun. She gazed at him. "Is this the best that you can do?"

"Mein schatz ... Darling, I am sorry, but I cannot leave Berlin right now to find something fitting for you in Paris."

"Really?" Magdaline's sarcasm sounded like much better bait than Celwyn could have hoped for.

Adalhard tried to hold her hand again, and she swatted him away.

"Darling, the Fuhrer himself has forbidden us to leave!"

The pout she developed deflated him like a toy balloon. The Nazi whined, "He thinks those fucking Englanders are going to invade France. Soon."

Ah, the magician thought.

Magdaline said, "You say you love me ... but..." She shrugged and turned away.

"I will have something wonderful next week. I promise you. The Englanders will attack before then and we will annihilate them. They will be finished. Then I will be all yours." With his hamster eyes, sweating face, and Aryan confidence, Adalhard leaned in for a kiss.

Too sickened to watch, the magician flew underneath the door and out of the building. He hoped Will had a strong stomach and the luck to leave without being discovered.

During the ride to Berchtesgaden, Celwyn sat in the rear of the Mercedes with Porky. Frackler drove. Lieutenant Dosher rode in a second car with other Nazis and announced she planned to rehearse her reports all the way there.

The magician couldn't remember the last time he felt ill as he did now, and as they traveled the twisting road, his stomach grew queasier with each mile. Frackler opened his window and inhaled the early morning air. Porky watched him a moment and spoke, "It is having too much rich food before riding in the backseat that causes this." He studied Frackler. "I'll be driving on the way back."

Celwyn nodded; he may or may not be returning to Berlin with him, but no matter what occurred, he would not be sitting in a horseless carriage that reeked of the Reich's finest.

Farther north, the road gradually climbed, and the air freshened further as they entered the mountains. The rock formations and trees became sparser.

The automobile in front of them slowed, made a 45° turn, and the driver urged the machine up the last 300 feet to a stronghold at the top of the hill. By the time they drove through massive gates, Celwyn had counted a regiment of soldiers and dozens of snarling dogs. A pair of soldiers approached the lead vehicle containing Lieutenant Dosher. Seconds more and they waved them ahead past granite fountains to a set of iron-banded doors. Celwyn estimated the entrance measured at least forty feet wide and nearly as tall.

Beyond the ramparts, the view took Celwyn's breath away and his imagination flew across the valley, above the treetops and fields of boulders, and down to the flatland below. Although he detected the scent of pine trees, he couldn't smell any evidence of people. The magician squinted, convinced that for miles the farmhouses had been abandoned and weeds, not crops, remained. A square-looking vehicle lay on its side in a ditch that ran parallel to the road. A skeleton crawling away in the mud wouldn't have surprised him.

Much closer, groups of the guards in the courtyard practiced dropping to a knee and pretending to fire before marching on. A single drummer accompanied them.

"Follow me please, Herr Linnsen." The Lieutenant ordered as she passed by the magician trailing a wisp of dusky perfume and a lingering look into his eyes.

Above them, crows flew in and out of the twin towers of the fortification. After their party had shown their identification to the guards inside, they searched everyone except the Lieutenant. The magician stifled the urge to make sure they found something interesting in Porky and Frackler's pockets.

Chapter 47

Back on the *Nautilus*

W HEN CELWYN OPENED HIS EYES and gazed at his audience in the study, the clock behind Bartholomew finished chiming the eleven o'clock hour; the magician realized he had been talking for a long time.

Granger had joined them, drinking coffee, and listening with a degree of nervousness. Nemo sat across from him on the other sofa, puffing on his pipe. Judging by the cloud of smoke, the Captain's agitation had increased, even though his eyes remained hooded as always.

"What the hell—" Professor Xiau Kang rarely cursed, but he did so now as he jumped to his feet and confronted Celwyn.

"You *are* going to finish the story, are you not?"

"Of course." The magician patted the air. "It is quite a bit to hear and understand, so I thought you would like to ask questions or simply comment on what I've said so far." Actually, Celwyn had stopped to decide what part of the story he should hold back—either for their safety—or for future endeavors. He mentally shrugged—or for when they meet Swango.

"I certainly hope so." The automat dropped back into his chair with an adorable glower. Celwyn would have missed Xiau and the rest of them very much if he had remained in the future with Porky and his nasty friends.

Bartholomew hid a grin behind his hand, but couldn't hold back for long, especially with Celwyn smiling at him. In seconds, he roared. "Jonas, Xiau is right though. At first, I suspected you were telling a tall tale or having a joke on us." As he spoke, suspicion filled his eyes until the big man asked slowly, "It is all true ... is it not?"

"Yes. But I wish it weren't."

"I wouldn't worry too much." Tara pinched his cheek. "And we'll discuss your Valkyrie later."

Although stated with calmness, the twinkle in her eye promised him a lively conversation. With a weak smile in return, the magician went back to thinking ... what he had yet to disclose about the Nazis floated in and out of his memory. Celwyn gazed at them and spoke with care.

"The things I haven't mentioned yet concern the atrocities of the Nazis. History won't treat those murderers kindly. And I will not talk of it now, other than to say that they were a scourge upon mankind.

I only know of part of their crimes because I deliberately avoided learning most of what they did." He controlled his fury. "You may have noticed that when I become angry, I break things and can't think clearly."

That brought a reaction from the automat and eye rolls from the rest. "You don't say?" Kang asked.

"I do. And you should know, Swango conveniently cleaned out my memory for his own benefit concerning much of what happened."

Tara eyed him. "You never mentioned any of this before." Her tone didn't sound irritated or hurt, more of curiosity than anything else. "Before now, you never talked about what the future holds."

"As a rule, I really don't want to know." Celwyn scanned the room. "With the provision that you understand that I am telling you what I know and that there will be gaps, I will continue." He produced a plateful of cookies and edged it across the table to the automat.

As he made his first selection, Kang said, "Chocolate with nuts. Go ahead."

Chapter 48

Berchtesgaden

HEAVY CLOUDS THE COLOR OF spoiled milk raced toward them from the west, blocking the sun and covering the foyer of the fortress in gloom. Guards switched on lamps as the doors behind the visitors opened again to admit newcomers.

Porky and Frackler huddled into their overcoats, and the magician did the same. A cold breeze pushed a serious woman of about sixty and another man half her age into the room. She wore wire-rimmed spectacles, but her companion removed his at the sight of Lieutenant Dosher. For her part, the Lieutenant ignored his admiring glances and addressed the woman.

"It is good to see you again, Frau Ubrecht."

"Likewise." She raised her open hand in the air. "Heil Hitler!" Her gesture caused the others to salute, including the guards.

Out of curiosity, the magician toured the Frau's mind and found she had traveled here to perform translation duties for Hitler. She hated the place and worried about her career. Celwyn agreed with her opinion of the slick man next to her. Frau Ubrecht had convinced herself Ludolf Mayer had been assigned to test her loyalty to the Reich. Celwyn wondered what the grandmotherly woman planned to do to the weasel if she got an opportunity. Apparently, he had been sending back unfavorable reports about her. Mayer inched his way closer to Dosher.

While the guards searched the translators for contraband, Celwyn toured Mayer's thoughts and wished the guards could search there as well. The Frau displayed astuteness; Mayer represented everything she suspected and more. The man's utmost thoughts centered on how to ingratiate himself to the Lieutenant and Hitler by selling out his fellow translator.

As everyone crossed to the far corner of the foyer, the storm arrived and pounded the windows with fury. In the courtyard, the platoon of guards soldiered on, splashing along in three-quarter-time as they marched onward.

Dosher asked, "Is there anything special on your agenda today, Herr Mayer?"

A buzzer made everyone jump, and the panels in the wall opened to reveal a padded box containing a uniformed guard. Everyone crowded inside, propelling the magician forward. He ended up squeezed between Frackler and the Lieutenant. Porky stood even closer to them, indecently so. The magician sniffed; someone smelled divine, and the other like burned sausages.

Like an unseen angel closed them, the doors shut, and then with a jerk, the box shuddered and started its descent. As it swayed and corrected again, everyone inside did also, in silence. The farther they went, the engine under their feet strained under the load. As the minutes went by, Celwyn wondered how deep underground they would travel. He trusted his magic, but what if something happened far below the surface? He had never been in this position before.

"Another minute," the guard intoned. "Then you will experience a bump when we stop."

Lieutenant Dosher swiveled to Celwyn. "We are descending to the 12th floor. This installation can withstand any bombing."

"Thank you," Celwyn said. "I congratulate your people on their ingenuity and the foresight involved."

"Of course." She nodded like she would like to add something, but checked it and pivoted back again.

He expected the bump signaling their arrival, but it felt like more than that—perhaps a drop of two feet, and yet the engine continued to vibrate with reassurance. Frackler stifled a yelp, and a sheen of perspiration covered his face, even over his little pink ears.

"This way." The guard led them down a poorly lit corridor infused with the smell of moist earth.

Everything here reminded the magician of his recent visit to the Capuchin Catacombs. Some of the guests would be reminded of the similarity soon.

As the concrete under their feet changed to gravel, the ceiling rose high under an earthen shaft supported by wooden beams and lit by lanterns. Celwyn enjoyed his view from behind the Lieutenant as she strode along; a walking illustration of why not to believe the outside before knowing the inside. By the time they had crossed a short distance, Porky wheezed from the effort, and Mayer trod on his heels to keep him moving.

Of a sudden, the guard halted and stooped to answer his radio. The squawking from it sounded far away as he waved them into a wide amphitheater about fifty feet square. Cross beams held up the ceiling a score of feet above them, and fully lit ornate chandeliers dangled from it, making the chamber as bright as day.

Before them, stuccoed walls framed an underground courtyard of comfortable benches and pots of hothouse plants. The magician sniffed the air; yes, he detected spicy roses and something else he didn't recognize filling scores of tall vases. They looked porcelain, similar to the ones he had last seen at Versailles. Possibly Hitler replicated what he admired, but the magician suspected he just stole it. Soon, it would not matter.

As they gathered outside the main doors to the inner sanctum, Celwyn enjoyed what he heard. From somewhere inside the room, Wagner's "Ride of the

Valkyries" played, sounding beautiful. He turned up the volume.

"The Fuhrer loves that opera," Frackler said. "Although he doesn't usually have it so loud."

"It is magnificent," Celwyn agreed and made it louder still.

Guards ushered them inside and down a hallway to a series of sofas arranged in a square. About a dozen people sat there, including Hitler, who ignored the Gestapo until they had sat down. The magician marveled that such a tiny man could cause so much trouble. This time, he found himself sitting next to Lieutenant Dosher and an arm's length from Porky, who dripped sweat. In contrast, Frackler yawned and leaned back, perfectly at ease. One of the aides nodded vigorously at the little dictator's instructions and scrambled to the far corner to the phonograph player. A chill passed through the magician as he remembered seeing one of those machines in Swango's mind, and even what it was called.

It didn't take long to recognize some of the field generals, such as Himmler, and other men from the newspaper accounts the magician had read. He spied a fluffy blonde woman with a masculine face sitting on Hitler's right.

Frackler whispered to the Lieutenant, "Why are those men here?" He gestured at the north corner of the room, where a trio of men in wrinkled suits waited.

"American scientists. Defectors."

Meanwhile, the aide turned, shouting at one of the generals over the thunder of the opera while they both examined the phonograph. They couldn't turn it down. Minutes passed and then the general raised the machine in the air and flung it to the floor. The magician killed the opera at the same time; he didn't need the unexplained to be of greater importance than setting the stage for the Fuhrer.

Dosher ignored the interruption.

"I've seen a dossier on the American atomic program. Those men defected from it a few weeks ago." While the Nazi warrior maintained a smile for the room, the magician saw another possibility to win the wager … he loved the freedom to change his ideas at whim and not have Xiau argue with him about it.

Celwyn asked Porky, "Who is that woman?"

"Eva Braun." He kept an agreeable expression on his face as he added, "She has Hitler's ear and penis, and is not to be trusted at all. Watch yourself with her. Your actions reflect upon us." He lowered his voice. "Don't you see her looking at you?"

"Yes."

"God help you, if she wants you." He shuddered.

It would be a cold day in the Hell, Celwyn thought. "I'll be on my guard."

Himler called for quiet, and for the next hour they listened to Hitler's ramblings about the Jews and speculations about Gypsies and the Americans' eating habits—especially the idea of rare roast beef. No translation accompanied him as he went along, even though both translators had taken seats near the little tyrant. Most of the audience could decipher the Fuhrer's intent as he described the Nazi losses.

Surprisingly, Celwyn heard the truth—not the slop given to the German newspapers. The magician made a note to discover what "verdammte schweine" meant in English.

Lieutenant Dosher wiggled seductively next to him and regarded the Fuhrer, seeming mesmerized as he screamed—not spoke—a speech about the inferiority of the Russians. This time Mayer translated. The magician couldn't help himself; a woolen scarf in bands of white, blue, and red of the Russian flag appeared around Hitler's neck. If anyone present did not recognize the significance, the colors also applied to the Americans.

The gasps from the audience grew until one of his aides rose and gingerly approached Hitler. Goring waved the aide and Himler away and leaned closer to whisper in Hitler's ear. He lay a hand on the Fuhrer's shoulder, and with a deft movement, yanked the scarf off Hitler's neck, flinging it behind his chair. The room breathed again.

Soon, the time came for the guests to perform.

The magician monitored the Americans' thoughts; Doctor Grunwald's attention centered more on his politics, particularly his fascination with Hitler than on his scientific work. The man sitting next to him reminded Celwyn of a young boy inside a man's suit of clothes; soft face, soft hands, and when Celwyn checked his thoughts, he found Doctor Lutz's only concern lay in how much the Nazis would pay him.

Mayer translated for the room, speaking slowly so that the American scientists could keep up. From the nervous glances Himmler sent their way, these guests appeared to be important to the Reich, and the magician wondered why.

Meanwhile, the Fuhrer and Mayer droned on with invented glories interspersed with Hitler's fantasies. Murmurings colored the room when Eva allowed Doctor Lutz to light her cigarette and blow smoke toward Hitler. Several of the generals worked on their pipes, making the room even murkier. Like a metaphorical butterfly, Celwyn flitted through the air, checking for anything they worried about or planned until he stopped in front of Hitler.

What he discovered amazed the magician, and that did not adequately describe the interesting things embedded in the dictator's brain. Herr Crazy Pants only listened to the first few words from whoever spoke before his attention fluttered else-where, such as wondering if Himmler dyed his hair and admiring the shoes the translator wore. Then came the beloved pictures of a "concentration camp." When the bastard heard the report about a suc-cessful Allied sea battle, the extraneous thoughts evaporated like water in the sun, and he spewed a new tirade.

Celwyn's glance at the delectable lieutenant held a degree of amusement as she listened to Himmler's report. The magician changed a few key phrases and outcomes as the translator began his interpretation of Himmler's report.

"The battle at the Sary Sin fortress—"

The magician entered the translator's mind and replaced a few other things. Mayer frowned in his confusion but repeated it.

The Americans stared, open-mouthed, as did everyone else, and none dared look at Hitler.

The Fuhrer asked, "Are you certain of this?"

Mayer answered him in German, "Yes."

"Just as I thought." Hitler went back to day-dreaming about crowds saluting him.

Chapter 49

A Tea Interlude

THE GONGS IN THE *NAUTILUS* ECHOED faintly, like underwater church bells.

"That's it?" the automat demanded.

"No." Celwyn poured a fresh cup of Earl Grey. "I'm thirsty." He wasn't used to talking so much. As he sipped, Bartholomew giggled, and the automat's patience evaporated.

"Why have we never heard about Swango and the Nazis before?"

The magician shrugged. "It did not come up in conversation, and it is also complex and not easy to listen to. Or to accept."

Kang sounded annoyed and like his old self. "How do you know what I accept?"

"When I finish the story, we'll see if it does." Celwyn covered a yawn. "Care to place a wager on how it turns out?" He grinned at Kang.

"I might." Bartholomew laughed. "What will I win?"

Granger's eyes twinkled. "We need to know more." He relit his pipe, puffed, and added, "I have several questions, and they are not expectations."

"Mine are that the fantastic things we're hearing are explained," Kang said. "And your involvement," he favored the magician with a pointed look, "is completely explained."

"Is that all?" Celwyn teased him.

"I second what the Professor says." Tara regarded him. "How dangerous did this become?"

The magician felt lucky they did not know all the Nazi's history. Extremely so. A few of them would want a different ending than what he would soon supply, and then complain about it constantly. None of them would be happy until they personally dealt Hitler a death blow.

"As you can see, I am alive and well, and fully capable of entertaining you and myself ... unless something unusual happens or if Wye joins us and scares Bartholomew."

"Funny, Jonas," the big man said. "But I think Miss McFein and Xiau's concerns are about the oddities and technology you found in the future. Perhaps they think there is a reason you never mentioned this before."

The magician frowned and decided the simplest explanation would be the best.

"I respectfully suggest that I finish the tale and then hear your questions. As for why I've never mentioned the horseless carriages or the rest, it bothered me seeing it then because I did not understand it. I'm not an engineer," he nodded at Bartholomew, "or a tactician or military visionary," and nodded at Nemo.

"You just weren't all that curious, were you?" Tara spoke slowly.

He squeezed her hand, once again reminded of her intuitiveness and intelligence.

"Oh, for God's sake." The automat threw up his hands. "Just get on with it."

Chapter 50

BACK IN THE ELABORATE BUNKER, Celwyn observed the participants as the meeting shifted to one of socializing. Champagne corks popped and soldiers arrived loaded with trays of food that most of Germany did not have access to. The magician selected a leg of lamb, considered the source, and wondered if he could eat it.

While Porky gobbled meat as fast as he could, Frackler had no trouble with the cakes and ended up with frosting on his upper lip. To balance the effect, the magician dotted the man's eyebrows with it as well. (Until he finished with Hitler, he would do only things that could be attributed to natural causes.) From what Celwyn had discovered, the dictator's phobias and fears made him unstable enough without anything else to distract him, and the magician would need a certain amount of clarity from him.

Over the next half-hour, the party continued with a few of the guests brave enough to do more than figuratively curtsy in front of Hitler. The Lieutenant sipped wine and watched the scene until the last bootlicker drifted away. She signaled Celwyn, and they approached Hitler.

The magician dutifully waited for the most feared man in the world to notice him and speak first—that had been a most definitive request from the Lieutenant. When he did, the little corporal's voice reminded Celwyn of an organ grinder he'd met in Lyon.

"So, you are Herr Elmo Linnsen from the Hague." He sneered. "An American too?" When he laughed at his joke, others nearby dutifully did as well. Hitler narrowed his eyes at Celwyn. "Tell me about your mother. Was she a whore?"

Dosher had told the magician to expect something like this.

"No."

For the next minute or so, the Fuhrer stared at him as if peeling away his skin to see inside. It did not surprise Celwyn. In something the magician had read, the man really did save pieces of skin from his enemies for amusement ... or revenge. The scrutiny went on long enough to cause the magician to curse Swango. Was this the price to win the bet?

"My aide tells me you could be very useful to the Reich." Hitler accepted a glass of water from a waiter and washed down a pair of pills. While he swallowed, Goring entertained the room with a ribald joke.

Celwyn listened to Hitler's thoughts until they made him stop still, unable to move or think. When he could listen again, Celwyn managed his fear but couldn't shake off what he'd learned. It took minutes, but he pushed beyond his disgust, and it took even longer before he could concentrate on the other discussions in the room.

The Fuhrer addressed Celwyn, "Have you been to Rome before? I could use another person there that is not one of us."

I bet you could, the magician thought.

"No, I haven't, but I am expanding my business, and will perhaps visit the city in the future."

Hitler leaned closer and whispered with a deadly kind of certainty, "You will visit there soon." His eyes caressed Celwyn. "The Lieutenant will make the arrangements."

We'll see about that.

This close, the magician noted the man's dilated pupils and nearly black circles under his eyes. He appeared to be under the influence of some sort of drug. The information from both Schultz and the pastor had alluded to this.

Dosher tugged on the magician's arm to leave. Celwyn held up a hand to wait. As Himler took the floor, reporting about the construction of an "advanced medical" facility, others nearby listened with a morbid kind of fascination, which caused Celwyn to wonder why this made Hitler's eyes dance in glee. When he checked the Lieutenant's thoughts, despite his resolve not to alarm the Nazis, the lights dimmed in the amphitheater and the chandeliers shook as his restraint evaporated and rage grew. Rows of crystal glasses shattered like hard rain, spraying the Nazis as Celwyn tried to control his temper.

As the tension in the room rocketed, several of the generals surrounded Hitler and shielded him with their bodies as if they'd rehearsed it many times. Guards advanced. The magician breathed deeply and pictured the automat telling him to calm down. It worked. Remembering how Bartholomew would just start shooting at them brought a smile. No one knew how close he'd come to a much more destructive reaction.

Several generals suggested that they had just experienced an underground earthquake. Hitler nodded and stood, and both translators followed him out of the room.

Celwyn asked Frackler, "Where are they going?"

"His office. It is two o'clock and Mussolini is making his call to the Fuhrer. They must translate." Frackler spat. "Mussolini speaks our language so badly no one can understand him. It is on purpose."

The magician might have sounded a bit distracted as he thanked him and excused himself. A guard directed him to the gentlemen's room. Soon, a handsome moth rode on one of the aides' collars.

Hitler's office seemed surprisingly empty—no medals, pictures of dead enemies, not even a brick from a destroyed building. Only a table with a telephone and chairs gave any indication of what occurred here. When they were seated, with a translator on each side of Hitler, the aide arranged earmuffs with cords on their heads and left the room.

Celwyn caused the translator, Frau Utrecht, to yawn widely and without any embarrassment. Her eyes drooped until she nodded off. Mayer smirked. "As I reported last week, I think it is time the Frau retired. This is too much for her."

The dictator said nothing. He waved the guards out as the call came in with a loud crackling noise. Hitler flung his earmuffs on the table and began speaking; at first annoyed, then in a rapid-fire staccato tantrum.

Every time Mussolini started to speak, the room heard Mayer's translation in Celwyn's words. Mayer was no longer in the room, having been stuffed into a convenient closet down the hall. Celwyn's effigy gave a translation that flowed with the kind of misinformation that would guarantee the Nazis would lose the invasion battle with the Allies in a few days.

Hitler sounded skeptical, and his little mustache twitched as he quizzed Mussolini. The magician spewed information over the telephone to him, even throwing in a few invented insults from the Fascist before the call ended.

Hitler slammed a palm on the table.

"Everyone out! I must think." He shouted, "Take the sleeping Frau with you! Out!"

When the last guard reached the door, he did not look worried about leaving the supreme leader alone; he couldn't hide his relief to go.

From his position atop the filing cabinet, the magician closed his wings and watched Hitler for several minutes, trying to reconcile the Nazi world with his own, and what he already knew.

During this timeframe, the world appeared to have so many changes, not just the war. Advances in science and medicine. Something called "vaccines" to stop plagues. Horseless carriages and cameras seemed useful, but the revealing dresses on women, inelegant hairstyles on the men, and speech patterns? Politics and suspenders? He cared little, except when they hurt others. He studied the bastard in front of him. Here sat the source of the monumental destruction of thousands, injured directly or indirectly. Celwyn resolved to act, wager or not. And in the back of his mind, he knew killing Hitler would not be enough. This kind of evil is hidden in many hearts.

A bluish mist became distinct, gathering and thickening in front of Hitler. As it solidified, the Fuhrer backed up and reached for the contraption on the wall to call someone. His hand closed over it just as it dissolved. When Hitler turned around, Celwyn stood before him.

"How did you get in here? Get out!"

The magician stared at him, visualizing everything from the gas chambers to the experiments on Afrikaans, the children and the elderly. Hitler's greed and hate went deep. Celwyn had seen it before and wondered why a man's skin color caused so much fear and jealousy.

"*What do you want?*" The tyrant stalked to the far wall and back like a toy soldier who couldn't bend his legs. "When my guards find you, I won't let them shoot you ... no. There are special rooms dedicated to people like you."

Hitler's irrationality gave Celwyn a headache. He needed something else to worry about.

"Pick up that instrument." Celwyn pointed at the remaining telephone. "And tell your generals to stop working on the concentration camp." When Hitler goggled at him, the magician gestured, slinging the Nazi across the room and back. He brought the receiver next to his face. Hitler knocked it away, and without touching it, Celwyn brought it back to him. They both heard a voice coming from it, requesting orders.

In Hitler's voice, Celwyn said, "My orders are to stop work on all concentration camps. Release all detainees." He listened to a protest and screamed, "I mean what I say! Do it!"

The magician told Hitler, "We won't be needing this anymore." When the telephone became a wildcat, stalking back and forth in front of them, Hitler squirmed, but the magician held him down and asked, "I heard there are no offices or anything below this level. Is that true?"

The magician already knew the answer but waited.

"Is that true?" Celwyn repeated.

"You will die for this!"

"Someday."

The wildcat licked his face and opened its mouth wide.

"Yes! This is the last floor. Get it off me!"

Someone tried the door from the corridor. The magician waved a hand, and the door dissolved. Yelling came from the other side.

"Time to go, my Führer." The magician patted his cheek and backed away from the middle of the room.

Celwyn executed a sarcastic Nazi salute as the floor under their feet shimmered and opened into an endless pit. From deep below, a chorus of horns played the Wagner march the Fuhrer loved, and steam rose upward; sweet and wet, like decay. The pounding from the corridor resumed with force until Celwyn stared at it and it stopped.

He gave Hitler a little push into the pit and floated down after him. A low hiss reached them and then a five-headed snake swung out of the blackness from only inches away and confronted Hitler. Its long teeth were slick with venom and even in the low light, its scales had an iridescent quality. A series of short shrieks came from Hitler as the nearest snake head moved closer and grazed his chin. When the music reached a crescendo, its skin rippled up and down its back with a metal tinkling as its scales shifted.

Celwyn brought them to a cave-like room with beds that continued to infinity. Each bed contained a form with a white sheet tucked under its chin. The eyes above the sheets burned with hatred as they registered Hitler's presence.

A woman materialized from the shadows to approach the Nazi.

Her eyes looked huge, like black pebbles floating in a pool. In Roma, she addressed Hitler. "You will die soon, my Führer." She ran long fingernails across his face. "Like my family. You remember them?"

Hitler turned away, but each time, the woman again appeared at his side. She whispered, "You killed them. Even my babies." She drew closer and screamed, "Because you hate Romanis!"

Example after example confronted him. As Celwyn watched the scene, he detected no remorse in Hitler and did not expect any. It would take much more than this for the bastard to feel fear.

When the Fuhrer blinked, the five-headed snake and thousands of victims had disappeared, leaving them under a cloudless night sky sprinkled with stars. Hitler lay on his back, tied to the top of the fortress turret. All the soldiers and staff were gone. A wispy breeze embraced them, bringing the faint scent from the forest below. Soon, a rolling chorus of voices raised in song swelled from the bottom of the valley, the music plaintive as it reached them.

The bastard struggled to free himself and scanned the courtyard, finding no one. Scores of flutes arrived as a lone figure approached from across the courtyard. Hitler tracked his progress between the ribbons of moonlight and swaths of inky blackness. The music of the flutes grew louder and hundreds more of them joined in.

The figure no longer walked, instead lifting off the ground with a tremendous whoosh of air and the flapping of large wings. Celwyn circled the towers of the fortress languidly, dipping low and then flying higher. Again, he swooped downward to visit Hitler, this time close enough to scrape his wings through the Nazi's hair.

The magician moved closer and breathed on Hitler. "Do you hear that?"

Hitler couldn't take his eyes off Celwyn.

"No?" Celwyn asked. "Perhaps you should listen again."

This time, a low hum reached them becoming a rumble in the night sky.

"Ah. I see that you do hear it." Celwyn asked, "How many of them do you think there are?" The engines grew louder as Hitler franticly searched the courtyard for his men.

"It's too late for that." Celwyn hovered in the air next to him. "They will be here soon."

By now, pin-prick light from the bombers could be seen a few miles out, and the hum of their engines drowned out the flutes, but not Hitler's terror.

"Only five planes? Perhaps there should be more since this place is so big and deep." Instantly, the noise blossomed, and the number of planes doubled. They flew in formation, straight toward them, their lights emerging from under a cloud deck.

"I thought you should hear and feel what the citizens of London do every night." He caused squadrons of air raid sirens to commence, heightening Hitler's frantic tries to escape. "It would be helpful to bring your generals up here to see the show; they are just as guilty as you are."

Before he finished speaking, Himmler, Goring, and the rest dangled by ropes from the battlements, able to watch the sky as the line of bombers grew nearer. "The Americans make a handsome machine, do they not?" He patted Hitler's head. By now, the roar of the bombers thundered as their bomb chutes opened.

"Auf Wiedersehen, you bastard." The magician flew by the generals before streaking away toward the trees to the south. The last thing he heard was Hitler screaming at last as the sky blossomed, became a brilliant gold and orange when the ground broke open like a giant rose, unfolding as the bombs exploded leaving a deep crater where the Nazis had plotted so much misery and destruction.

"No!"

The magician hopped out of the trees and blinked. He couldn't believe it.

Only seconds ago, Hitler and the Nazis had been blown apart. Yet, now the compound had returned, looking exactly as before, sitting there in the middle of a sunny day as if nothing had ever happened.

"Damnation!"

Celwyn flew upward and over the courtyard. Small figures marched in formation as before. He cursed and fumed and raised his arms. He would do this again!

Laughter, low and taunting, reached him from below. Without looking, the magician growled in his throat, knowing who it belonged to. As he descended to the ground, Swango sauntered toward him with a bottle of wine to his lips.

"Really?"

Swango laughed louder. "But of course." He offered Celwyn the bottle.

The magician grabbed it and drank deeply. "What the hell!"

"You lost the bet."

Celwyn rounded on him. "I did not!"

"You were not allowed to alter history, my friend." He gestured at the fortress. Swango laughed harder and wiped wine off his shirt. "I, of course, had to restore everything."

"Why?"

"Because … you shouldn't alter history or *time*." He regarded the magician. "Your solution killed everyone from Hitler to your new friend, Porky. Many of the victims would have had offspring, who would also reproduce, and so on and so on across the world. Everything they will touch will affect millions, eventually. Didn't you know that?"

Celwyn finished the wine and glowered at him. Something felt warm in his pocket. He withdrew the silver mouse he'd obtained more than 50 years ago at the market in London. It felt smooth in his hand, and for some reason he remembered the old man standing in front of his cart who had smiled at him and insisted he take the mouse. "Oh, my god—" Now, he knew why what happened in Prague seemed familiar. Celwyn wondered if the ornament possessed any other surprises.

"That is an adorable toy. But it won't change the outcome today." Swango flung a hand toward the compound behind them. "You had no compunction at killing all the people here?" The beat of the drums that accompanied the marching soldiers reached them, followed by a chorus of barking from the dogs.

"To a point, certainly."

"And the delectable Lieutenant Dosher? And her men?"

The magician swiveled and eyed Swango. "Why are you smiling?"

"Because."

As Celwyn watched, Swango's features melted into something softer and his expression became evasive. Speechless, Celwyn squinted at Lieutenant Dosher who stood in front of him. In Swango's irritating voice, she said, "Come now, I'd be delighted to hear your love poem again. So touching and infantile."

Chapter 51

In the comfort of the *Nautilus*

A S CELWYN FINISHED THE STORY, A proverbial pin could have been dropped into the stunned silence of the study. From beside him, Tara whispered, "Oh my," and tried not to laugh.

Bartholomew shook his head, thinking, and when he had it worked out, his eyes grew wide, and he held his sides and roared. The others reacted, including the broad smile that developed across Captain Nemo's face.

The automat laughed so hard he fell off the sofa. Qing didn't understand, but flew to the magician and rubbed his beak along his jaw, either in sympathy or for attention. Verne put everything into a question.

"If I understand all of this correctly, you visited the future and came back unhurt and resumed your normal activities?"

The big man snickered. "I can imagine what those were."

A red gelatinous frog landed in Bartholomew's lap. He yelped and shook it off, and Qing dove after it. Xiau stopped his hilarity long enough to crawl back onto the sofa and demand, "Don't you have anything to say?"

"I answered everything I was asked." Celwyn shrugged and produced his tea service.

Nemo had his reaction under control and nodded politely at Tara. "I think I speak for everyone in requesting that you tell us more." He opened his hand. "This Swango will be on my ship in two days' time, and we need to know what else to expect."

"Also, what exactly happened?" The automat eyed him. "For instance, did you pay off on the bet?"

"We need to know, Jonas." Bartholomew's eyes gleamed.

"There is not a lot to tell you." The magician inhaled the steam from his tea. "We traded a few appropriate insults while he kept insisting that I lost the bet. When I looked up again, he had disappeared and did not make a further demand I pay off the wager. So I assumed it was a draw and that no one won."

"Is that so?" Verne sounded disappointed. "Did he go back to England?"

Celwyn shook his head. "I do not know. I made my way to the nearest village, appearing to them as an elderly priest. When I awoke the next morning, I found myself more than a hundred years in the past where everything had started. I made it back to London and resumed my activities. Swango was right. Perhaps neither of us could say we won. But it still rankled after I put in so much effort to win."

"Your uncontrolled emotions are your undoing," the automat observed. "Don't take out your temper on my ears. It's true."

Tara had been quiet for so long, Celwyn wondered what she thought. Later, he would find out privately. For now, she asked, "Why did you say he won? Earlier you related how Hitler had been misled about the American's invasion. That alone may have turned the tide on the war. Correct?"

Nemo shook his head.

"Perhaps." Celwyn's frown deepened. "At the time I knew Swango had manipulated me, just as he had the time frame, the locations, the people, everything. I felt like a puppet left to flop around in the mud." A growl escaped him. "Especially when I figured out that Hitler's evil and the rest of the Nazis would continue for years after that. And I think they were active even further into the future."

"That is barbaric!" Bartholomew exclaimed.

"There are other things; in less than forty years from now, a horrible plague will descend on all of Europe. There is nothing I can do to stop it!"

"I wish I could make you feel better." Tara brushed fingertips across his hand.

The ever-logical automat asked him, "You can't stop it because Swango won't allow it?"

"Because I did not know how to control time. He does."

"Had you thought about convincing him or tricking him into stopping people like Hitler?" Tara asked.

Again, her perception amazed him. "During the two times I've encountered Swango since 1805, I haven't been able to figure out how to do so."

"Interesting. A circular conundrum." Nemo rubbed his chin in thought. "Question: the medical facility that the Nazis mentioned they built ... perhaps it has a connection to our current situation with Doctor Lazlo's genetic experiments?"

"A very good question, sir, but I did not hear enough to know."

"We need to explore that idea." Bartholomew frowned.

Tara said, "You say Swango isn't a magician, yet your descriptions sound like he is."

"I can recognize magic in all its forms." Celwyn decided against more tea for now, he was too angry to enjoy it. "He is not a magician, and I do not know how he does what I saw in Germany." He shook his head. "Or why he lives for so long."

"Let's set that aside for a moment. We must make a final decision." Nemo stared at him from under lowered brows. "Is it dangerous to have him on my ship?"

"An excellent question," Kang said. "Well, Jonas?" He put his hands on his hips, always a sign of an adorable lecture.

"Yes. However, he is not malicious like Pelaez. He likes to win and play games more than anything. He is honorable, especially if one pays attention to everything he says. I believe it is safe to have him here." Nemo did not look convinced, and his frown remained. Celwyn added, "He is not dangerous, just impish." He yawned. When Celwyn focused again, Qing's bright diamond gaze was the first thing he saw, and he patted the bird's metallic feathers.

"Are you saying that despite everything occurring in the future, you were aware of us? Of everything that is occurring now?" Tara's eyes looked as wide as he'd ever seen them.

Verne popped out of his chair and ran across the room to him. "Is that true? Oh my God, this is wonderful!"

"Yes, it is true about some things." The magician didn't feel completely sure about that. "But not about others. It depends on what Swango erased the last time I saw him. Everything between now, 1877, and that Nazi's business is unknown to me. And yes, when the bet between Swango and I transpired, I thought about all of you." He faced the automat. "And your favorite things to say and tease me about. Of course, I didn't remember things I don't agree with." He eyed the automat.

Kang appeared speechless for a moment, finally drawling, "I'm surprised you have survived this long, Jonas."

"Are you saying that if there is a fact or a scene," Bartholomew's brows touched in confusion, "that happened after Swango sent you to the future, much of what occurred between those two points you were aware of? And it doesn't bother you?"

"I suppose not. It also seemed natural to think of all of you as things came up. Just as natural as remembering something that happened in 1825. It came and went, nothing constant."

"Did you already know about what occurred in, say, 1906? Or happenings between 1871 and 1944?" Nemo asked.

Celwyn couldn't help it. He checked Nemo's worry. Out loud, he said, "No, I still do not know anything from that timeframe. But I suggest staying away from both San Francisco and Spain in 1906. That date occurred several times in one of the German papers I read, but I do not recall why."

At this point, the layers of what he'd seen, and the implications piled upon each other as he gazed at Nemo in a horrific fascination. He tried to control a shiver that wouldn't stop.

Now the magician knew the answer to what would happen to Nemo and to Bartholomew. *Oh, my …* but the answer did not come from Swango. It came from the random and silent visit just now from Thales. He held his hands together so no one would see them shaking. Minutes went by and Thales said nothing more.

"What is the matter?" Tara asked.

Celwyn tried to grin at them, felt his face flush, and said, "Isn't it time for our evening game of bridge?"

As ever a wise owl in elfin ears, Kang tilted his head at him and asked, "It's obvious. What did Thales say?"

The magician inhaled and wished he were back in Nazi Germany.

"Not now." He had to think about this, alone, not even with Tara beside him. Also, he refused to worry them.

As ever the man of tact, Verne asked, "Did you discover anything about our fates?"

This wouldn't stop soon, the magician decided. "Again, not now. But I can report that I saw nothing about Pelaez. Heard nothing."

He couldn't say the same about Wolfgang, their father. As usual, the Captain stared at him with understanding.

Into the silence, Nemo addressed the room.

"We pick up Mr. Soriano early tomorrow, then this Mr. Swango. I suggest everyone get some sleep. Our battle with Jurik Lazlo is about to begin."

Book club questions

1. Did you like the way the Celwyn series changed direction in book 6? Do you agree that it adds a new genre to the mix?

2. Is Celwyn becoming more likable, unpredictable, or more dangerous? Is Bartholomew becoming a stronger character?

3. Is the romance between Celwyn and Tara interesting, or does it get in the way of the action in the book?

4. Do you expect Tara to take a leading role with book 6? Or 7? Why or why not?

5. Have you ever encountered a bad character (like Pelaez) who did heroic acts (like saving Kang and the others) before doing something despicable?

6. In the previous book, Elizabeth, Mrs. Xiau Kang, was murdered. Her death is avenged in this book. Should Professor Kang remarry?

7. Again, in this book, Celwyn brings up the subject of what to do if Bartholomew is ever mortally wounded or becomes very old. Should they talk him into becoming a vampire to keep him alive and with them? Same question for Captain Nemo.

8. Will Swango help or hurt them in book 7?

Author Bio

LOU'S EARLY WORK WAS HORROR AND suspense. Later, her work morphed into a combination of magical realism, mystery, and adventure, painted with horrific elements as needed.

Lou is one of those writers who doesn't plan a plot—no outlines, no clue, and she sometimes writes herself into a corner. Atmospheric music in the background helps, especially "Black" by Pearl Jam.

More information is available at LouKemp.com. She'd love to hear from you and what you think of Celwyn, Bartholomew, and Professor Xiau Kang.

Milestones:

2009 The anthology story Sherlock's Opera appears in Seattle Noir, edited by Curt Colbert, Akashic Books. Available through Amazon or Barnes and

Noble online. Booklist published a favorable review of Lou Kemp's contribution to the anthology.

2010 The story, In Memory of the Sibylline, is accepted into the best-selling MWA anthology Crimes by Moonlight, edited by Charlaine Harris. The immortal magician Celwyn makes his first appearance in print in the story In Memory of the Sybilline.

2018 The story, The Violins Played before Junstan, is published in the MWA anthology Odd Partners, edited by Anne Perry. The Celwyn series begins.

2022 The partnership with 4 Horsemen Publications begins. Book 1, The Violins Played before Junstan is published.

2023 Book 2 of the Celwyn series, Music Shall Untune the Sky.

2023 Book 3, The Raven and the Pig.

June 2023 The companion book, The Sea of the Vanities.

December 2023 Book 4, The Pirate Danced and the Automat Died.

January 2024 Book 5 The Wyvern, the Pirate and the Madman.

Late 2024 Book 6 Swango (the Translator Lied)

Discover more at
4HorsemenPublications.com

10% off using HORSEMEN10

9 798823 204262